NERVE

Dick Francis has written more than forty international bestsellers and is widely acclaimed as one of the world's finest thriller writers. His awards include the Crime Writers' Association's Cartier Diamond Dagger for his outstanding contribution to the crime genre, and an honorary Doctorate of Humane Letters from Tufts University of Boston. In 1996 Dick Francis was made a Mystery Writers of America Grand Master for a lifetime's achievement and in 2000 he was awarded the CBE in the Queen's Birthday Honours list.

Dick Francis

NERVE

PAN BOOKS

First published in Great Britain 1964 by Michael Joseph Ltd

First published in paperback 1976 by Pan Books

This edition published 2007 by Pan Books
an imprint of Pan Macmillan Ltd
Pan Macmillan, 20 New Wharf Road, London N1 9RR
Basingstoke and Oxford
Associated companies throughout the world
www.panmacmillan.com

ISBN 978-0-330-45040-9

5 7 9 8 6 4

A CIP catalogue record for this book is available from
the British Library.

Printed and bound in the UK by
CPI Mackays, Chatham ME5 8TD

CHAPTER ONE

Art Mathews shot himself, loudly and messily, in the centre of the parade ring at Dunstable races.

I was standing only six feet away from him, but he did it so quickly that had it been only six inches I would not have had time to stop him.

He had walked out of the changing-room ahead of me, his narrow shoulders hunched inside the khaki jerkin he had put on over his racing colours, and his head down on his chest as if he were deep in thought. I noticed him stumble slightly down the two steps from the weighing-room to the path; and when someone spoke to him on the short walk to the parade ring, he gave absolutely no sign of having heard. But it was just another walk from the weighing-room to the parade ring, just another race like a hundred others. There was nothing to suggest that when he had stood talking for two or three minutes with the owner and trainer of the horse he was due to ride, he would take off his jerkin, produce from under it as he dropped it to the ground a large automatic pistol, place the barrel against his temple and squeeze the trigger.

Unhesitating. No pause for a final weighing-up. No goodbyes. The casualness of his movement was as shocking as its effect.

He hadn't even shut his eyes, and they were still open as he fell forwards to the ground, his face hitting the grass with an audible thud and his helmet rolling off. The bullet had passed straight through his skull, and the exit wound lay open to the sky, a tangled, bloody mess of skin and hair and brain, with splinters of bone sticking out.

The crack of the gunshot echoed round the paddock, amplified by the high back wall of the stands. Heads turned searchingly and the busy buzz and hum of conversation from the three-deep railside racegoers grew hushed and finally silent as they took in the appalling, unbelievable, indisputable fact that what remained of Art Mathews lay face downwards on the bright green turf.

Mr John Brewar, the owner of Art's prospective mount, stood with his middle-aged mouth stretched open in a soundless oval, his eyes glazed with surprise. His plump, well-preserved wife toppled to the ground in the graceless sprawl of a genuine faint, and Corin Kellar, the trainer for whom both Art and I had been about to ride, went down on one knee and shook Art by the shoulder, as if he could still awaken one whose head was half blown away.

The sun shone brightly. The blue and orange silk on Art's back gleamed: his white breeches were spotless, and his racing boots had been polished into a clean, soft shine. I thought inconsequentially that he would have been glad that – from the neck down at least – he looked as immaculate as ever.

The two stewards hurried over and stood stock-still, staring at Art's head. Horror dragged down their jaws and narrowed their eyes. It was part of their responsibility at a meeting to stand in the parade ring while the horses were led round before each race, so that they should be both witnesses and adjudicators if anything irregular should occur. Nothing as irregular as a public suicide of a top-notch steeplechase jockey had ever, I imagined, required their attention before.

The elder of them, Lord Tirrold, a tall, thin man with an executive mind, bent over Art for a closer inspection. I saw the muscles bunch along his jaw, and he looked up at me across Art's body and said quietly, 'Finn . . . fetch a rug.'

I walked twenty steps down the parade ring to where one of the horses due to run in the race stood in a little group with his owner, trainer and jockey. Without a word the trainer took the rug off the horse and held it out to me.

'Mathews?' he said incredulously.

I nodded unhappily and thanked him for the rug, and went back with it.

The other steward, a sour-tempered hulk named

Ballerton, was, I was meanly pleased to see, losing his cherished dignity by vomiting up his lunch.

Mr Brewar pulled down his unconscious wife's rucked-up skirt and began anxiously to feel her pulse. Corin Kellar kept passing his hand over his face from forehead to chin, still down on one knee beside his jockey. His face was colourless, his hand shaking. He was taking it badly.

I handed one end of the rug to Lord Tirrold and we opened it out and spread it gently over the dead man. Lord Tirrold stood for a moment looking down at the motionless brown shape, then glanced round at the little silent groups of the people who had runners in the race. He went over and spoke to one or two, and presently the stable lads led all the horses out from the parade ring and back to the saddling boxes.

I stood looking down at Corin Kellar and his distress, which I thought he thoroughly deserved. I wondered how it felt to know one had driven a man to kill himself.

There was a click, and a voice announced over the loud-speaker system that owing to a serious accident in the parade ring the last two races would be abandoned. Tomorrow's meeting would be held as planned, it said, and would everyone please go home. As far as the growing crowd of racegoers round the ring were concerned, this might never have been said, for they remained glued to the rails with all eyes on the concealing rug. Nothing rivets human attention as hungrily as a bloody disaster, I thought tolerantly, picking up Art's helmet and whip from the grass.

Poor Art. Poor badgered, beleaguered Art, rubbing out his misery with a scrap of lead.

I turned away from his body and walked thoughtfully back to the weighing-room.

While we changed back from riding kit into our normal clothes the atmosphere down our end of the changing-room was one of irreverence covering shock. Art, occupying by general consent the position of elder statesman among jockeys, though he was not actually at thirty-five by any means the eldest, had been much deferred to and respected. Distant in manner sometimes, withdrawn even, but an honest man and a good jockey. His one noticeable weakness, at which we usually smiled indulgently, was his conviction that a lost race was always due to some deficiency in his horse or its training, and never to a mistake on his own part. We all knew perfectly well that Art was no exception to the rule that every jockey misjudges things once in a while, but he would never admit a fault, and could put up a persuasive defence every time if called to account.

'Thank the Lord,' said Tick-Tock Ingersoll, stripping off his blue and black checked jersey, 'that Art was considerate enough to let us all weigh out for the race before bumping himself off.' Tick-Tock's face emerged from the woolly folds with a wide grin which faded comically when no one laughed.

'Well,' he said, dropping his jersey absentmindedly in a heap on the floor. 'If he'd done it an hour ago we'd all have been ten quid out of pocket.'

He was right. Our fees for each race were technically earned once we had sat on the scales and been checked out as carrying the correct weight, and they would be automatically paid whether we ran the race or not.

'In that case,' said Peter Cloony, 'we should put half of it into a fund for his widow.' He was a small, quiet young man prone to over-emotional, quickly roused and quickly spent bouts of pity both for others and for himself.

'Not ruddy likely,' said Tick-Tock, who disliked him openly. 'Ten quid's ten quid to me, and Mrs Art's rolling in it. And snooty with it. Catch me giving her the time of day, you'll be lucky.'

'It's a mark of respect,' said Peter obstinately, looking round at us with rather damp large eyes and carefully refraining from returning young Tick-Tock's belligerent glare.

I sympathized with Tick-Tock. I needed the money, too. Besides, Mrs Art had treated me, along with all the other rank-and-file jockeys, with her own particularly arctic brand of coolness. Giving her a fiver in Art's memory wouldn't thaw her. Pale, straw-haired, light-eyed, she was the original ice maiden, I thought.

'Mrs Art doesn't need our money,' I said. 'Remember how she bought herself a mink coat last winter and used it as a hedge against all of us who didn't measure up to her standards? She hardly knows two of us by name. Let's just buy Art a wreath, and perhaps a useful memorial, something he would have appreciated, like some hot showers in the washroom here.'

Tick-Tock's angular young face registered delight. Peter Cloony bent on me a look of sorrowful reproof. But from the others came nods of agreement.

Grant Oldfield said violently, 'He probably shot himself because that whey-faced bitch short-changed him in bed.'

There was a curious little silence. A year ago, I reflected, a year ago we might have laughed. But a year ago Grant Oldfield would have said the same thing amusingly and perhaps vulgarly, but not with this ugly unsmiling venom.

I was aware, we all were, that he didn't know or care a jot about the private practices of Art's marriage; but in the past months Grant had seemed more and more to be consumed by some inner rage, and lately he could scarcely make the most commonplace remark without in some way giving vent to it. It was caused, we thought, by the fact that he was going down the ladder again without ever having got to the top. He had always been ambitious and ruthless in character, and had developed a riding style to match. But at the vital point when he had attracted public attention with a string of successes and had begun to ride regularly for James Axminster, one of the very top trainers, something had happened to spoil it. He had lost the Axminster job, and other trainers booked him less and less. The race we had not run was his only engagement that day.

Grant was a dark, hairy, thick-set man of thirty, with high cheek-bones and a wide-nostrilled nose bent permanently out of shape. I endured a great deal more of his company than I would have liked because my peg in the changing-room at nearly all racecourses was next to his, since both our kit was looked after by the same racecourse valet. He borrowed my things freely without asking first or thanking afterwards, and if he had broken something, denied he had used it. When I first met him I had been amused by his pawky humour, but two years later, by the day Art died, I was heartily sick of his thunderous moods, his roughness and his vile temper.

Once or twice in the six weeks since the new season had begun I had found him standing with his head thrust forward looking round him in bewilderment, like a bull played out by a matador. A bull exhausted by fighting a piece of cloth, a bull baffled and broken, all his magnificent strength wasted on something he could not pin down with his horns. At such times I could pity Grant all right, but at all others I kept out of his way as much as I could.

Peter Cloony, paying him no attention as usual, indicated the peg on which Art's everyday clothes hung, and said, 'What do you think we had better do with these?'

We all looked at them, the well-cut tweed suit neatly arranged on a hanger, with the small grip which contained his folded shirt and underclothes standing on the bench beneath. His almost obsessive tidiness was so familiar to us that it aroused no comment, but now that he was dead I was struck afresh by it. Everyone else hung up their jackets by the loop at the back of the neck, hooked their braces on to the pegs, and piled their other clothes into the tops of their trousers. Only Art had insisted on a hanger, and had provided his valet with one to bring for him.

Before we had got any further than an obscene suggestion from Grant, a racecourse official threaded his way down the changing-room, spotted me, and shouted, 'Finn, the stewards want you.'

'Now?' I said, standing in shirt and underpants.

'At once.' He grinned.

'All right.' I finished dressing quickly, brushed my hair, walked through the weighing-room, and knocked on the stewards' door. They said to come in, and in I went.

All three stewards were there, also the clerk of the course, and Corin Kellar. They were sitting in uncomfortable-looking, straight-backed chairs around a large, oblong table.

Lord Tirrold said, 'Come along in and close the door.'

I did as he said.

He went on, 'I know you were near Mathews when he ... er ... shot himself. Did you actually see him do it? I mean, did you see him take the pistol out and aim it, or did you look at him when you heard the shot?'

'I saw him take out the pistol and aim it, sir,' I said.

'Very well. In that case the police may wish to take a statement from you; please do not leave the weighing-room building until they have seen you. We are waiting now for the inspector to come back from the first-aid room.'

He nodded to dismiss me, but when I had my hand on the door-knob he said, 'Finn ... do you know of any reason why Mathews should have wished to end his life?'

I hesitated a fraction too long before I turned round, so that a plain 'No' would have been unconvincing. I looked at Corin Kellar, who was busy studying his fingernails.

'Mr Kellar might know,' I said, non-committally.

The stewards exchanged glances. Mr Ballerton, still pallid from his bout of sickness by Art's body, made a pushing away gesture with his hand, and said, 'You're not asking us to believe that Mathews killed himself merely because Kellar was dissatisfied with his riding?' He turned to the other stewards. 'Really,' he added forcefully, 'if these jockeys get so big for their boots that they can't take a little well-earned criticism, it is time they looked about for other employment. But to suggest that Mathews killed himself because of a few hard words is irresponsible mischief.'

At that point I remembered that Ballerton himself owned a horse which Corin Kellar trained. 'Dissatisfied with his riding,' the colourless phrase he had used to describe the recent series of acrimonious post-race arguments between Art and the trainer suddenly seemed to me a deliberate attempt at oiling troubled waters. You know why Art killed himself, I thought; you helped to cause it, and you won't admit it.

I shifted my gaze back to Lord Tirrold and found him regarding me with speculation.

'That will be all, Finn,' he said.

'Yes, sir,' I said.

I went out and this time they did not call me back, but before I had crossed the weighing-room the door opened again and shut and I heard Corin's voice behind me.

'Rob.'

I turned round and waited for him.

'Thanks very much,' he said sarcastically, 'for tossing that little bomb into my lap.'

'You had told them already,' I said.

'Yes, and just as well.'

He still looked shocked, his thin face deeply lined with worry. He was an exceptionally clever trainer but a nervous, undependable man who offered you life-long friendship one day and cut you dead the next. Just then, it appeared, he needed reassurance.

He said, 'Surely you and the other jockeys don't believe Art killed himself because... er... I had decided to employ him less? He must have had another reason.'

'Today was supposed to be his last as your jockey in any case, wasn't it?' I said.

He hesitated and then nodded, surprised at my knowing what had not been published. I didn't tell him that I had bumped into Art in the car park the evening before, and that Art, bitterly despairing and smarting from a corroding sense of injustice, had lowered the customary guard on his tongue enough to tell me that his job with Kellar was finished.

I said only, 'He killed himself because you gave him the sack, and he did it in front of you to cause you the maximum amount of remorse. And that, if you want my opinion, is that.'

'But people don't kill themselves because they've lost their jobs,' he said, with a tinge of exasperation.

'Not if they're normal, no,' I agreed.

'Every jockey knows he'll have to retire some time. And Art was getting too old... he must have been mad.'

'Yes, I suppose so,' I said.

I left him standing there, trying to convince himself that he was in no way responsible for Art's death.

Back in the changing-room the discussion on what

to do with Art's clothes had been ended by his valet taking charge of them, and Grant Oldfield, I was glad to find, had finished dressing and gone home. Most of the other jockeys had gone also, and the valets were busy tidying up the chaos they had left behind, sorting dirty white breeches into kit bags, and piling helmets, boots, whips and other gear into large wicker hampers. It had been a dry sunny day, and for once there was no mud to wash off.

I reflected as I watched the quick, neat way they flipped the things into the baskets, ready to take the dirty ones home, clean them and return them laundered and polished on the following day, that possibly they did deserve the very large fees we had to pay them for the service. I knew I would loathe, after a day of travelling and of dressing jockeys, to have to face those hampers and bags when I reached home; take out the grubby piles and set to work. Ugh.

I had often seen Art paying his valet, counting through a wad of notes. At the height of the season it always amounted to over twenty pounds each week. My own valet, Young Mike (in his middle forties), twitched my helmet up from the bench and smiled at me as he went by. He earned more than most of the dozen or so jockeys he regularly looked after, and decidedly more than I did. But all the same ... ugh!

Tick-Tock, whistling the latest hit tune between his teeth, sat on the bench and pulled on a pair of very fancy yellow socks. On top of those went smooth, slim-toed shoes reaching up to the ankle bone. He shook down the slender legs of his dark tweed trousers (no turn-ups), and feeling my gaze upon him looked up and grinned at me across the room.

He said, 'Look your fill on the "Tailor and Cutter's" dream boy.'

'My father in his time,' I said blandly, 'was a Twelve Best Dressed man.'

'My grandfather had vicuna linings in his raincoats.'

'My mother,' I said, dredging for it, 'has a Pucci shirt.'

'Mine,' he said carefully, 'cooks in hers.'

At this infantile exchange we regarded each other with high good humour. Five minutes of Tick-Tock's company were as cheering as rum punch in a snowstorm, and some of his happy-go-lucky enjoyment of living always rubbed off on to the next man. Let Art die of shame, let the murk spread in Grant Oldfield's soul; surely nothing could be really wrong in the racing world, I thought, while young Ingersoll ticked so gaily.

He waved his hand at me, adjusted his Tyrolean trilby, said 'See you tomorrow,' and was gone.

But all the same there *was* something wrong in the racing world. Very wrong. I didn't know what; I could see only the symptoms, and see them all the more clearly perhaps, since I had been only two years in the game. Between trainers and jockeys there seemed to be an all-round edginess, sudden outbursts of rancour, and an ebbing and flowing undercurrent of resentment and distrust. There was more to it, I thought, than the usual jungle beneath the surface of any fiercely competitive business, more to it than the equivalent of grey-flannel-suit manoeuvring in the world of jodhpurs and hacking jackets; but Tick-Tock, to whom alone I had in any way suggested my misgivings, had brushed the whole thing aside.

'You must be on the wrong wavelength, pal,' he said. 'Look around you. Those are smiles you can see, boy. Smiles. It's an O.K. life by me.'

The last few pieces of kit were disappearing into the hampers and some of the lids were already down. I drank a second cup of sugarless tea, lukewarm, and eyed the moist looking pieces of fruit cake. As usual it took a good deal of resolution not to eat one. Being constantly hungry was the one thing I did not enjoy about race riding, and September was always a bad time of the year, with the remains of the summer's fat still having to be starved off. I sighed, averted my eyes from the cake, and tried to console myself that in another month my appetite would have shrunk back to its winter level.

Young Mike shouted down the room from the doorway through which he had been staggering with a hamper, 'Rob, there's a copper here to see you.'

I put down the cup and went out into the weighing-room. A middle-aged, undistinguished-looking policeman in a peaked cap was waiting for me with a notebook in his hand.

'Robert Finn?' he asked.

'Yes,' I said.

'I understand from Lord Tirrold that you saw Arthur Mathews put the pistol against his temple and pull the trigger?'

'Yes,' I agreed.

He made a note: then he said, 'It's a very straightforward case of suicide. There won't be any need for more than one witness at the inquest, apart from the doctor, and that will probably be Mr Kellar. I don't think we will need to trouble you any further.' He smiled briefly, shut the notebook and put it in his pocket.

'That's all?' I asked rather blankly.

'Yes, that's all. When a man kills himself as publicly as this there's no question of accident or homicide. The only thing for the coroner to decide is the wording of his verdict.'

'Unsound mind and so on?' I said.

'Yes,' he said. 'Thank you for waiting, though it was your stewards' idea, not mine. Good afternoon, then.' He nodded at me, turned, and walked across towards the stewards' room.

I collected my hat and binoculars and walked down to the racecourse station. The train was already waiting and full, and the only seat I could find was in a compartment packed with bookmakers' clerks playing

16

cards on a suitcase balanced across their knees. They invited me to join them, and between Luton and St Pancras I fear I repaid their kindness by winning from them the cost of the journey.

CHAPTER TWO

The flat in Kensington was empty. There were a few
letters from the day's second post in the wire basket
on the inner side of the door, and I fished them out
and walked through into the sitting-room, sorting
out the two which were addressed to me.

As usual, the place looked as if it had lately
received the attentions of a minor tornado. My
mother's grand piano lay inches deep in piano scores,
several of which had cascaded to the floor. Two music-
stands leant at a drunken angle against the wall with
a violin bow hooked on to one of them. The violin
itself was propped up in an armchair, with its case
open on the floor beside it. A 'cello and another music-
stand rested side by side like lovers along the length
of the sofa. An oboe and two clarinets lay on a table
beside another untidy pile of music, and round the
room and on all the bedroom chairs which filled most
of the floor space lay a profusion of white silk
handkerchiefs, rosin, coffee cups and batons.

Running a practised eye over the chaos I diagnosed

the recent presence of my parents, two uncles and a cousin. As they never travelled far without their instruments, it was safe to predict that the whole circus was within walking distance and would return in a very short while. I had, I was thankful to realize, struck the interval.

I threaded a path to the window and looked out. No sign of returning Finns. The flat was at the top of a house two or three streets back from Hyde Park, and across the rooftops I could see the evening sunlight striking on the green dome of the Albert Hall. The Royal Institute of Music, where one of my uncles taught, rose in a solid dark mass beside it. The large airy apartment which was the headquarters of the Finn family was held by my father to be an economy, as it was within walking distance of where so many of them from time to time worked.

I was the odd one out. The talents with which both my parents' families had been lavishly endowed had not descended to me. This had become painfully clear to them when at the age of four I had failed to distinguish between the notes of an oboe and a *cor anglais*. To the uninitiated there may not seem to be much difference between them, but my father happened to be an oboist of international reputation, against whom other oboists were measured. Also, high musical talent, if it exists, is apparent in a child from an extremely early age, earlier than any other form of inborn ability, and at three years (when Mozart began

19

composing), concertos and symphonies made less impression on me than the noise of the men emptying the dustbins.

By the time I was five my shattered parents had reluctantly faced the fact that the child they had bred by mistake (I had caused an important American tour to be cancelled) was unmusical. Unmusical, that is, in their pure sense. I was not tone deaf and soaring flights of melody had drawn from me childish tears, but I never had, and still have not, their complete understanding, intellectual, emotional, technical and spiritual, of the effect of putting certain sounds in certain orders.

My mother never being one to do things by halves, I had henceforth been shuffled off from London between school terms to a succession of long holidays on farms, ostensibly for my health, but in reality, I knew later, to free my parents for the complicated and lengthy concert tours in which they were engaged. I grew up into a sort of truce with them, in which it was tacitly agreed that as they had not intended to have a child in the first place, and as he had proved to be less than a (musical) credit to them in the second, the less we saw of each other the better.

They disapproved of my venture into jockeyship for no other reason than that racing had nothing to do with music. It was no use my pointing out that the one thing I had learned on the various holiday farms was how to ride (for I was enough my father's son for farming itself to bore me stiff), and that my present occupation was directly due to their actions in the past. To what they did not want to hear my acute-eared parents were sublimely deaf.

There was still no sign of them down in the street, nor of the uncle who lived with us who played the 'cello, nor the visiting uncle and cousin, violin and clarinet.

I opened my two letters. The first informed me that my income tax returns were overdue. I slit the second envelope with a smiling and complacent anticipation of enjoyment, which just shows how often life can get up and slap you when you least expect it. In a familiar childish hand the letter said:

Dearest Rob,
I am afraid this may come as a surprise to you, but I am getting married. He is Sir Morton Henge, who you may have heard of, and he is very sweet and kind and no cracks from you about him being old enough to be my father etc. I don't think I had better ask you to the reception, do you? Morton doesn't know about you and you will be a great dear not to let on to anybody about us, if you don't mind. I shall never forget you, dearest Rob, and all the sweet times we had together. Thank you for everything, and goodbye.
Your loving Paulina.

Sir Morton Henge, middle-aged widower and canning tycoon. Well, well. I wondered sardonically how his serious-minded son, whom I knew slightly, would enjoy the prospect of a cuddly twenty-year-old model for a stepmother. But being in a lopsided way able to laugh at Paulina's catch made it no less of a blow.

In the eighteen months since I had first met her she had progressed from mousy-haired obscurity to blonde blossoming on the cover of at least one glossy magazine a week. In the last month her radiant eyes had smiled at me (and eight million other men) from a cigarette advertisement in every underground station in London. I had known that it was inevitable that one day she would forsake me if she struck gold in her profession, and our whole relationship had from the start been based on that assumption; but a future without her happy inanity and her generous love-making seemed all of a sudden more bleak than I had expected.

I went through to my bedroom and putting down Paulina's letter on the chest of drawers, caught sight of myself in the oval mirror on the wall above it. That is the face, I thought, that she has been pleased to see beside her on her pillow, but which was no match for a title and a canning fortune. Looking objectively at my reflection I noted the black hair, black eyebrows and lashes, brown eyes . . . not a distinguished face, nor handsome; too thin perhaps. Not bad, not good. Just a face.

I turned away and looked around the little sloping-ceilinged room which had been converted for me from a lumber room when I came home from my travels. There was very little in it; a bed, the chest of drawers, an armchair and a bedside table with a lamp on it. One picture, an impressionistic sketch of racing horses, hung on the wall facing my bed. There were no other ornaments, few books, no clutter. In six years of wandering round the world I had become so used to living with a minimum of possessions that although I had now occupied this little room on and off for two years, I had amassed nothing to put in it.

A clothes cupboard had been built for me across one end of the room. I opened the door and tried to look at its contents as Paulina must have looked, the twice she had been there. One good dark grey suit, one evening jacket with black trousers, one hacking jacket, two pairs of grey slacks, and a pair of jodhpurs. I took off the suit I was wearing and hung it at the end of the meagre row, a tweed mixture of browns. They were enough for me, those clothes. They covered every situation. Sir Morton Henge probably counted his suits in dozens and had a manservant to look after them. I shrugged my shoulders. There was no profit in this melancholy stocktaking. Paulina was gone, and that was that.

Picking up a pair of black sneakers, I shut the

cupboard door and changed into jeans and an old checked shirt. That done, I contemplated the desert of time between then and the next day's racing. The trouble with me was that steeplechasing had got into my blood like a drug addiction, so that all the normal pleasures of life, and even Paulina herself, had become merely ways of passing as quickly as possible the hours away from it.

My stomach gave an extra twist, which I would like to have believed was due to romantic desolation at my blasted love life, but which I knew very well was only the effect of not having eaten for twenty-three hours. Admitting wryly that being jettisoned had not spoiled my appetite, I made for the kitchen. Before I reached it, however, the front door of the flat banged open and in trooped my parents, uncles and cousin.

'Hello, darling,' said my mother, presenting a smooth sweet-smelling cheek for a kiss. It was her usual greeting to everyone from impresarios to back row chorus singers, and when applied to me still utterly lacked any maternal quality. She was not a motherly person in any way. Tall, slender and immensely chic in a style that looked casual but was the result of much thought and expenditure, she was becoming more and more a 'presence' as she approached fifty. As a woman I knew her to be passionate and temperamental; as an artist to be a first-class interpretative vehicle for the genius of Haydn, whose piano concertos she poured out with magical, meticulous, ecstatic precision. I had seen hardened music critics leave her performances with tears in their eyes. So I had never expected a broad motherly bosom to comfort my childish woes, nor a sock-darning, cake-making mum to come home to.

My father, who treated me always with polite friendliness, said as a form of greeting, 'Did you have a good day?' He always asked. I usually answered briefly yes or no, knowing that he was not really interested.

I said, 'I saw a man kill himself. No, it wasn't a good day.'

Five heads swivelled towards me.

My mother said, 'Darling, what do you mean?'

'A jockey shot himself at the races. He was only six feet away from me. It was a mess.' All five of them stood there looking at me with their mouths open. I wished I hadn't told them, for it seemed even more horrible in memory than it had done at the time.

But they were unaffected. The 'cello uncle shut his mouth with a snap, shrugged, and went on into the sitting-room, saying over his shoulder, 'Well, if you will go in for these peculiar pursuits . . .'

My mother followed him with her eyes. There was a bass twang as he picked up his instrument from the sofa, and as if drawn by an irresistible magnet the others drifted after him. Only my cousin stayed long enough to spare Art a thought, then he too went back to his clarinet.

I listened to them re-tuning and setting up the music stands. They began to play a jigging piece for strings and woodwind that I particularly disliked. The flat was suddenly intolerable. I went out and down into the street and began to walk.

There was only one place to go if I wanted a certain kind of peace, and I didn't care to go there too often for fear of wearing out my welcome. But it was a full month since I had seen my cousin Joanna, and I needed some more of her company. Need. That was the only word for it.

She opened the door with her usual air of good humoured invitation.

'Well, hello,' she said, smiling. I followed her into the big converted mews garage which served her as sitting-room, bedroom and rehearsal room all in one. Half of the roof was a sloping skylight, through which the remains of the evening sun still shone. The size and comparative bareness of the room gave it unusual acoustic qualities; if one spoke ordinarily it was like any other room; if one sang, as Joanna did, there was a satisfying illusion of distance and some good amplification from concrete walls.

Joanna's voice was deep and clear and resonant. When she liked, in singing dramatic passages, she could colour it with the suggestion of graininess, a very effective hint of a crack in the bell. She could have made a fortune as a blues singer; but having been born a true classical Finn, so commercial a use of her talent

26

was out of the question. Instead she preferred songs which were to me unmelódic and unrewarding, though she seemed to be amassing a fair-sized reputation with them among people who enjoyed that sort of thing.

She had greeted me in a pair of jeans as old as my own and a black sweater streaked here and there with paint. On an easel stood a half-finished portrait of a man, with some brushes and paints on a table beside it.

'I'm trying my hand at oils,' she said, picking up a brush and making a tentative dab at the picture, 'but it's not going very well, damn it.'

'Stick to charcoal, then,' I said. She had drawn with flowing lines the racing horses which hung in my bedroom, short on anatomy, but full of life and movement.

'I'll finish this, at least,' she said.

I stood and watched her. She squeezed out some carmine.

Without looking at me she said, 'What's the matter?'

I didn't answer. She paused with her brushes in the air and turned and regarded me calmly for some seconds.

'There's some steak in the kitchen,' she said.

A mind reader, my cousin Joanna. I grinned at her and went out into the long narrow lean-to where she both took her bath and did her cooking. It was rump steak, thick and dark. I grilled it with a couple of tomatoes and made some french dressing for a lettuce

I found already prepared in a wooden bowl. When the steak was done I divided it on to two plates and took the whole lot back to Joanna. It smelt wonderful.

She put down her brush and came to eat, wiping her hands on the seat of her pants.

'I'll say one thing for you, Rob. You cook a mean steak,' she said, after her first mouthful.

'Thanks for nothing,' I said, with my mouth full.

We ate every scrap. I finished first, and sat back and watched her. She had a fascinating face, full of strength and character, with straight dark eyebrows and, that night, no lipstick. She had tucked her short wavy hair in a no-nonsense style behind her ears, but on top it still curled forward on to her forehead in an untidy fringe.

My cousin Joanna was the reason I was still a bachelor, if one can be said to need a reason at twenty-six years of age. She was three months older than I, which had given her an advantage over me all our lives, and this was a pity, since I had been in love with her from the cradle. I had several times asked her to marry me, but she always said no. First cousins, she explained firmly, were too closely related. Besides which, she added, I didn't stir her blood.

Two other men, however, had done that for her. Both were musicians. And each of them in their turn in a most friendly way had told me how greatly having Joanna for a lover had deepened their appreciation of living, given new impetus to their musical inspiration, opened new vistas, and so on and so on. They were both rather intense brooding men with undeniably handsome faces, and I didn't like hearing what they had to say. On the first occasion, when I was eighteen, I departed in speed and grief to foreign lands, and somehow had not returned for six years. On the second occasion I went straight to a wild party, got thoroughly drunk for the first and only time in my life, and woke up in Paulina's bed. Both adventures had turned out to be satisfying and educational. But they had not cured me of Joanna.

She pushed away her empty plate and said, 'Now, what's the matter?'

I told her about Art. She listened seriously and when I had finished she said, 'The poor man. And his poor wife ... Why did he do it, do you know?'

'I think it was because he lost his job,' I said. 'Art was such a perfectionist in everything. He was too proud ... He would never admit he had done anything wrong in a race ... And I think he simply couldn't face everyone knowing he'd been given the sack. But the odd thing is, Joanna, that he looked as good as ever to me. I know he was thirty-five, but that's not really old for a jockey, and although it was obvious that he and Corin Kellar, the trainer who retained him, were always having rows when their horses didn't win, he hadn't lost any of his style. Someone else would have employed him, even if not one of the top stables like Corin's.'

'And there you have it, I should think,' she said. 'Death was preferable to decline.'

'Yes, it looks like it.'

'I hope that when your time comes to retire you will do it less drastically,' she said. I smiled, and she added, 'And just what will you do when you retire?'

'Retire? I have only just started,' I said.

'And in fourteen years' time you'll be a second-rate, battered, bitter forty, too old to make anything of your life and with nothing to live on but horsy memories that no one wants to listen to.' She sounded quite annoyed at the prospect.

'You, on the other hand,' I said, 'will be a fat, middle-aged, contralto's understudy, scared stiff of losing your looks and aware that those precious vocal cords are growing less flexible every year.'

She laughed. 'How gloomy. But I see your point. From now on I'll try not to disapprove of your job because it lacks a future.'

'But you'll go on disapproving for other reasons?'

'Certainly. It's basically frivolous, unproductive, escapist, and it encourages people to waste time and money on inessentials.'

'Like music,' I said.

She glared at me. 'For that you shall do the washing up,' she said, getting to her feet and putting the plates together.

While I did my penance for the worst heresy possibly in the Finn family she went back to her portrait, but it was nearly dusk, and when I brought in a peace offering of some freshly-made coffee she gave it up for the day.

'Is your television set working?' I asked, handing her a cup.

'Yes, I think so.'

'Do you mind if we have it on for a quarter of an hour?'

'Who's playing?' she asked automatically.

I sighed. 'No one. It's a racing programme.'

'Oh, very well. If you must.' But she smiled.

I switched on, and we saw the end of the variety show. I enjoyed the songs of the last performer, a vivacious blonde, but Joanna, technique-minded, said her breath control creaked. A batch of advertisements followed, and then the fluttering urgent opening bars of 'The Galloping Major', accompanied by speeded-up superimposed views of horses racing, announced the weekly fifteen minutes of *Turf Talk*.

The well-known good-looking face of Maurice Kemp-Lore came on the screen, smiling and casual. He began in his easy charming way to introduce his guest of the evening, a prominent bookmaker, and his topic of the evening, the mathematics involved in making a book.

'But first,' he said, 'I would like to pay a tribute to the steeplechase jockey, Art Mathews, who died today by his own hand at Dunstable races. Many of you have watched him ride ... I expect nearly all of you have seen televised races in which he has appeared ... and you will feel with me a great sense of shock that such a long and successful career should end in a tragedy of this sort. Although never actually champion jockey, Art was acknowledged to be one of the six best steeplechase riders in the country, and his upright incorruptible character has been a splendid example to young jockeys just starting in the game ...'

Joanna lifted an eyebrow at me, and Maurice Kemp-Lore, neatly finishing off Art's glowing obituary, reintroduced the bookmaker, who gave a clear and fascinating demonstration of how to come out on the winning side. His talk, illustrated with films and animated charts, described the minute by minute decisions made daily in a big London starting price office, and was well up to the high standard of all the Kemp-Lore programmes.

Kemp-Lore thanked him and rounded off the quarter of an hour with a review of the following week's racing, not tipping particular animals to win but giving snippets of information about people and horses on the basis that there would be more interest in the outcome of a race if the public already knew something of the background of the contestants. His anecdotes were always interesting or amusing, and I had heard him called the despair of racing journalists since he so often beat them to a good story.

He said finally, 'See you all next week at the same time,' and 'The Galloping Major' faded him out.

I switched off the set. Joanna said, 'Do you watch that every week?'

'Yes, if I can,' I said. 'It's a racing must. It's so full of things one ought not to miss, and quite often his guest is someone I've met.'

'Mr Kemp-Lore knows his onions, then?' she said.

'He does indeed. He was brought up to it. His father rode a Grand National winner back in the thirties and is now a big noise on the National Hunt Committee; which,' I went on, seeing her blank look, 'is the ruling body of steeplechasing.'

'Oh. And has Mr Kemp-Lore ridden any Grand National winners himself?' she asked.

'No,' I said. 'I don't think he rides much at all. Horses give him asthma, or something like that. I'm not sure ... I only know him by sight. He is often at the races but I have never spoken to him.'

Joanna's interest in racing, never very strong, subsided entirely at this point, and for an hour or so we gossiped amicably and aimlessly about how the world wagged.

The door bell rang. She went to answer it and came back followed by the man whose portrait she was attempting, the second of her two blood stirrers, still stirring away. He put his arm possessively round her waist and kissed her. He nodded to me.

'How did the concert go?' she asked. He played a first violin in the London Symphony Orchestra.

'So so,' he said; 'the Mozart B flat went all right

except that some fool in the audience started clapping after the slow movement and ruined the transition to the allegro.'

My cousin made sympathetic noises. I stood up. I did not enjoy seeing them so cosily together.

'Going?' asked Joanna, detaching herself.

'Yes.'

'Good night, Rob,' he said, yawning. He took off his black tie and loosened the neck of his shirt.

I said politely, 'Good night, Brian.' And may you rot, I thought.

Joanna came with me to the door and opened it, and I stepped out into the dark cobbled mews and turned to say good-bye. She was silhouetted against the warm light in the studio room where Brian, I could see, was sitting down and taking off his shoes.

I said flatly, 'Thank you for the steak... and the television.'

'Come again,' she said.

'Yes. Well, good night.'

'Good night,' she said, and then in an afterthought added, 'How is Paulina?'

'She is going to marry,' I said, 'Sir Morton Henge.'

I am not sure what I expected in the way of sympathy, but I should have known. Joanna laughed.

CHAPTER THREE

Two weeks after Art died I stayed a night in Peter Cloony's house.

It was the first Cheltenham meeting of the season, and having no car I went down as usual on the race train, carrying some overnight things in a small suitcase. I had been engaged for two races at the meeting, one on each day, and intended to find a back street pub whose charges would make the smallest possible dent in my pocket. But Peter, seeing the case, asked me if I were fixed up for the night, and offered me a bed. It was kind of him, for we were not particularly close friends, and I thanked him and accepted.

From my point of view it was an unexciting day. My one ride, a novice hurdler revoltingly called Neddikins, had no chance of winning. His past form was a sorry record of falls and unfinished races. Tailed-off and pulled-up figured largely. I wondered why on earth the owner bothered with the wretched animal, but at the same time rehearsed in advance some

35

complimentary things to say about it. I had long ago discovered that owners hated to be told their horses were useless and often would not employ again a jockey who spoke too much unpalatable truth. It was wiser not to answer the typical question, 'What do you think we should do with beautiful Neddikins next?' with an unequivocal 'Shoot it.'

By working hard from start to finish I managed to wake Neddikins up slightly, so that although we finished plainly last, we were not exactly tailed off. A triumph, I considered it, to have got round at all, and to my surprise this was also the opinion of his trainer, who clapped me on the shoulder and offered me another novice hurdler on the following day.

Neddikins was the first horse I rode for James Axminster, and I knew I had been asked because he had not wanted to risk injury to his usual jockey. A good many of that sort of ride came my way, but I was glad to have them. I reckoned if I could gain enough experience on bad horses when nothing much was expected of me, it would stand me in good stead if ever I found myself on better ones.

At the end of the afternoon I joined Peter and we drove off in his sedate family saloon. He lived in a small village, scarcely more than a hamlet, in a hollow in the Cotswold Hills about twenty miles from Cheltenham. We turned off the main road into a narrow secondary road bordered on each side by thick hedges. It seemed to stretch interminably across bare farm land, but eventually, turning a corner, it came to the edge of the plateau and one could see a whole village spread out in the small valley below.

Peter pointed. 'That bungalow down there is where I live. The one with the white windows.'

I followed his finger. I had time to see a neatly-fenced little garden round a new-looking house before a curve in the road hid it from view. We slid down the hill, rounded several blind corners with a good deal of necessary horn blowing, and at the beginning of the village curled into an even smaller lane and drew up outside Peter's house. It was modern, brick-built, and freshly attractive, with neatly-edged flower beds and shaven squares of lawn.

Peter's wife opened the white front door and came down the path to meet us. She was, I saw, very soon to have a child. She herself looked hardly old enough to have left school. She spoke shyly.

'Do come in,' she said, shaking my hand. 'Peter telephoned to say you were coming, and everything is ready.'

I followed her into the bungalow. It was extremely neat and clean and smelled of furniture polish. All the floors were covered with mottled soft blue linoleum with a few terra-cotta rugs scattered about. Peter's wife, she told me during the evening, had made the rugs herself.

In the sitting-room there was only a sofa, a television set, and a dining-table with four chairs. The bareness of the room was to some extent disguised by one wall being almost completely covered in photographs. They had been framed by Peter himself and were edged in passe-partout in several different bright colours, so that the effect was gay and cheerful. Peter showed them to me while his wife cooked the dinner.

They were clearly devoted to each other. It showed in every glance, every word, every touch. They seemed very well matched; good natured, quickly moved to sympathy, sensitive, and with not a vestige of a sense of humour between them.

'How long have you two been married?' I asked, biting into a wedge of cheese.

Peter said, 'Nine months,' and his wife blushed beguilingly.

We cleared away the dishes and washed them, and spent the evening watching television and talking about racing. When we went to bed they apologized for the state of my bedroom.

'We haven't furnished it properly yet,' said Peter's wife, looking at me with anxious eyes.

'I'll be very comfortable indeed,' I said. 'You are so kind to have had me at all.' She smiled happily.

The bedroom contained a bed and a chair only. There was the blue linoleum on the floor, with a terra-cotta rug. A small mirror on the wall, some thin rust-coloured curtains at the window, and a hook and two hangers on the back of the door to serve as a wardrobe. I slept well.

In the morning, after breakfast, Peter did a lot of household jobs while his wife showed me round the small garden. She seemed to know every flower and growing vegetable individually. The plants were cherished as thoroughly as the house.

'Peter does most of my housework just now,' she said, looking fondly back to the house. 'The baby is due in six days. He says I mustn't strain myself.'

'He is a most considerate husband,' I said.

'The best in the world,' she said fervently.

It was because Peter insisted at the last minute on driving down to the village shop to fetch a loaf of bread to save his wife the walk that we started out for Cheltenham later than we had intended.

We wound up the twisty hill too fast for prudence, but nothing luckily was on its way down. At least, it seemed to be lucky until we had streaked across the farm land and were slowing down to approach the turn into the main road. That was when we first saw the tank carrier. It was slewed across the road diagonally, completely blocking the way.

Peter's urgent tooting on the horn produced one soldier, who ambled over to the car and spoke soothingly.

'I'm very sorry, sir, but we were looking for the road to Timberley.'

'You turned too soon. It's the next road on the right,' said Peter impatiently.

'Yes, I know,' said the soldier. 'We realized we had turned too soon, and my mate tried to back out again, but he made a right mess of it, and we've hit the hedge on the other side. As a matter of fact,' he said casually, 'we're ruddy well stuck. My mate's just hitched a lorry to go and ring up our H.Q. about it.'

We both got out of the car to have a look, but it was true. The great unwieldy articulated tank carrier was solidly jammed across the mouth of the narrow lane, and the driver had gone.

Pale and grim, Peter climbed back into his seat with me beside him. He had to reverse for a quarter of a mile before we came to a gateway he could turn the car in: then we backtracked down the long bend-ridden hill, raced through the village and out on to the road on the far side. It led south, away from Cheltenham, and we had to make a long detour to get back to the right direction. Altogether the tank carrier put at least twelve miles on to our journey.

Several times Peter said, 'I'll be late,' in a despairing tone of voice. He was, I knew, due to ride in the first race, and the trainer for whom he rode liked him to report to him in the weighing-room an hour earlier. Trainers had to state the name of the jockey who would be riding their horse at least three-quarters of an hour before the event: if they took a chance and declared a jockey who had not arrived and then he did not arrive at all, however good the reason, the trainer was in trouble with the stewards. Peter rode for a man who never took this risk. If his jockey was not there an hour before the race, he found a substitute; and since Peter was his jockey, the rule was a good one, because he was by nature a last-minute rusher who left no time margin for things to go wrong.

We reached the racecourse just forty-three minutes before the first race. Peter sprinted from the car park, but he had some way to go and we both knew that he wouldn't do it. As I followed him more slowly and walked across the big expanse of tarmac towards the weighing-room I heard the click of the loud speakers being turned on, and the announcer began to recite the runners and riders of the first race. P. Cloony was not among them.

I found him in the changing-room, sitting on the bench with his head in his hands.

'He didn't wait,' he said miserably. 'He didn't wait. I knew he wouldn't. I knew it. He's put Ingersoll up instead.'

I looked across the room to where Tick-Tock was pulling his boots up over his nylon stockings. He already wore the scarlet jersey which should have been Peter's. He caught my eye and grimaced and shook his head in sympathy: but it was not his fault he had been given the ride, and he had no need to be too apologetic.

The worst of it was that Tick-Tock won. I was

standing beside Peter on the jockeys' stand when the scarlet colours skated by the winning post, and he made a choking sound as if he were about to burst into tears. He managed not to, but there was a certain dampness about his eyes and his face had changed to a bloodless, greyish white.

'Never mind,' I said awkwardly, embarrassed for him. 'It's not the end of the world.'

It had been unfortunate that we had arrived so late, but the trainer he rode for was a reasonable man, if impatient, and there was no question of his not engaging him in future. Peter did in fact ride for him again that same afternoon, but the horse ran less well than was expected, and pulled up lame. My last glimpse of him showed a face still dragged down in lines of disappointment and he was boring everyone in the weighing-room by harping on the tank carrier over and over again.

For myself, things went slightly better. The novice chaser fell at the water jump, but went down slowly and I suffered nothing but grass stains on my breeches.

The young hurdler I was to ride for James Axminster in the last race on the card had as vile a reputation as his stablemate the previous day and I had made completing the race my sole target. But for some reason the wayward animal and I got on very well together from the start, and to my surprise, an emotion shared by every single person present, we came over the last hurdle in second place and passed the leading horse on the uphill stretch to the winning post. The odds-on favourite finished fourth. It was my second win of the season, and my first ever at Cheltenham: and it was greeted with dead silence.

I found myself trying to explain it away to James Axminster in the winner's unsaddling enclosure.

'I'm very sorry, sir,' I said. 'I couldn't help it.'

I knew he hadn't had a penny on it, and the owner had not even bothered to come to see the horse run.

He looked at me broodingly without answering, and I thought that there was one trainer who would not employ me again in a hurry. Sometimes it is as bad to win unexpectedly as to lose on a certainty.

I unbuckled the girths, pulled the saddle off over my arm and stood waiting for the storm to break.

'Well, go along and weigh in,' he said abruptly. 'And when you're dressed I want to talk to you.'

When I came out of the changing-room he was standing just inside the weighing-room door talking to Lord Tirrold, whose horse he trained. They stopped talking and turned towards me as I went over to them, but I could not see their expressions clearly as they had their backs to the light.

James Axminster said, 'What stable do you ride for most?'

I said, 'I ride mainly for farmers who train their own horses. I haven't a steady job with a public trainer, but I have ridden for several when they have asked me. Mr Kellar has put me up a few times.' And that,

I thought a little wryly, is the true picture of the smallness of the impression I had made in the racing world.

'I have heard one or two trainers say,' said Lord Tirrold, speaking directly to Axminster, 'that for their really bad horses they can always get Finn.'

Axminster grinned back at him. 'Just what I did today, and look at the result! How am I going to convince the owner it was as much a surprise to me as it will be to him when he hears about it? I've told him often that the horse is pretty useless.' He turned to me. 'You have made me look a proper fool, you know.'

'I'm sorry, sir,' I said again: and I meant it.

'Don't look so glum about it. I'll give you another chance; several in fact. There's a slow old plug you can ride for me on Saturday, if you're not booked already for that race, and two or three others next week. After that . . . we'll see.'

'Thank you,' I said dazedly. 'Thank you very much.' It was as if he had thrust a gold brick into my hands when I had expected a scorpion: if I acquitted myself at all well on his horses he might use me regularly as a second-string jockey. That would be, for me, a giant step up.

He smiled a warm, almost mischievous smile which crinkled the skin round his eyes and said, 'Geranium in the handicap chase at Hereford on Saturday, then. Are you free?'

'Yes,' I said.

'And you can do the weight? Ten stone?'

'Yes,' I said. I'd need to lose another three pounds in the two days, but starvation had never seemed so attractive.

'Very well. I'll see you there.'

'Yes, sir,' I said.

He and Lord Tirrold turned away and went out of the weighing-room together, and I heard them laugh. I watched them go, the thin angular Lord Tirrold and the even taller trainer, a pair who had between them won almost every important event in the National Hunt calendar.

James Axminster was a big man in every sense. Six foot four and solidly bulky, he moved and spoke and made decisions with easy assurance. He had a big face with a prominent nose and a square-looking heavy lower jaw. When he smiled his lower teeth showed in front of the upper ones, and they were good strong teeth, evenly set and unusually white.

His stable was one of the six largest in the country: his jockey, Pip Pankhurst, had been champion for the past two seasons; and his horses, about sixty of them, included some of the best alive. To have been offered a toe-hold in this set-up was almost as frightening as it was miraculous. If I messed up this chance, I thought, I might as well follow Art into oblivion.

I spent most of the next day running round Hyde Park in three sweaters and a wind-cheater and resisting the temptation to drink pints of water to replace what

I had sweated off. Some of the other jockeys used dehydrating pills to rid their bodies of fluid (which weighs more than fat and is easier to shift) but I had found, the only time I took some, that they left me feeling almost too weak to ride.

At about six o'clock I boiled three eggs and ate them without salt or bread, and then removed myself hurriedly, for my mother was entertaining some friends to dinner, and the girl who came to cook for us on these occasions was beginning to fill the kitchen with demoralizing savoury smells. I decided to go to the pictures to take my mind off my stomach; but it wasn't a great success as I chose the film somewhat carelessly, and found myself watching three men staggering on their parched way through a blazing desert sharing their rations into ever dwindling morsels.

After that I went to the Turkish baths in Jermyn Street and spent the whole night there, sweating gently all evening and again when I woke in the morning. Then I went back to the flat and ate three more boiled eggs, which I no longer cared for very much, and at last made my way to Hereford.

The needle quivered when I sat on the scales with the lightest possible saddle and thin boots. It swung up over the ten stone mark and pendulumed down and finally settled a hair's breadth on the right side.

'Ten stone,' said the clerk of the scales in a surprised voice. 'What have you been doing? Sandpapering it off?'

'More or less,' I grinned.

In the parade ring James Axminster looked at the number boards where the weights the horses carried were recorded, if they differed from those printed in the race cards. He turned back to me.

'No overweight?' he asked.

'No, sir,' I said matter-of-factly, as if it were the easiest thing in the world.

'Hm.' He beckoned the lad who was leading round the slow old plug I was to ride and said, 'You'll have to kick this old mare along a bit. She's lazy. A good jumper, but that's about all.'

I was used to kicking lazy horses. I kicked, and the mare jumped: and we finished third.

'Hm,' said Axminster again as I unbuckled the girths. I took my saddle and weighed in – half a pound lighter – and changed into the colours of the other horse I had been engaged to ride that afternoon, and when I walked out into the weighing-room, Axminster was waiting for me. He had a paper in his hand. He gave it to me without a word.

It was a list of five horses running in various races during the following week. Against each horse's name he had put the weight it had to carry and the race it was to run in. I read through them.

'Well?' he said. 'Can you ride them?'

'I can ride four of them,' I said. 'But I'm already booked for that novice chase on Wednesday.'

'Is it important? Can you get off?' he asked.

I would dearly have liked to say yes. The paper I held was an invitation to my personal paradise, and there was always the chance that if I refused one of his mounts, the man who got it might corner all the future ones.

'I . . . no,' I said, 'I ought not to. It's for the farmer who gave me my first few rides . . .'

Axminster smiled faintly, the lower teeth showing in front. 'Very well. Ride the other four.'

I said, 'Thank you, sir. I'd be glad to.' He turned away, and I folded up the precious list and put it in my pocket.

My other ride later that afternoon was for Corin Kellar. Since Art's death he had employed several different jockeys and moaned to them about the inconvenience of not having a first-class man always on call. As it was his treatment of Art which had driven a first-class man to leave him in the most drastic possible way, Tick-Tock and I considered him a case for psychiatry; but both of us were glad enough to ride his horses, and Tick-Tock had ridden more of them than anyone else.

'If Corin asks you,' I said as we collected our saddles and helmets ready to weigh out for the race, 'will you accept Art's job?'

'If he asks me, yes,' said Tick-Tock. 'He won't harass *me* into the hereafter.' He looked up slantwise from under his rakishly tilted eyebrows, the thin-lipped, wide mouth stretched in a carefree grin. A vivid, almost aggressive sanity moulded the angular planes of his face, and for a moment he seemed to me more than ever to have been born too soon. He was what I pictured twenty-first century man should be – intensely alive, curiously innocent, with no taint of apathy or anger or greed. He made me feel old. He was nineteen.

We went out together to the parade ring.

'Paste on a toothy leer,' he said. 'The eye of the world has swivelled our way.'

I glanced up. From its draughty platform a television camera swung its square snout towards us as it followed the progress of a grey horse round the ring. It tracked briefly over us and moved on.

'I'd forgotten we were on the air,' I said indifferently.

'Oh, yes,' said Tick-Tock, 'and the great man himself is here somewhere too, the one and only M. Kemp-Lore, no less. Puff pastry, that man is.'

'How do you mean?' I asked.

'A quick riser. And full of hot air. But rich, man, and tasty. A good crisp flavour, nice and crunchy.'

I laughed. We joined Corin and he began to give us both our instructions for the race. Tick-Tock's mount was a good one, but I was as usual riding a horse of whom little was expected, and quite rightly, as it turned out. We trailed in a long way behind, and I saw from the numbers going up in the frame that Corin's other horse had won.

Corin and Tick-Tock and the horse's owner were

conducting a mutual admiration session in the winner's enclosure when I walked back to the weighing-room with my saddle, but Corin caught me by the arm as I went past and asked me to come straight out again, when I had dumped my saddle and helmet, to tell him how the horse had run.

When I rejoined him he was talking to a man who had his back towards me. I hovered, not wanting to interrupt, but Corin saw me and beckoned, and I walked across to them. The man turned round. He was in his early thirties, I judged. Of average height and slim build, with good features and light hair. It never ceases to be disconcerting, meeting for the first time in the flesh a man whose face is as familiar to you as a brother's. It was Maurice Kemp-Lore.

Television is unflattering to everybody. It fattens the body and flattens the personality, so that to sparkle from the small screen an entertainer must be positively incandescent in real life, and Kemp-Lore was no exception. The charm which came over gradually in his programme was instantly compelling when one met him. Intensely blue eyes looked at me from a firm, sun-tanned face; his hand-shake was quick and strong, his smile, infectious and warm, indicated his delight in meeting me. But it was a professional delight, and even as I responded to him I recognized that the effect he had on me was calculated. His stock in trade. All good interviewers know how to give people confidence so that they expand and flower, and Kemp-Lore was a master of his art. Dull men had shone as wits in his programme, taciturn men chattered, bigoted men thought again.

'I see you were last in the race,' he said. 'Bad luck.'

'Bad horse,' said Corin, put into smiling good humour by his presence.

'I've been wanting for some time to do a programme on – if you'll forgive me – an unsuccessful jockey.' His smile took the sting out of his words. 'Or at least, a jockey who is not yet successful. Perhaps that would be a fairer way of putting it?' His blue eyes twinkled. 'Would you consider coming on my programme and telling viewers what sort of life you lead? I have in mind your financial position, your reliance on chance rides, insecurity . . . that sort of thing. Just to give the public the reverse side of the coin. They know all about big retainers and fat presents and jockeys who win important races. I want to show them how a jockey who seldom wins even unimportant races manages to live. A jockey on the fringe.' He smiled his warm smile. 'Will you do it?'

'Yes,' I said, 'certainly. But I'm not really typical. I . . .'

He interrupted me. 'Don't tell me anything now,' he said, 'I know enough about your career to find you suitable for what I have in mind, but I always prefer not to know the answers to my specific questions until we are actually on the air. It makes the whole thing more spontaneous. I have found that if I rehearse with

my subject what we are going to say the programme
comes over stiffly and unconvincingly. Instead, I will
send you a list of the sort of questions I will be asking,
and you can think out your replies. 'O.K.?'

'Yes,' I said. 'All right.'

'Good. Next Friday then. The programme goes out
at nine o'clock. Get to the studios by seven-thirty, will
you? That gives time for seeing to lighting, make-up,
and so on, and perhaps for a drink beforehand. Here
is a card which will tell you how to get there.' He
produced a card which had 'Universal Telecast' printed
in large capitals on one side and a simplified map of
Willesden on the other.

'Oh, and by the way, there will be a fee, of course,
and your expenses.' He smiled sympathetically, letting
me know that he knew that that was good news.

'Thank you,' I smiled back. 'I'll be there.'

He spoke a word to Corin and strolled away. I
turned to Corin and caught on his face as he watched
the retreating figure of Kemp-Lore, the same
expression that I saw so often on hangers-on round
my parents. The smug, fawning smirk which meant 'I
am on speaking terms with a famous person, clever
me.' It would have been more impressive, I thought,
if like most other trainers he had taken knowing the
illustrious Kemp-Lore entirely for granted.

'I know Maurice quite well,' said Corin aloud, in a
self-satisfied voice. 'He asked my advice about whether

you'd be any good as his – er – unsuccessful jockey, and I told him to go ahead.'

'Thanks,' I said, as he waited for it.

'Yes, a grand fellow, Maurice. Good family, you know. His father won the National – an amateur of course – and his sister is the best lady point-to-point rider there has been for years. Poor old Maurice, though, he hardly rises at all. Doesn't even hunt. Horses give him the most ghastly asthma, you know. He's very cut-up about it. Still, he'd never have taken to broadcasting if he'd been able to race, so perhaps it's all for the best.'

'I dare say,' I said. I was still in lightweight silk colours and breeches and the afternoon was growing cool. I dragged the conversation back to the horse I had just come last on, got the post-mortem over, and eventually went back to the weighing-room to change.

The jockeys had already gone out for the last race, but several others were standing about in various stages of undress, gossiping and putting on their street clothes. As I went down the room I saw Grant Oldfield standing by my peg, holding a paper in his hand, and I was annoyed to find, drawing nearer, that it was the list of horses James Axminster had given me. Grant had been going through my pockets.

My protest was never uttered. Without a word, without any warning, Grant swung his fist and punched me heavily in the nose.

CHAPTER FOUR

The amount of blood which resulted would have done credit to a clinic full of donors. It splashed in a scarlet stain down the front of my pale green silk shirt and made big uneven blotches on the white breeches. There were large spots of it on the bench and on the floor and it was all over my hands where I had tried to wipe it out of my mouth.

'For God's sake, lay him down on his back,' said one of the valets, hurrying over. His advice was almost unnecessary, since I was already lying down, mostly on the floor but half propped up by the leg of the bench. It was where that one blow, catching me off balance, had felled me.

Grant stood at my feet, looking down as if surprised to have caused so much mess. I could have laughed if I had not been so busy swallowing what seemed like cupfuls of my own blood.

Young Mike thrust a saddle under my shoulders and pushed my head backwards over it. A second later he was piling a cold, wet towel across the bridge of my nose; and gradually the breath-clogging bleeding lessened and stopped.

'You'd better stay there for a bit,' said Mike. 'I'll go and get one of the first-aid men to see to you.'

'Don't bother,' I said. 'Please don't bother, it's all right now.'

He came back irresolutely from the door and stood by my head. He looked upside down to me, as my eyes were level with his ankles.

'What the hell did you do that for?' he said to Grant.

I wanted to hear his answer too, but Grant did not reply. He scowled down at me, then turned on his heel and pushed his way out of the changing-room against the incoming tide of the jockeys returning from the last race. The list of Axminster horses fluttered to the floor in his wake. Mike picked it up and put it into my outstretched hand.

Tick-Tock dumped his saddle on the bench, tipped back his helmet, and put his hands on his hips.

'What have we here? A blood bath?' he said.

'Nose bleed,' I said.

'You don't say.'

The others began crowding round and I decided I'd been lying down long enough. I lifted the towel off my face and stood up gingerly. All was well. The fountains had dried up.

'Grant socked him one,' said one of the jockeys who had been there all the time.

'Why?'

'Ask me another,' I said. 'Or ask Grant.'

'You ought to report it to the stewards.'

'It's not worth it,' I said.

I cleaned myself up and changed, and walked down to the station with Tick-Tock.

'You must know why he hit you,' he said. 'Or was it merely target practice?'

I handed him Axminster's list. He read it and gave it back.

'Yes, I see. Hatred, envy and jealousy. You're stepping into the shoes he couldn't fill himself. He had his chance there, and he muffed it.'

'What happened?' I asked. 'Why did Axminster drop him?'

'I don't honestly know,' Tick-Tock said, 'you'd better ask Grant and find out what mistakes not to make.' He grinned. 'Your nose looks like a vulgar seaside postcard.'

'It's good enough for the goggle box,' I said. I told him about Maurice Kemp-Lore's invitation.

'My dear sir,' he said, sweeping off his Tyrolean hat, and making me a mocking bow. 'I am impressed.'

'You're a fool,' I said, grinning.

'Thank God.'

We went our ways, Tick-Tock to his digs in Berkshire and I to Kensington. The flat was empty, the usual state of affairs on Saturday evenings, a busy night for concerts. I took half the ice cubes from the refrigerator, wrapped them in a plastic bag and a tea towel and lay down on the bed with the ice bag balanced on my forehead. My nose felt like a jelly. Grant's fist had had the power of severe mental disturbance behind it.

I shut my eyes and thought about them, Grant and Art; two disintegrated people. One had been driven to violence against himself, and the other had turned violent against the world. Poor things, I thought rather too complacently, they were not stable enough to deal with whatever had undermined them: and I remembered that easy pity, later on.

On the following Wednesday Peter Cloony came to the races bubbling over with happiness. The baby was a boy, his wife was fine, everything was rosy. He slapped us all on the back and told us we didn't know what we were missing. The horse he rode that afternoon started favourite and ran badly, but it didn't damp his spirits.

The next day he was due to ride in the first race, and he was late. We knew before he arrived that he had missed his chance, because five minutes before the deadline for declaring jockeys his trainer had sent an official into the changing-room to find out if he was there, and he wasn't.

I was standing outside the weighing-room when Peter finally came, forty minutes before the first race.

He was running over the grass, anxiety clear on his face even from a distance. His trainer detached himself from the group of people had he been talking to and intercepted him. Fragments of angry remarks floated across to me.

'Is this your idea of an hour before the first? . . . I've had to get another jockey . . . very stupid of you . . . second time in a week . . . irresponsible . . . not the way to go on if you want to keep your job with me . . .' He stalked away.

Peter brushed past me, white, trembling and looking sick, and when I went back into the changing-room a short time later he was sitting on a bench with his head in his hands.

'What happened this time?' I asked. 'Is your wife all right? And the baby?' I thought he must have been so busy attending to them that he had forgotten to watch the clock.

'They're fine,' he said miserably. 'My mother-in-law is staying with us to look after them. I wasn't late setting out . . . only five minutes or so . . . but . . .' he stood up and gazed at me with his large, moist-looking eyes, '. . . you'll never believe it but there was something else stuck across the lane, and I had to go miles round again, even further than last time . . .' His voice trailed off as I looked at him in disbelief.

'Not another tank carrier?' I asked incredulously.

'No, a car. An old car, one of those heavy old Jaguars. It had its nose in the hedge and one front wheel in the ditch, and it was jammed tight, right across the lane.'

'You couldn't have helped its driver push it straight again?' I asked.

'There wasn't any driver. No one at all. And the car doors were locked, and the hand-brake was full on, and he'd left the thing in gear. The stinking bastard.' Peter seldom used such strong language. 'Another man had driven up the hill behind me and we both tried to shift the Jag, but it was absolutely hopeless. We had to reverse again for miles, and he had to go first, and he wouldn't hurry a yard . . . he had a new car and he was afraid of scratching it.'

'It's very bad luck,' I said inadequately.

'Bad luck!' he repeated explosively, apparently near to tears. 'It's more than bad luck it's – it's awful. I can't afford . . . I need the money . . .' He stopped talking and swallowed several times, and sniffed, 'We've got a mortgage to pay off,' he said, 'and I didn't know babies could cost so much. And my wife had to stop working, which we hadn't reckoned on . . . we didn't mean to have a baby so soon.'

I remembered vividly the new little bungalow with its cheap, blue linoleum, its home-made terra-cotta rugs, it bare, bare furnishings. And he had a car to run and now a child to keep. I saw that the loss of a ten guinea riding fee was a calamity.

He had not been booked for any other ride that afternoon, and he spent the whole day mooching about the weighing-room so as to be under the eye of any trainers looking hurriedly for a jockey. He wore a desperate, hunted look all the time, and I knew that that alone would have discouraged me, had I been a trainer. He left, unemployed and disconsolate, just before the fifth race, having done himself no good at all in the eyes of every trainer at the meeting.

I watched him trailing off to the car park as I walked down from the weighing-room to the parade ring for my own one-and-only ride of the day, and I felt a surge of irritation against him. Why couldn't he pretend a little, make light of his misfortune, shrug it off? And why above all didn't he leave himself a margin for error on his journeys, when unprompt arrivals cost him so much? A punctured tyre, a windscreen shattered by a flying stone, anything might make him late. It didn't have to be as unforeseeable as a tank carrier or a locked Jaguar wedged immovably across his path. And what a dismal coincidence, I reflected, that it should have happened twice in a week.

James Axminster smiled his disconcerting, heavy-jawed smile in the parade ring and introduced me to the owner of the horse I was to ride. He shook hands and we made the usual desultory pre-race conversation. The middle-aged handicap hurdler plodding sleepily round the ring was the third Axminster horse I had ridden during the week, and I had already grown to appreciate the sleekness and slickness of his organization. His horses were well schooled and beautifully turned out, and there was nothing makeshift or second-best in any of his equipment. Success and prosperity spoke from every brightly initialled horse rug, every top quality bridle, every brush, bandage and bucket that came to the meetings.

In the two earlier races that week I had been riding the stable's second string while Pip Pankhurst took his usual place on the better horses. Thursday's handicap hurdle, however, was all my own because Pip could not do the weight.

'Anything under ten stone six, and it's yours,' he told me, cheerfully, when he found I was riding some of his stable's horses. 'Anything under ten six is hardly worth riding, anyway.'

By eating and drinking very little I had managed to keep my riding weight down to ten stone for a whole week. This meant a body weight of nine stone eight, which was a strain at my height, but with Pip in that ungrudging frame of mind it was well worth it.

James Axminster said, 'At the fourth hurdle, you want to be somewhere in the middle. About three from home, providing they're not too strung out, you want to lie about fourth. He takes some time to get into top gear, so start him moving going into the second last. Keep him going, try to come up to the leader at the last and see how much you can gain in the air there. This horse is a great jumper, but has

61

no finishing speed. Very one-paced. See what you can do, anyway.'

He had not given me such detailed instructions before, and it was the first time he had mentioned anything about what to do at the last obstacle. I felt a deep quiver of excitement in my stomach. At last I was about to ride a horse whose trainer would not be thoroughly surprised if he won.

I followed my instructions to the letter, and coming into the last hurdle level with two other horses I kicked my old mount with all the determination I could muster. He responded with a zipping leap which sped him clean past the other horses in mid-air and landed us a good two lengths clear of them. I heard the clatter of the hurdles as the others rapped them, and basely hoped they had made stumbling, time-wasting landings. It was true that the old hurdler could not quicken. I got him balanced and ran him straight to the winning post, using my whip hardly at all and concentrating mainly on sitting still and not disturbing him. He held on gamely, and still had half a length in hand when we passed the post. It was a gorgeous moment.

'Well done,' said Axminster matter-of-factly. Winners were nothing out of the ordinary to him. I unbuckled the girths and slid the saddle off over my arm, and patted the hurdler's sweating neck.

The owner was delighted. 'Well done, well done,' he said to the horse, Axminster and me indiscriminately. 'I never thought he'd pull it off, James, even though I took your advice and backed him.'

I looked quickly at Axminster. His piercingly blue eyes regarded me quizzically.

'Do you want the job?' he asked. 'Second to Pip, regular?'

I nodded and dragged in a deep breath, and said, 'Yes.' It sounded like a croak.

The hurdler's owner laughed. 'It's Finn's lucky week. John Ballerton tells me Maurice is interviewing him on his television programme tomorrow evening.'

'Really?' Axminster said. 'I'll try and watch it.'

I went to weigh in and change, and when I came out Axminster gave me another list of horses, four of them, which he wanted me to ride the following week.

'From now on,' he said, 'I don't want you to accept any rides without finding out first if I need you. All right?'

'Yes, sir,' I said, trying not to show too much of the idiotic delight I was feeling. But he knew. He was too old a hand not to. His eyes glimmered with understanding and friendliness and promise.

I telephoned to Joanna. 'How about dinner? I want to celebrate.'

'What?' she asked economically.

'A winner. A new job. All's right with the world,' I said.

'You sound as if you've been celebrating already.'

'No,' I said. 'Any drunkenness you can hear in my voice is due to being hit on the head by good luck.'

She laughed. 'All right then. Where?'

'Hennibert's,' I said. It was a small restaurant in St James's Street with a standard of cooking to match its address, and prices to match both.

'Oh yes,' said Joanna. 'Shall I come in my golden coach?'

'I mean it,' I said. 'I've earned forty pounds this week. I want to spend some of it. And besides, I'm hungry.'

'You won't get a table,' she said.

'It's booked.'

'I'm sold,' she said. 'I'll be there at eight.'

She came in a taxi, a compliment to me as she was a girl who liked walking. She wore a dress I had not seen before, a slender straight affair made of a firm, deep-blue material which moved with a faint shimmer when the light fell on it. Her springy dark hair curved neatly down on to the nape of her neck, and the slanting outward tapering lines she had drawn on her eyelids made her black eyes look bigger and deep set and mysterious. Every male head turned to look at her as we walked down the room: yet she was not pretty, not eye-catchingly glamorous, not even notably well dressed. She looked ... I surprised myself with the word ... intelligent.

We ate avocados with french dressing and *boeuf stroganoff* with spinach, and late crop strawberries and cream, and a mushroom and bacon and prune savoury. For me, after so many bird-sized meals, it was a feast. We took a long time eating and drank a bottle of wine, and sat over our coffee talking with the ease of a friendship which stretched back to childhood. Most of the time, after so much practice, I could keep my more uncousinly feelings for Joanna well concealed from her; and it was necessary to conceal them because I knew from past experience that if I even approached the subject of love she would begin to fidget and avoid my eyes, and would very soon find a good reason for leaving. If I wanted to enjoy her company, it had to be on her terms.

She seemed genuinely pleased about the James Axminster job. Even though racing didn't interest her, she saw clearly what it meant to me.

'It's like the day the musical director at the Handel Society picked me out of the choir to sing my first recitative. I felt like a pouter pigeon and so full of air that I thought I would need guy-ropes to keep my feet on the ground.'

'Heady stuff,' I agreed. My first elation had settled down to a warm cosy glow of satisfaction. I did not remember ever having felt so content.

I told her about the television programme.

'Tomorrow?' she said. 'Good, I think I'll be free to watch you. You don't do things by halves, do you?'

I grinned. 'This is just the start,' I said. I almost believed it.

We walked all the way back to Joanna's studio. It was a clear crisp night with the stars blazing coldly in the black sky. Depth upon depth of infinity. We stopped in the dark mews outside Joanna's door and looked up.

'They put things into proportion, don't they?' she said.

'Yes.' I wondered what it was that she needed to see in proportion. I looked at her. It was a mistake. The up-tilted face with starlight reflected in the shadowy eyes, the dark hair tousled again by our walk, the strong line of throat, the jut of breasts close to my arm, they swept me ruthlessly into the turmoil I had been suppressing all evening.

'Thank you for coming,' I said abruptly. 'Good night, Joanna.'

She said, surprised, 'Wouldn't you like some more coffee . . . or something?'

Or something. Yes.

I said, 'I couldn't eat or drink another thing. Anyway . . . there's Brian . . .'

'Brian's in Manchester, on tour,' she said. But it was a statement of fact, not an invitation.

'Oh. Well, all the same, I think I'd better get some sleep,' I said.

'All right, then.' She was undisturbed. 'A lovely dinner, Rob. Thank you.' She put her hand for a moment on my shoulder in a friendly fashion and smiled good night. She put the key in her door and opened it and waved briefly to me as I turned and started back down the mews. She shut her door. I swore violently, aloud. It wasn't much relief. I looked up at the sky. The stars went on whizzing round in their courses, uncaring and cold.

CHAPTER FIVE

They gave me what in the Finn family was known as
F.I.P. treatment at the Universal Telecast Studios.
Fairly Important Person. It meant being met by
someone well enough up in the hierarchy of the
organization for it to be clear that trouble was being
taken, but not so high that he needed to be supported
by lieutenants.

My mother was a connoisseur of all the shades
between V.I.P. and F.I.P. and invariably noticed every
detail of the pains or lack of them taken to make her
feel comfortable. Her awareness had rubbed off on to
me at a very early age and the whole gambit caused me
a lot of quiet amusement when I grew up. Years of
being a U.I.P. (Unimportant Person) had only
sharpened my appreciation.

I went through the swinging glass doors into the
large echoing entrance hall and asked the girl at
the reception desk where I should go. She smiled
kindly. Would I sit down, she said, gesturing to a near-

68

by sofa. I sat. She spoke down the telephone, 'Mr Finn is here, Gordon.'

Within ten seconds a burly young man with freckles and a rising-young-executive, navy-blue, pin-striped suit advanced briskly from one of the corridors.

'Mr Finn?' he said expansively, holding out a hand protruding from a snowy, gold-linked shirt cuff.

'Yes,' I said, standing up and shaking hands.

'Glad to have you here. I am Gordon Kildare, Associate Producer. Maurice is up in the studio running over the last-minute details, so I suggest we go along and have a drink and a sandwich first.' He led the way down the corridor he had come from and we turned in through an open door into a small impersonal reception room. On the table stood bottles and glasses and four plates of fat freshly-cut and appetizing-looking sandwiches.

'What will you have?' he asked hospitably, his hands hovering over the bottles.

'Nothing, thank you,' I said.

He was not put out. 'Perhaps afterwards, then?' He poured some whisky into a glass, added soda and raised it to me, smiling. 'Good luck,' he said. 'Is this your first time on television?'

I nodded.

'The great thing is to be natural.' He picked up a sandwich with a pink filling and took a squelchy bite.

The door opened and two more men came in. Introduced to me as Dan something and Paul something, they were a shade less carefully dressed than Gordon Kildare, to whom they deferred. They too dug into the sandwiches and filled their glasses, and wished me luck and told me to be natural.

Maurice Kemp-Lore strode briskly in with a couple of sports-jacketed assistants in tow.

'My dear chap,' he greeted me, shaking me warmly by the hand. 'Glad to see you're here in good time. Has Gordon been looking after you? That's right. Now, what are you drinking?'

'Nothing just now,' I said.

'Oh? Oh well, never mind. Perhaps afterwards? You got the list of questions all right?'

I nodded.

'Have you thought out some answers?'

'Yes,' I said.

'Good, good. That's fine,' he said.

Gordon handed him a well-filled glass and offered him the sandwiches. The assistants helped themselves. It dawned on me that the refreshments provided for the entertainment of visitors probably served all of them as their main evening meal.

Kemp-Lore looked at his watch. 'Our other guest is cutting it rather fine.' As he spoke, the telephone rang. Gordon answered it, listened briefly, said 'He's here, Maurice,' and opened the door.

Kemp-Lore went out first, followed by Gordon and either Dan or Paul, who looked very much alike. It was a more impressive welcoming committee than had been accorded me: I smiled to think of what my mother would have said.

A sports-jacketed assistant offered me sandwiches.

'No?' he said. 'Oh, well, a lot of people feel like that beforehand. You'll be very hungry afterwards.' He put two sandwiches carefully together and stretched open his mouth to bite them.

The voice of Kemp-Lore could be heard coming back along the corridor talking with someone who spoke in a harsh voice with a nasal twang. I wondered idly who the other guest would be and whether I knew him. At the doorway Kemp-Lore stood respectfully back to let his guest precede him into the room. My spirits sank. Paunch and horn-rims well to the fore, Mr John Ballerton allowed himself to be ushered in.

Kemp-Lore introduced all the television men to him. 'And Rob Finn, of course, you know?' he said.

Ballerton nodded coldly in my direction without meeting my eyes. Evidently it still rankled with him that I had seen him sicking up beside Art's body. Perhaps he knew that I had not kept it a secret from the other jockeys.

'It's time we went up to the studio, I think,' Kemp-Lore said, looking enquiringly at Gordon, who nodded.

We all filed out into the corridor, and as I passed the table I noticed the sandwich plates now held nothing but crumbs and a few straggly pieces of cress.

The smallish studio held a chaotic-looking tangle of cameras trailing their thick cables over the floor. To one side there was a shallow carpet-covered platform on which stood three low-slung chairs and a coffee table. A tray with three cups, cream jug and sugar basin shared the table with three empty balloon brandy glasses, a silver cigarette box and two large glass ash-trays.

Kemp-Lore took Ballerton and me towards this arrangement.

'We want to look as informal as possible,' he said pleasantly. 'As if we had just had dinner and were talking over coffee and brandy and cigars.'

He asked Ballerton to sit in the left-hand chair and me in the right, and then took his place between us. Set in front and slightly to one side stood a monitor set with a blank screen; and in a semicircle a battery of cameras converged their menacing black lenses in our direction.

Gordon and his assistants spent some time checking their lights, which dazed us with a dazzling intensity for a few moments, and then tested for sound while the three of us made stilted conversation over the empty cups. When he was satisfied, Gordon came over to us. 'You all need make-up,' he said. 'Maurice, you'll see to yours as usual? Then Mr Ballerton and Mr Finn, I'll show you where to go, if you will follow me?'

He led us to a small room off one corner of the studio. There were two girls in pink overalls and bright smiles.

'It won't take long,' they said, smoothing coloured

cream into our skins. 'Just a little darkener under the
eyes ... that's right. Now powder ...' They patted
the powder on with pads of cotton wool, carefully
flicking off the excess. 'That's all.'

I looked in the mirror. The make-up softened and
blurred both the outlines of the face and texture of
the skin. I didn't much care for it.

'You'd look ill on television without it,' the girls
assured us. 'You need make-up to look natural and
healthy.'

Ballerton frowned and complained as one of them
powdered the bald patch on his head. The girl insisted
politely. 'It'll shine too much otherwise, you see,' she
said, and went on patting his head with the cotton
wool.

He caught me grinning at him and it clearly made
him furious, raising a dark flush under the sun-tone
make-up. There was no question of his ever sharing a
rueful joke at his own expense, and I should have
known it. I sighed to myself. This made twice that I
had seen him at what he considered a disadvantage,
and though I had not meant at all to antagonize him,
it seemed that I had made a thorough job of it.

We went back into the studio and Kemp-Lore
beckoned to us to take our places in the chairs on the
platform.

'I'll just run through the order of the programme,'
he said, 'so that you will know what to expect. After
the introductory music I am going to talk to you first,

73

John, along the lines we discussed. After that, Rob will tell us what his sort of life entails. We have some film of a race you rode in, Rob, which we are using as an illustration, and I plan to fit that in fairly near the beginning of our talk. It will be thrown on to that screen over there.' He pointed.

'For the last few minutes, John will have a chance to comment on what you have said and we might have a final word or two from you. We'll see how it goes. Now, the great thing is to talk naturally. I've explained that too much rehearsal spoils the spontaneity of a programme like this, but it means that a lot of the success of the next quarter of an hour depends on you. I'm sure you will both do splendidly.' He finished his pep talk with a cheerful grin, and I did in fact feel confidence flowing into me from him.

One of the sports-jacketed assistants stepped on to the shallow platform with a coffee pot in one hand and a brandy bottle in the other. He poured hot black coffee into the three cups, and put the pot down on the tray. Then he uncorked the brandy and wet the bottom of the balloon glasses.

'No expense spared,' he said cheerfully. He produced three cigars from the breast pocket of the sports jacket and offered them to us. Ballerton accepted one and sniffed it and rolled it between his fingers, curving his bad-tempered mouth into what passed with him for a smile.

'Two minutes,' shouted a voice.

The spotlights flashed on, dazzling as before, blacking out everything in the studio. For a moment the monitor set showed a close-up of the coffee cups: then it went dark and the next picture on it was an animated cartoon advertising petrol. It was tuned now to what was actually being transmitted.

'Thirty seconds. Quiet please. Quiet please,' Gordon said.

A hush fell over the whole area. I glanced at the monitor set in front of us. It was busy with a silent advertisement for soap flakes. Dimly seen beyond the lights, Gordon stood with his hand raised. There was dead silence. Steam rose gently from the three coffee cups. Everyone waited. Kemp-Lore beside me arranged his features in the well-known smile, looking straight ahead at the round black lens of the camera. The smile stayed in position for ten seconds without wavering.

On the monitor set the superimposed horses galloped and faded. Gordon's hand swept down briskly. The camera in front of Kemp-Lore developed a shining red eye and he began to speak, pleasantly, intimately, straight into a million sitting-rooms.

'Good evening . . . tonight I am going to introduce you to two people who are both deeply involved with National Hunt racing, but who look at it, so to speak, from opposite poles. First, here is Mr John Ballerton . . .' He gave him a good build-up but overdid the importance. There were about forty-nine other members of the National Hunt Committee, including Kemp-Lore's own father, all at least as active and devoted as the fat man now basking in praise.

Skilfully guided by Kemp-Lore, he talked about his duties as one of the three stewards at a race meeting. It involved, he said, hearing both sides if there was an objection to a winner and awarding the race justly to the more deserving, and yes, summoning jockeys and trainers for minor infringements of the rules and fining them a fiver or a tenner a time.

I watched him on the monitor set. I had to admit he looked a solid, sober, responsible citizen with right on his side. The aggressive horn rims gave him, on the screen, a definite air of authority; also for the occasion his habitually sour expression had given way to a rather persuasive geniality. No one watching the performance Kemp-Lore coaxed out of him would have suspected him to be the bigoted, pompous bully we knew on the racecourse. I understood at last how he had come to be voted on to the National Hunt Committee.

Before I expected it, Kemp-Lore was turning round to me. I swallowed convulsively. He smiled at the camera.

'And now,' he said with the air of one producing a treat, 'here is Rob Finn. This is a young steeplechase jockey just scratching the surface of his career. Few of you will have heard of him. He has won no big races, nor ridden any well-known horses, and that is why I have invited him here tonight to meet you, to give us all a glimpse of what it is like to break into a highly competitive sport . . .'

The red light was burning on the camera pointing at me. I smiled at it faintly. My tongue stuck to the roof of my mouth.

'First,' he went on, 'here is a piece of film which shows Finn in action. He is the rider with the white cap, fourth from last.'

We watched on the monitor set. I was all too easy to pick out. It was one of the first races I ever rode in, and my inexperience showed sorely. During the few seconds the film lasted the white cap lost two places, and as an illustration of an unsuccessful jockey it could not have been bettered.

The film faded out and Kemp-Lore said, smiling, 'How did you set about starting to be a jockey, once you had decided on it?'

I said, 'I knew three farmers who owned and trained their own horses, and I asked them to let me try my hand in a race.'

'And they did?'

'Yes, in the end,' I agreed. I could have added, 'After I had promised to return the riding fees and not even ask for expenses'; but the method I had used to persuade a string of farmers to give me rides was strictly against the rules.

'Usually,' Kemp-Lore said, turning towards the camera which immediately glowed with its red eye, 'jumping jockeys either start as amateur steeplechase riders or as apprentices on the flat, but I understand that you did neither of these things, Rob?'

'No,' I said. 'I started too old to be an apprentice and couldn't be an amateur because I had earned my living riding horses.'

'As a stable lad?' He put it in the form of a question but from his intonation he clearly expected me to say yes. It was, after all by far the commonest background of jockeys riding as few races as I had been doing.

'No,' I said.

He was waiting for me to go on, his eyebrows a fraction raised in a tinge of surprise mingled with what looked like the beginning of apprehension. Well, I thought in amusement, you wouldn't listen when I said I was hardly typical, so if my answers are not what you expect, it's entirely your own fault.

I said, 'I was away from England for some years, wandering round the world, you know? Mainly in Australia and South America. Most of the time I got jobs as a stockman, but I spent a year in New South Wales working as a hand in a travelling rodeo. Ten seconds on the bucking bronc: that sort of thing.' I grinned.

'Oh.' The eyebrows rose another fraction, and there was a perceptible pause before he said, 'How very interesting.' He sounded as if he meant it. He went on, 'I wish we had more time to hear about your experiences, but I want to give viewers a picture of the economics of a jockey in your position ... trying to make a living on a race or two a week. Now, your fee is ten guineas a time, that's right? ...'

He took me at some length through my finances, which didn't sound too good when dissected into travelling expenses, valets' fees, replacement of kit, and so on. It emerged quite clearly that my net income over the last two years was less than I could have earned driving a delivery van, and that my future prospects were not demonstrably much better. I could almost feel the thought clicking into the viewers' heads that I was a fool.

Kemp-Lore turned deferentially to Ballerton. 'John, have you any comment to make on what we have been hearing from Rob?'

A trace of purely malicious pleasure crept into Ballerton's man-of-authority smile.

'All these young jockeys complain too much,' he stated in his harsh voice, ignoring the fact that I had not complained at all. 'If they aren't very good at their job they shouldn't expect to be highly paid. Racehorse owners don't want to waste their money and their horses' chances by putting up jockeys in whom they have no confidence. I speak as an owner myself, of course.'

'Eh ... of course,' said Kemp-Lore. 'But surely every jockey has to make a start? And there must always be large numbers of jockeys who never quite reach the top grade, but who have a living to make, and families to support.'

'They'd be better off in a factory, earning a fair wage on a production line,' said Ballerton, with heavy, reasonable-sounding humour. 'If they can't endure the fact that they are unsuccessful without snivelling about how poor they are, they ought to get out of racing altogether. Not many of them do,' he added with an unkind chuckle, 'because they like wearing those bright silks. People turn to look at them as they go by, and it flatters their little egos.'

There was a gasp somewhere out in the dark studio at this ungentlemanly blow below the belt, and I saw out of the corner of my eye that the red spot on the camera pointing at me was glowing. What expression it had initially caught on my face I did not know, but I raised a smile for Mr Ballerton then, as sweet and cheerful and forgiving a smile as ever turned the other cheek. It was made easier by the certain knowledge that wearing bright shirts was if anything an embarrassment to me, not a gratification.

Kemp-Lore's head switched to me. 'And what do you say to that, Rob?'

I spoke truthfully, vehemently, and straight from the heart. 'Give me a horse and a race to ride it in, and I don't care if I wear silks or ... or ... pyjamas. I don't care if there's anyone watching or not. I don't care if I don't earn much money, or if I break my bones, or if I have to starve to keep my weight down. All I care about is racing ... racing ... and winning, if I can.'

There was a small silence.

'I can't explain it,' I said.

Both of them were staring at me. John Ballerton looked as if a squashed wasp had revived and stung him, and his earlier animosity settled and deepened into a scowl. And Kemp-Lore? There was an expression on his face that I could not read at all. There were only a few empty seconds before he turned smoothly back to his camera and slid the familiar smile into place, but I felt irrationally that something important had taken place in them. I found it oddly disturbing not to have the slightest clue to what it was.

Kemp-Lore launched into his usual review of the following week's racing, and was very soon closing the programme with the customary words, 'See you all next week at the same time ...'

The image on the monitor faded on Kemp-Lore's smile and changed to another soap advertisement. The hot spotlight flicked off and my eyes began to get used to not being dazzled.

Gordon strode up beaming. 'A very good programme. It came over well. Just what they like, an argument with an edge to it. Well done, well done, Mr Ballerton, Mr Finn. Splendid.' He shook us both by the hand.

Kemp-Lore stood up and stretched and grinned around at us all. 'Well, John. Well, Rob. Thank you both very much.' He bent down, picked up my brandy glass and handed it to me. 'Drink it,' he said, 'you deserve it.' He smiled warmly. He crackled with released tension.

I smiled back and drank the brandy, and reflected again how superlative he was at his job. By encouraging Ballerton to needle me he had drawn from me, for the ears of a few million strangers, a more soul-baring statement than I would ever have made privately to a close friend.

A good deal of back-slapping followed, and more plates of sandwiches were dealt with downstairs in the reception room before I left the television building and went back to Kensington. In view of the approval which had been generously, if undeservedly, heaped upon Ballerton and me after the show, I wondered why it was that I felt more apprehensive than I had before I started.

CHAPTER SIX

Three weeks and a day after the broadcast, Pip Pankhurst broke his leg. His horse, falling with him and on him at the last hurdle of the second race on a dreary, drizzly mid-November Saturday afternoon, made a thorough job of putting the champion jockey out of action for the bulk of the 'chasing season.

The first-aid men beside the hurdle were slow to move him into the ambulance for the good reason that a sharp arrow of shin bone was sticking out at a crazy angle through a tear in the thin leather racing boot; and they finally managed to lift him on to a stretcher, one of them told me later, only because Pip slid off into a dead faint.

From the stands I saw only the white flag waving, the ambulance creeping down over the bumpy ground, and the flat, ominously unmoving figure of Pip on the grass. It would be untrue to say that I went down the stairs to the weighing-room with a calm heart. However sincere my pity for his plight might be, the faint chance that I might take his place in the following race was playing hop, skip and jump with my pulse.

It was the big race of the day, the big race of the week, a three-mile chase with a substantial prize put up by a firm of brewers. It had attracted a good number of top horses and had been well discussed on the sports pages of all the day's papers. Pip's mount, which belonged to Lord Tirrold, was the rising star of the Axminster stable; a stringy six-year-old brown gelding with nothing much to recommend him at first sight, but intelligent, fast, and a battler. He had all the qualities of a world beater, and his best years lay ahead. At present he was still reckoned 'promising'. He was called Template.

Stifling hope is a hopeless business. As I went into the weighing-room I saw James Axminster talking to Pip's close friend, another leading jockey. The jockey shook his head, and across the room I watched his lips say, 'No, I can't.'

Axminster turned slowly round looking at faces. I stood still and waited. Gradually his head came round and he saw me. He looked at me steadily, pondering, unsmiling. Then his eyes were past me and focused on someone to my left. He came to a decision and walked briskly past me.

Well, what did I expect? I had ridden for him for only four weeks. Three winners. A dozen also-rans. During the past fortnight I had taken digs in the village near his stable and ridden out at exercise on his horses every morning; but I was still the new boy, the unknown, unsuccessful jockey of the television programme. I began to walk disconsolately over to the changing room door.

'Rob,' he said in my ear. 'Lord Tirrold says you can ride his horse. You'd better tell Pip's valet; he has the colours.'

I half-turned towards them. They stood together, the two tall men, looking at me appraisingly, knowing they were giving me the chance of a lifetime, but not sure that I was up to it.

'Yes, sir,' I said; and I went on into the changing-room, queerly steadied by having believed that I had been passed over.

I rode better than I had ever done before, but that was probably because Template was the best horse I had ever ridden. He was smooth and steely, and his rocketing spring over the first fence had me gasping; but I was ready for it at the second, and exulted in it at the third; and by the fourth I knew I had entered a new dimension of racing.

Neither Axminster nor Lord Tirrold had given me any orders in the paddock on how to shape the race. They had been too concerned about Pip, whom they had just briefly visited. The sight of his shattered leg had left them upset and preoccupied.

Axminster said only, 'Do the best you can, Rob,' and Lord Tirrold, unusually tactless for so diplomatic a man, said gloomily, 'I put a hundred on Template this morning. Oh, well, it's too late to cancel it, I suppose.' Then seeing my rueful amusement, added, 'I beg your pardon, Rob. I'm sure you'll do splendidly.' But he did not sound convinced.

As the pattern of the race shifted and changed, I concentrated solely on keeping Template lying in about fourth position in the field of twelve runners. To be farther back meant leaving him a lot to do at the end, and to be farther forward meant that one could not see how well or how badly everyone else was going. Template jumped himself into third place at the second last fence, and was still not under pressure. Coming towards the last I brought him to the outside, to give him a clear view, and urged him on. His stride immediately quickened. He took off so far in front of the fence that for a heart-breaking second I was sure he would land squarely on top of it, but I had underestimated his power. He landed yards out on the far side, collecting himself without faltering and surged ahead towards the winning post.

One of the two horses close in front had been passed in mid-air over the fence. There remained only a chestnut to be beaten. Only. Only the favourite, the choice of the critics, the public and the press. No disgrace, I fleetingly thought, to be beaten only by him.

I dug my knees into Template's sides and gave him two taps with the whip down his shoulder. He needed only this signal, I found, to put every ounce into getting to the front. He stretched his neck out and flattened his stride, and I knelt on his withers and squeezed him and moved with his rhythm, and kept my whip still for fear of disturbing him. He put his head in front of the chestnut's five strides from the winning post, and kept it there.

I was almost too exhausted to unbuckle the saddle. There was a cheer as we went into the unsaddling enclosure, and a lot of smiling faces, and some complimentary things were said, but I felt too weak and breathless to enjoy them. No race had ever before taken so much out of me. Nor given me so much, either.

Surprisingly Lord Tirrold and Axminster were almost subdued.

'That was all right, then,' said Axminster, the lower teeth glimmering in a smile.

'He's a wonderful horse,' I said fervently.

'Yes,' said Lord Tirrold, 'he is.' He patted the dark sweating neck.

Axminster said, 'Don't hang about then, Rob. Go and weigh in. You haven't any time to waste. You're riding in the next race. And the one after.'

I stared at him.

'Well, what did you expect?' he said. 'Pip's obviously going to be unfit for months. I took you on to ride second to him, and you will stand in for him until he comes back.'

*

Tick-Tock said, 'Some people would climb out of a septic tank smelling of lavender.'

He was waiting for me to change at the end of the afternoon.

'Six weeks ago you were scrounging rides. Then you get yourself on television as a failure and make it obvious you aren't one. Sunday newspapers write columns about you and your version of the creed gets a splash in *The Times* as well. Now you do the understudy-into-star routine, and all that jazz. And properly too. Three winners in one afternoon. What a nerve.'

I grinned at him. 'What goes up must come down. You can pick up the pieces later on.'

I tied my tie and brushed my hair, and looked in the mirror at the fatuous smile I could not remove from my face. Days like this don't happen very often, I thought.

'Let's go and see Pip,' I said abruptly, turning round.

'Okay,' he agreed.

We asked the first-aid men where Pip had been taken, and as they were leaving in any case they gave us a lift to the hospital in the ambulance. It was not until they told us that we realized how seriously the leg was broken.

We saw Pip only for a few moments. He lay in a cubicle in the casualty department, a cradle over his leg and blankets up to his chin. A brisk nurse told us he was going to the operating theatre within minutes and not to disturb the patient, as he had been given his pre-med. 'But you can say hello,' she said, 'as you've come.'

Hello was just about all we did say. Pip looked terribly pale and his eyes were fuzzy, but he said weakly, 'Who won the big race?'

'Template,' I said, almost apologetically.

'You?'

I nodded. He smiled faintly. 'You'll ride the lot now, then.'

'I'll keep them warm for you,' I said. 'You won't be long.'

'Three bloody months.' He shut his eyes. 'Three bloody months.'

The nurse came back with a stretcher trolley and two khaki-overalled porters, and asked us to leave. We waited outside in the hall, and saw them trundle Pip off towards the open lift.

'He'll be four months at least with a leg like that,' said Tick-Tock. 'He might just be ready for Cheltenham in March. Just in time to take back all the horses and do you out of a chance in the Champion Hurdle and the Gold Cup.'

'It can't be helped,' I said. 'It's only fair. And anything can happen before then.'

I think Axminster had trouble persuading some of his

owners that I was capable of taking Pip's place, because I didn't ride all of the stable's horses, not at first. But gradually as the weeks went by and I seemed to make no unforgivable bloomers, fewer and fewer other jockeys were engaged. I became used to seeing my name continually in the number boards, to riding three or four races a day, to going back to my digs contentedly tired in body and mind and waking the next morning with energy and eagerness. In some ways, I even became used to winning. It was no longer a rarity for me to be led into the first's enclosure, or to talk to delighted owners, or to see my picture in the sporting papers.

I began earning a good deal of money, but I spent very little of it. There was always the knowledge, hovering in the background, that my prosperity was temporary. Pip's leg was mending. Tick-Tock and I decided, however, to share the cost of buying a car. It was a second-hand cream-coloured Mini-Cooper which did forty miles to the gallon on a long run and could shift along at a steady seventy on the flat, and a friend of Tick-Tock's who kept a garage had recommended it to him as a bargain.

'All we want now are some leopard-skin seat covers and a couple of blondes in the back,' said Tick-Tock, as we dusted the small vehicle parked outside my digs, 'and we'll look like one of those gracious living advertisements in the *Tatler*.' He lifted up the bonnet and took at least his tenth look at the engine. 'A beautiful job of design,' he said fondly.

Gracious living, good design or not, the little car smoothed our paths considerably, and within a fortnight I could not imagine how we had ever managed without it. Tick-Tock kept it where he lived, seven miles away, near the stable he rode for, and came to collect me whenever Axminster himself was not taking me to meetings in his own car. Race trains came and went without any further support from either of us as we whizzed homewards through the black December afternoons in our cosy box on wheels.

While the Gods heaped good fortune on my head, others fared badly.

Grant had offered neither explanation nor apology for hitting me on the nose. He had not, in fact, spoken one word to me since that day, but, as at the same time he had also stopped borrowing my kit, I was not sure that I minded. He withdrew more and more into himself. The inner volcano of violence showed itself only in the stiffness of his body and the tightness of his lips, which seemed always to be compressed in fury. He loathed to be touched, even accidentally, and would swing round threateningly if anyone bumped into him in the changing-room. With my peg at most meetings still next to his I had knocked into him several times, for however hard I tried it was impossible in those cramped quarters not to, and the glare he gave me each time was frankly murderous.

It was not only to me that he had stopped speaking. He no longer said much at all. The trainers and owners who still employed him could get him neither to discuss a race beforehand nor explain what had happened afterwards. He listened to his orders in silence and left the trainer to draw his own conclusions through his race-glasses about how the horse had run. When he did speak, his remarks were laden with such a burden of obscenity that even the hardened inmates of the changing-room shifted uncomfortably.

Oddly enough Grant's riding skill had not degenerated with his character. He rode the same rough, tough race as always; but he had, we knew, begun to let out his anger on his mounts, and twice during November he was called before the stewards for 'excessive use of the whip'. The horses in question had each come in from their races with raw red weals on their flanks.

The Oldfield volcano erupted, as far as I was concerned, one cold afternoon in the jockeys' and trainers' car park at Warwick. I was late leaving the meeting as I had won the last race and had been taken off to the bar afterwards by the elated owner, one of my farmer friends. Tick-Tock had gone to a different meeting, and I had the car. By the time I got there the park was empty except for the Mini-Cooper and another car which was standing almost next to it, and two or three cars further on down the row.

I went towards the Mini still smiling to myself with

the pleasure of this latest win, and I did not see Grant until I was quite close to him. I was approaching the cars from behind, with Grant's on the right of mine. His near hind wheel lay on the grass, surrounded by a collection of implements spilling out of a holdall tool bag. A jack held up the bare axle of his black saloon and he was kneeling beside it with the spare wheel in his hand.

He saw me coming, and he saw me smiling, and he thought I was laughing at him for having a puncture. I could actually see the uncontrollable fury rise in his face. He got to his feet and stood rigidly, his thickset body hunched with belligerence, the strong shoulders bunching under his coat, his arms hanging down. Then he bent forward and from among the mess of tools picked up a tyre lever. He swished it through the air, his eyes on me.

'I'll help you with your puncture, if you like,' I said mildly.

For answer he took a step sideways, swung his arm in a sort of backwards chop, and smashed the tyre lever through the back window of the Mini-Cooper. The glass crashed and tinkled into the car, leaving only a fringe of jagged peaks round the frame.

Tick-Tock and I had had the car barely three weeks. My own anger rose quick and hot and I took a step towards Grant to save my most precious possession from further damage. He turned to face me squarely and lifted the tyre lever again.

'Put it down,' I said, reasonably, standing still. We were now about four feet apart. He told me to do something which was biologically impossible.

'Don't be an ass, Grant,' I said. 'Put that thing down and let's get on with changing your tyre.'

'You—' he said, 'you took my job.'

'No,' I said. It was pointless to add more, not least because if he was going to try to hit me I wanted to have all my concentration focused on what he was doing, not on what I was saying.

His eyes were red-rimmed above the high cheek bones. The big nostrils flared open like black pits. With his wild face, his bursting anger, and the upheld quivering tyre lever, he was a pretty frightening sight.

He slashed forward and downward at my head.

I think that at that moment he must have been truly insane, for had the blow connected he would surely have killed me, and he couldn't have hoped to get away with it with his car standing there with the wheel off. He was beyond thought.

I saw his arm go up a fraction before it came down and it gave me time to duck sideways. The lever whistled past my right ear. His arm returned in a backhand, again aiming at my head. I ducked again underneath it, and this time, as his arm swung wide and his body lay open to me, I stepped close and hit him hard with my fist just below his breast bone. He grunted as the wind rushed out of his lungs, and the arm with the tyre lever dropped and his head came

94

forward. I took a half pace to the right and hit him on the side of the neck with the edge of my hand.

He went down on his hands and knees, and then weakly sprawled on the grass. I took the tyre lever from his slack fingers and put it with all the other tools into the holdall, and shut the whole thing into the boot of his car.

It was getting very cold and the early dusk was turning colours to black and grey. I squatted beside Grant. He was hovering on the edge of consciousness, breathing heavily and moaning slightly.

I said conversationally, close to his ear, 'Grant, why did you get the sack from Axminster?'

He mumbled something I could not hear. I repeated my question. He said nothing. I sighed and stood up. It had been only a faint chance, after all.

Then he said distinctly, 'He said I passed on the message.'

'What message?'

'Passed on the message,' he said, less clearly. I bent down and asked him again, 'What message?' But although his lips moved he said nothing more.

I decided that in spite of everything I could not just drive off and leave him lying there in the cold. I took out the tools again, and sorting out the brace, put the spare wheel on and tightened up the nuts. Then I pumped-up the tyre, let the jack down and slung it with the punctured wheel into the boot on top of the tools.

Grant was still not properly conscious. I knew I hadn't hit him hard enough to account for such a long semi-waking state, and it occurred to me that perhaps his disturbed brain was finding this a helpful way to dodge reality. I bent down and shook his shoulder and called his name. He opened his eyes. For a split second it seemed as though the old Grant smiled out of them, and then the resentment and bitterness flooded back as he remembered what had happened. I helped him sit up, and propped him against his car. He looked desperately tired, utterly worn out.

'O God,' he said, 'O God.' It sounded like a true prayer, and it came from lips which usually blasphemed without thought.

'If you went to see a psychiatrist,' I said gently, 'you could get some help.'

He didn't answer; but neither did he resist when I helped him into the passenger seat of the Mini-Cooper. He was in no state to drive his own car, and there was no one else about to look after him. I asked him where he lived, and he told me. His car was safe enough where it was, and I remarked that he could fetch it on the following day. He made no reply.

Luckily he lived only thirty miles away, and I drew up where he told me outside a semi-detached featureless house on the outskirts of a small country town. There were no lights in the windows.

'Isn't your wife in?' I asked.

'She left me,' he said absently. Then his jaw tensed

and he said, 'Mind your own — business.' He jerked the door open and climbed out and slammed it noisily. He shouted, 'Take your bloody do-gooding off and — it. I don't want your help, you — '. He appeared to be back to his usual frame of mind, which was a pity, but there didn't seem to be any point in staying to hear more so I let in the clutch and drove off: but I had gone only half a mile down the road when I reluctantly came to the conclusion that he shouldn't be left alone in an empty house.

I was at that point in the centre of the little town whose brightly lit shops were closing their doors for the day, and I stopped and asked an elderly woman with a shopping basket where I could find a doctor. She directed me to a large house in a quiet side street, and I parked outside and rang the door bell.

A pretty girl appeared and said, 'Surgery at six,' and began to close the door again.

'If the doctor is in, please let me speak to him,' I said quickly, 'it's not a case for the surgery.'

'Well, all right,' she said and went away. Children's voices sounded noisily somewhere in the house. Presently, a youngish, chubby, capable-looking man appeared, munching at a piece of cream-filled chocolate cake and wearing the resigned, enquiring expression of a doctor called to duty during his free time.

'Are you by any chance Grant Oldfield's doctor?' I

asked. If he weren't, I thought, he could tell me where else to go.

But he said at once, 'Yes, I am. Has he had another fall?'

'Not exactly,' I said, 'but could you please come and take a look at him?'

'Now?'

'Yes, please,' I said. 'He ... er ... he was knocked out at the races.'

'Half a mo,' he said and went back to the house, reappearing with his medical bag and another piece of cake. 'Can you run me down there? Save me getting my car out again for those few yards.'

We went out to the Mini-Cooper and as soon as he sat in it he made a remark about the broken window, not unreasonably, since gusts of December wind blowing through it were freezing our necks. I told him that Grant had smashed it and explained how I had come to bring him home.

He listened in silence, licking the cream as it oozed out of the side of the cake. Then he said, 'Why did he attack you?'

'He seems to believe I took his job.'

'And did you?'

'No,' I said. 'He lost it months before it was offered to me.'

'Are you a jockey too, then?' he asked, looking at me curiously, and I nodded and told him my name. He said his was Parnell. I started the car and drove the few hundred yards back to Grant's house. It was still in complete darkness.

'I left him here not ten minutes ago,' I said as we went up the path to the front door. The small front garden was ragged and uncared for, with rotting dead leaves and mournful grass-grown flower beds dimly visible in the light from the street lamp. We rang the bell. It sounded shrilly in the house, but produced no other results. We rang again. The doctor finished his cake and licked his fingers.

There was a faint rustle in the darkness of the patch of garden. The doctor unclipped from his breast pocket the pen-shaped torch he normally used for peering into eyes and down throats, and directed its tiny beam round the bordering privet hedge. It revealed first some pathetic rose bushes choked with last summer's unmown grass; but in the corner where the hedge dividing the garden from the next door one met the hedge bordering the road, the pin point of light steadied on the hunched shape of a man.

We went over to him. He was sitting on the ground, huddling back into the hedge, with his knees drawn up to his chin and his head resting on his folded arms.

'Come along old chap,' said the doctor encouragingly, and half-helped, half-pulled him to his feet. He felt in Grant's pockets, found a bunch of keys, and handed them to me. I went over and unlocked the front door and turned on the lights in the hall. The doctor guided Grant through the hall and into the first room we came to, which happened to be a dining-room. Everything in it was covered with a thick layer of dust.

Grant collapsed in a heap on a dining chair and laid his head down on the dirty table. The doctor examined him, feeling his pulse, lifting up his eyelid and running both hands round the thick neck and the base of the skull. Grant moved irritably when Parnell's fingers touched the place where I had hit him and he said crossly, 'Go away, go away.'

Parnell stepped back a pace and sucked his teeth. 'There's nothing physically wrong with him as far as I can see, except for what is going to be a stiff neck. We'd better get him into bed and I'll give him something to keep him quiet, and in the morning I'll arrange for him to see someone who can sort out his troubles for him. You'd better give me a ring during the evening if there's any change in his condition.'

'I?' I said. 'I'm not staying here all evening . . .'

'Oh yes, I think so, don't you?' he said cheerfully, his eyes shining sardonically in his round face. 'Who else? All night too, if you don't mind. After all, you hit him.'

'Yes, but,' I protested, 'that's not what's the matter with him.'

'Never mind. You cared enough to bring him home and fetch me. Be a good chap and finish the job. I do really think someone ought to stay here all night . . . someone strong enough to deal with him in a crisis.

It's not a job for elderly female relatives, even if we could rake one up so late in the day.'

Put like that, it was difficult to refuse. We took Grant upstairs, balancing his thick-set body between us as he stumbled up the treads. His bedroom was filthy. Dirty tangled sheets and blankets were piled in heaps on the unmade bed, dust lay thick on every surface, and soiled clothes were scattered over the floor and hung sordidly over chairs. The whole room smelled of sour sweat.

'We'd better put him somewhere else,' I said, switching on lights and opening all the other doors on the small landing. One door led into a bathroom whose squalor defied description. Another opened on to a linen cupboard which still contained a few sheets in a neat pile, and the last revealed an empty bedroom with bright pink rosebuds on the walls. Grant stood blinking on the landing while I fetched some sheets and made up the bed for him. There were no clean pyjamas. Doctor Parnell undressed Grant as far as his underpants and socks and made him get into the fresh bed. Then he went downstairs and returned with a glass of water, wearing so disgusted an expression that I knew without being told what state the kitchen must be in.

Opening his case, he shook two capsules on to his hand and told Grant to swallow them, which he docilely did. Grant at this time seemed as if he were sleep-walking; he was only a shell, his personality a blank. It was disturbing, but on the other hand it made the business of putting him to bed much easier than it might have been.

Parnell looked at his watch. 'I'm late for surgery,' he said as Grant lay back on his pillow and shut his eyes. 'Those pills ought to keep him quiet for a bit. Give him two more when he wakes up.' He handed me a small bottle. 'You know where to find me if you want me,' he added with a callous grin. 'Have a good night.'

I spent a miserable evening and dined off a pint of milk I found on the back doorstep. Nothing else in the stinking kitchen was any longer edible. There were no books and no radio to be found, and to pass the hours I made an effort to clean up some of the mess, but what that dreadful house really needed was a breezy spring day, lashings of disinfectant, and an army of strong-minded charwomen.

Several times I went softly in to see how Grant was doing, but he slept peacefully, flat on his back, until midnight. I found him then with his eyes open, but when I went close to him there was no recognition in them. He was still in a withdrawn blank state and he obediently, without a word, swallowed the capsules when I offered them to him. I waited until his eyes had closed again, then I locked his door and went downstairs and eventually fell uneasily asleep myself, wrapped in a travelling rug on a too short sofa. There was no sound from Grant all night, and when I went up to him at six in the morning he was still sleeping quietly.

Dr Parnell at least had the decency to release me at an early hour, arriving with a middle-aged male nurse at 7.30 in the freezing dawn. He had also brought a basket packed by his wife, containing eggs, bacon, bread, milk, and coffee, and from his medical bag he produced a powerful battery razor.

'All mod. cons,' he said cheerfully, his round face beaming.

So I went back to the races washed, shaved and fed. But thinking of the husk of a man I left behind me, not in a happy frame of mind.

CHAPTER SEVEN

'The trouble is, there's such a shortage of jockeys just now,' said James Axminster.

We were on our way to Sandown, discussing whom he should engage to ride for him the following week when he would be sending horses to two different places on the same day.

'You'd almost think there was a hoodoo on the whole tribe,' he said, expertly swinging his large car between a wobbly girl cyclist and an oncoming pantechnicon. 'Art shot himself, Pip's broken his leg, Grant's had a breakdown. Two or three others are out with more ordinary things like busted collar bones, and at least four quite useful chaps took that wretched Ballerton's misguided advice and are now churning out car bodies on assembly lines. There's Peter Cloony... but I've heard he's very unreliable and might not turn up in time; and Danny Higgs bets too much, they say, and Ingersoll doesn't always try, so I've been told...'

He slowed down while a mother pushed a

perambulator and three small children untidily across the road in front of us, and went on talking. 'Every time I think I've found a good up-and-coming jockey I seem to hear something to his disadvantage. With you, it was that film, the one they showed on that television programme. It was shocking, wasn't it? I watched it and thought, my God, what have I done, asking this clod to ride for me, however will I explain it away to the owners.' He grinned. 'I was on the point of ringing them all up and assuring them you'd not be on their horses after all. Luckily for you I remembered the way you had already ridden for me and I watched the rest of the programme first, and when it had finished I had changed my mind. I had even begun to think I had perhaps struck oil in annexing you. Nothing that has happened since,' he glanced at me sideways, smiling, 'has led me to alter that opinion.'

I smiled back. In the weeks since Pip broke his leg I had come to know him well, and liked him better with every day that passed. Not only was he a superb craftsman at his job and a tireless worker, but he was reliable in other ways. He was never moody: one did not have to approach him circumspectly every time to see if he were in a good or bad humour because he was always the same, neither boisterous nor irritable, just reasonable and receptive. He said directly what he thought, so that one never had to search for innuendoes or suspect hidden sarcasm and it made any relationship with him stable and free from worry. He was, on the other hand, in many ways thoroughly selfish. Unless it were a strictly business matter, his own comfort and convenience came first, second and third, and he would do a favour for someone else only if it caused him absolutely no personal sacrifice of time or effort. Even this was often a blessing to his stable lads since it was typical of him, if the occasion arose, to give them a generous travelling allowance out of his own pocket to visit their homes, rather than go five miles out of his way to drop them on their doorsteps.

He had seemed from the first to be as satisfied with my company as I was with his, and had quite soon told me to drop the 'sir' and stick to 'James'. Later the same week as he drove us back from Birmingham races, we passed some brightly lit posters advertising a concert which was to be held there that evening.

'Conductor, Sir Trelawny Finn,' he read aloud, the enormous lettering catching his eye. 'No relation, I suppose,' he said jokingly.

'Well, yes, as a matter of fact, he's my uncle,' I said.

There was a dead silence. Then he said, 'And Caspar Finn?'

'My father.' A pause.

'Anyone else?'

'Dame Olivia Cottin is my mother,' I said, matter-of-factly.

'Good God,' he said explosively.

I grinned.

'You keep it very quiet,' he said.

'It's really the other way round,' I said cheerfully. 'They like to keep me quiet. A jockey in the family is a disgrace to them, you see. It embarrasses them. They don't like the connexion to be noticed.

'All the same,' he said thoughtfully, 'it explains quite a lot about you that I had begun to wonder about. Where you got that air of confidence from ... and why you've said so little about yourself.'

I said, smiling, 'I'd be very glad ... James ... if you'd not let my parentage loose in the weighing-room, as a favour to them.'

He had said he would not, and he had kept his word, but he had accepted me more firmly as a friend from then on. So when he ran through the reported shortcomings of Peter Cloony, Danny Higgs and Tick-Tock, it was with some confidence that I said, 'You seem to have heard a great many rumours. Do you know all these things for a fact?'

'For a fact?' he repeated, surprised. 'Well, Peter Cloony definitely missed two races a few weeks back because he was late. That's a fact.'

I told him about Peter's atrocious luck in twice finding a vehicle stuck across the mouth of the narrow lane from his village to the main road. 'As far as I know,' I said, 'he hasn't been late since then. His reputation for lateness seems to be built mainly on those two days.'

'I've heard several times that he can't be trusted to turn up,' said James obstinately.

'Who from?' I asked curiously.

'Oh, I don't know. Corin Kellar for one. And of course Johnson who employs him. Ballerton too, though it's against my better judgement to pay too much attention to what he says. It's common knowledge though.'

'How about Danny Higgs, then?' I said. Danny was an irrepressible cockney, tiny in size, but ferociously brave.

'He bets too heavily,' James said positively.

'Who says so?' I asked. I knew Danny broke the regulations by backing horses, but from what he said in the changing-room, it was only in amounts of five or ten pounds, which would cause few trainers to look askance at him.

'Who says? I ... er ... Corin,' he finished lamely. 'Corin, come to think of it, has told me so several times. He says he never puts him up because of it.'

'And Tick-Tock?' I said. 'Who says Ingersoll doesn't always try?'

He didn't answer at once. Then he said, 'Why shouldn't I believe what Corin says? He has no axe to grind. He's an excellent trainer, but he depends as we all do on securing good jockeys. He certainly wouldn't deny himself the use of people like Cloony or Higgs if he didn't have a good reason.'

I thought for a few moments, and then said, 'I know it's really none of my business, but would you mind very much telling me why you dropped Grant

Oldfield? He told me himself that it was something to do with a message, but he wouldn't explain what.' I refrained from mentioning that he had been semi-conscious at the time.

'A message? Oh yes, he passed on the message, I couldn't have that.'

I still looked mystified. Axminster squeezed through the traffic lights on the amber and glanced sideways at me.

'The message,' he said impatiently, 'you know, the news. He was passing on the news. If we had a fancied runner he would tip off a professional backer. The owner of the horse didn't get good odds to his money because the professional was there before him and spoiled the market. Three of my owners were very angry about it – no fun for them having to take two or three to one when they expected sixes or sevens. So Grant had to go. It was a pity; he was a strong jockey, just what I needed.'

'How did you discover it was Grant passing on the information?'

'Maurice Kemp-Lore found out while he was working on one of those programmes of his. Something to do with how professional backers work, I think it was, and he found out about Grant more or less by accident. He told me very apologetically, and just said it would be wiser not to let Grant know too much. But you can't work properly with a jockey and keep secrets from him, it's a hopeless set-up.'

'What did Grant say when you sacked him?' I asked.

'He denied the whole thing very indignantly. But of course he would. No jockey would ever confess to selling information if he wanted another trainer to take him on.'

'Did you talk to the professional backer in question?' I asked.

'Yes I did, as a matter of fact,' he said. 'I didn't want to believe it, you see. But it was open and shut. I had to press him a bit, because it didn't reflect well on him, but Lubbock, the professional, did admit that Grant had been tipping him off over the telephone, and that he had been paying him ever since he had started to ride for me.'

It seemed conclusive enough, but I had an elusive feeling that I had missed something, somewhere.

I changed the subject. 'Going back to Art,' I said, 'why was he always having rows with Corin?'

'I don't really know,' James said reflectively. 'I heard Corin say once or twice that Art didn't ride to orders. Perhaps it was that.' He neatly passed two slow lorries on a round-about, and glanced at me again. 'What are you getting at?'

'It seems to me sometimes that there is too much of a pattern,' I said. 'Too many jockeys are affected by rumours. You said yourself that there seems to be a hoodoo on the whole tribe.'

'I didn't mean it seriously,' he protested. 'You're

imagining things. And as for rumours, what rumour made Art kill himself or broke Pip's leg, or made Grant sell information? Rumour didn't make Cloony late either.'

'Danny Higgs doesn't bet heavily,' I said, feeling I was fighting a rearguard action, 'and Ingersoll rides as honestly as anyone.'

'You can't know about Higgs,' he pointed out, 'and Ingersoll, let me remind you, was called in before the stewards last week for easing his mount out of third place. John Ballerton owned the horse and he was very annoyed about it, he told me so himself.'

I sighed. Tick-Tock's version was that since Corin had told him not to overwork the horse, which was not fully fit, he had decided that he ought not to drive the horse too hard just for the sake of finishing third. Better to save the horse's energy for winning next time, he had thought, adopting a view commonly held and acted on by at least half the jockeys and trainers engaged in the sport: but owners and members of the public who had backed the horse for a place were liable to disagree. After the enquiry, changing with the wind as usual, Corin had been heard condemning Tick-Tock for his action.

'I may be quite wrong about it all,' I said slowly, 'I hope so. Only . . .'

'Only?' he prompted as I paused.

'Only,' I finished lightly, 'if you ever hear any rumours about me, will you remember what I think . . .

and make utterly sure they're true before you believe them?'

'All right,' he said, humouring me. 'I think it's nonsense, but all right, I'll agree to that.' He drove in silence for a while, and then said with an impatient shake of his big head, 'No one stands to gain anything by trying to ruin jockeys. It's nonsense. Pointless.'

'I know,' I said. 'Pointless.'

We changed the subject.

Christmas came, and during the week before it, when there was no racing, I spent several days in Kensington. My parents greeted me with their usual friendly detachment and left me to my own devices. They were both preoccupied with crowded Christmas schedules, and my mother also spent each morning working at her piano on a new concerto which was to have its first performance in the New Year. She started daily at seven punctually, and played with short interruptions for coffee and thought until twelve-thirty. I awoke as so often during my life to the sound of warming up chromatics and wrist loosening arpeggios, and lay lazily in bed listening to her pick her way phrase by phrase through a dissonant modern score, repeating and repeating each section until she was satisfied she knew it, until the notes flowed easily in their intended order.

I could picture her exactly, dressed for work in a

cashmere sweater and ski pants, sitting upright on her special stool, with her head thrust forward as if to hear more from the piano than the notes themselves. She was digging the bones out of the piece, and I knew better than to interrupt her. Digging the bones, the essence, the composer's ultimate intention: and when she had these things firmly in her mind, she would begin the process of clothing them with her own interpretations, sharpening the contrasts of mood and tone, until the finished conception emerged clear and shining and memorable.

My mother might not have been a comforting refuge in my childhood nor take much loving interest in me now I was a man, but she had by her example shown me many qualities to admire and value. Professionalism, for instance; a tough-minded singleness of purpose; a refusal to be content with a low standard when a higher one could be achieved merely by working. I had become self-reliant young and thoroughly as a result of her rejection of motherhood, and because I saw the grind behind the gloss of her public performances, I grew up not expecting life's plums to be tossed into my lap without any effort from me. What mother could teach her son more?

Joanna's time was tangled inextricably with several performances in different places of the Christmas Oratorio. I managed to hook her only for one chilly morning's walk in the Park, which was not a success from my point of view since Bach easily shoved me into second place for her attention. She hummed bits of the Oratorio continuously from the Albert Gate to the Serpentine, and from the Serpentine to Bayswater Road. There I put her into a taxi and gave her a Christmassy lunch at the Savoy, where she appeared to restrain herself with difficulty from bursting into full song, as the acoustics in the entrance hall appealed to her. I couldn't decide whether or not she was being irritating on purpose, and if she was, why?

She was definitely a great deal less serene than usual, and there was a sort of brittleness in her manner which I didn't like and couldn't understand, until when we were half-way through some excellent mince pies it belatedly occurred to me that she might be unhappy. Unhappiness was not a state I had seen her in before, so I couldn't be sure. I waited until the coffee came, and then said, casually, 'What's up, Joanna?'

She looked at me, then she looked round the room, then at me again, then at her coffee.

Finally she said, 'Brian wants me to marry him.'

It wasn't what I expected, and it hurt. I found myself looking down at my own coffee: black and bitter, very appropriate, I thought.

'I don't know what to do,' she said. 'I was content as we were. Now I'm unsettled. Brian keeps talking about "living in sin" and "regularizing the position". He goes to church a lot now, and he can't reconcile our relationship with his religion. I never thought of

114

it as sinful, just as enjoyable and fruitful and . . . and comfortable. He is talking about buying a house and settling down, and sees me as the complete housewife, cleaning, mending, cooking, and so on. I'm not that sort of person. The thought appals me. If I marry him, I know I'll be miserable . . .' Her voice trailed off.

'And if you don't marry him?' I asked.

'I'll be miserable then, too, because he refuses to go on as we are. We're not easy together any more. We nearly have rows. He says it's irresponsible and childish not to want to marry at my age, and I say I'll gladly marry him if we live as we do now, with him coming and going from the studio when he likes, and me free to work and come and go as I please too. But he doesn't want that. He wants to be respectable and conventional and . . . and stuffy.' The last word came out explosively, steeped in contempt. There was a pause while she stirred her coffee vigorously. There was no sugar in it. I watched the nervous gesture, the long strong fingers with the pink varnished nails gripping the spoon too hard.

'How much do you love him?' I asked painfully.

'I don't know,' she said unhappily. 'I don't know any more what love is.' She looked straight across the little table. 'If it means that I want to spend my life attending to his creature comforts, then I don't love him. If it means being happy in bed, then I do.'

She saw the movement in my face, and said

abruptly, 'Oh hell . . . Rob, I'm sorry. It's so long since you said anything . . . I thought you didn't still . . .'

'Never mind,' I said. 'It can't be helped.'

'What . . . what do you think I should do?' she said after a pause, still fiddling with the coffee spoon.

'It's quite clear,' I said positively, 'that you should not marry Brian if you can't bear the prospect of the life he intends to lead. It wouldn't work for either of you.'

'So?' she said, in a small voice.

But I shook my head. The rest she would have to resolve for herself. No advice I could give her would be unbiased, and she must have known it.

She left presently to go to a rehearsal, and I paid the bill and wandered out into the festive streets. I bought some presents for my family on the way, walking slowly back to the flat. The sort of marriage which Joanna had offered Brian, and which he had spurned, was what I most wanted in the world. Why, I wondered disconsolately, was life so ruddy unfair.

On Boxing Day Template won the King 'Chase, one of the ten top races of the year. It put him conclusively into the star class and it didn't do me any harm either.

The race had been televised, and afterwards, as was his custom, Maurice Kemp-Lore interviewed me as the winning jockey before the cameras. Towards the end of the brief talk he invited me to say hullo directly to

Pip, who, he explained to viewers, was watching at home. I had seen Pip only a week or two earlier and had discussed big-race tactics with him, but I obligingly greeted him and said I hoped his leg was mending well. Kemp-Lore smilingly added, 'We all wish you a speedy recovery, Pip,' and the interview was over.

On the following day the sporting press was complimentary about the race, and a number of trainers I had not yet ridden for offered me mounts. I began to feel at last as though I were being accepted as a jockey in my own right, and not principally as a substitute for Pip. It even seemed likely that when Pip returned to his job I would not fade back into the wilderness, for two of the new trainers said they would put me up on their horses as often as I was free.

I had, of course, my share of falls during this period, for however fortunate I was I couldn't beat the law of averages: but no damage was done except for a few bruises here and there, and none of them was bad enough to stop me riding.

The worst fall from the spectators' point of view happened one Saturday afternoon in January, when the hurdler I was riding tripped over the flight of hurdles nearest to the grandstand and flung me off on to my head. I woke up dizzily as the first-aid men lifted me into the ambulance on a stretcher, and for a moment or two could not remember where I was.

James's face, looming over me, as they carried me

into the first-aid room, brought me back to earth with a click, and I asked him if his horse was all right.

'Yes,' he said, 'how about you?'

'Nothing broken,' I assured him, having explored my limbs rather drunkenly during the short trip back in the ambulance.

'He rolled on you,' he said.

'I'm not surprised.' I grinned up at him. 'I feel a bit squashed, come to think of it.'

I lay for a while on a bed in the first-aid room, but there was nothing wrong with me that a good sleep wouldn't cure, and at the end of the afternoon I went back to Berkshire with James as expected.

'Are you all right?' he asked once, on the way.

'Yes,' I said cheerfully. 'Fine.' Actually I felt dizzy now and then, and also shivery and unsettled, but concealing one's true state of health from trainers was an occupational habit, and I knew I would be fit again to ride on Monday.

The only person who was openly annoyed at the run of good luck I had had was John Ballerton, and I had caught him several times in the parade ring staring tight-lipped at me with a patent and most unstewardly animosity.

Since the day of our joint broadcast we had exchanged the fewest possible words, but I had heard from Corin, who repeated it to me with sly relish, that Ballerton had said loudly to him and Maurice Kemp-Lore in the members' bar at Kempton, 'Finn isn't worth all the fuss that's being made of him. He'll come down just as quickly as he's gone up, you'll see. And I for one won't weep about it.'

In view of this it was astonishing that on the day after my fall I should be offered a ride on one of his horses. At first I refused to take Corin seriously. His telephone call woke me on the Sunday morning, and I was inclined to think the concussion had returned.

'If it were a choice between me and a sack of potatoes,' I said sleepily, 'he'd choose the potatoes.'

'No, seriously Rob, he wants you to ride Shantytown at Dunstable tomorrow.' Corin's voice held no trace of humour. 'I must say, I don't really understand why, as he's been so set against you before. But he was quite definite on the telephone, not five minutes ago. Perhaps it's an olive branch.'

And perhaps not, I thought. My first instinct was to refuse to ride the horse, but I couldn't think of a reasonable excuse, as Corin had found out I was free for the race before he told me whose the horse was. A point-blank excuseless refusal was, while possible, a senseless course. It would give Ballerton a genuine grievance against me, and if he sincerely wanted to smooth over his hostility, which I doubted, I should only deepen it by spurning his offer.

Shantytown was no Template. Far, far from it. His uncertain temper and unreliable jumping were described to me in unreassuring terms by Tick-Tock on the way to Dunstable the following morning.

119

'A right one,' he said, putting his foot down on the Mini-Cooper's accelerator. 'A knacker's delight. Dog-meat on the hoof.'

'His form's not bad,' I protested mildly, having looked it up the previous day.

'Hmph. Any time he's won or been placed it's because he's dragged his jockey's arms out of the sockets by a blast-off start and kept right on going. Hang on and hope, that's how to ride him when he's in that mood. His mouth is as hard as Gibraltar. In fact I cannot,' finished Tick-Tock with satiric formality, 'I cannot instantly recall any horse who is less receptive of his jockey's ideas.'

There was no bitterness in his voice, but we were both aware that a few weeks ago riding Shantytown would have been his doubtful pleasure, not mine. Since his parade before the stewards for not pushing his horse all out into third place, had had been ignored by Corin Kellar. It was the sort of injustice typical of Corin, to sack a man who ran into trouble looking after his interests, and it had done nothing to lay the unfair rumour that Tick-Tock was a habitual non-trier.

Apart from abruptly lessening the number of races he rode in, the rumour had had little effect on Tick-Tock himself. He shrugged his shoulders, and with a determined look on his angular young face stated, 'They'll change their minds again in time. I'll mash every horse I ride into a pulp. I'll do my nut on every hopeless hack. No one henceforth will see me finish eighth when by bashing the beast I could be sixth.'

I had smiled to hear these fighting words from one whose chief asset was his lightness of touch, but was relieved, too, that he was intact in spirits. No suicides, no mental breakdowns for him.

Shantytown, when it came to the race, was not what I had been led to expect. The damp raw January afternoon had drawn only a small crowd of stalwarts to watch a second-class programme at a minor meeting, and as I watched the big chestnut plod round the parade ring I thought how well he matched the circumstances. Uninspiring.

But far from pulling my arms out of their sockets, Shantytown seemed to me to be in danger of falling asleep. The start caught him flat-footed, so little interest was he taking in it, and I had to boot him into the first fence. He rose to it fairly well, but was slow in his recovery, and it was the same at every jump. It was puzzling, after what Tick-Tock had said, but horses do have their off-days for no discernible reason, and I could only suppose that this was one of them.

We trailed round the entire three miles in the rear of the field, and finished ingloriously last. All my efforts to get him to quicken up the straight met with no response. Shantytown hadn't taken hold of his bit from the beginning and at the end he seemed to be dead beat.

A hostile reception met us on our return. John

Ballerton, with whom I had exchanged coldly polite 'Good afternoons' in the parade ring before the race, now glowered like a July thunderstorm. Corin, standing on one leg and wearing an anxious, placatory expression, was obviously going to use me as the scapegoat for the horse's failure, to save his face as its trainer. That was always one of the hazards to be run in riding Corin's horses.

'What the hell do you think you were doing?' Ballerton said aggressively, as I slid off on to the ground and begun to unbuckle the saddle girths.

'I'm sorry, sir,' I said. 'He wouldn't go any faster.'

'Don't talk such bloody rubbish,' he said, 'he always goes faster than that. I've never seen a more disgusting display of incompetence ... you couldn't ride in a cart with a pig net over it. If you ask me, the horse wasn't given a chance. You missed the start and couldn't be bothered to make it up.'

'I did say,' said Corin to me reproachfully, 'not to let him run away with you, and to keep tucked in behind for the first two miles. But I do think you carried my orders a bit too far ...'

'A bit too far!' interrupted Ballerton furiously. 'Were you afraid to let him go, or something? If you can't manage to ride a decent race on a horse which pulls, why the hell do you try to. Why not say straight out that you can't? Save us all a lot of time and money.'

I said, 'The horse didn't pull. There was no life in him.'

'Kellar,' Ballerton was nearly shouting. 'Is my horse a puller or is he not?'

'He is,' said Corin, not meeting my eyes.

'And you told me he was fit. On his toes.'

'Yes,' said Corin. 'I thought he'd win.'

They looked at me accusingly. Corin must have known that the horse had run listlessly because he had seen the race with experienced eyes, but he was not going to admit it. If I had to ride often for Corin, I thought wryly, I would soon have as many rows with him as Art had had.

Ballerton narrowed his eyes and said to me, 'I asked you to ride Shantytown against my better judgement and only because Maurice Kemp-Lore insisted I had been misjudging you and that you were really a reliable man who would ride a genuine race. Well, I'm going to tell him he is wrong. Very wrong. You'll never ride another horse of mine, I promise you that.'

He turned on his heel and stalked off, followed by Corin. My chief feeling, as I went back to the weighing-room, was of irritation that I hadn't relied on instinct and refused to ride for him in the first place.

By the end of the afternoon the puzzlement I had felt over Shantytown's dead running had changed to a vague uneasiness, for neither of the other two horses I rode afterwards did anything like as well as had been expected. Both were well backed, and both finished nearly last, and although their owners were a great deal nicer about it than Ballerton had been, their disappointment was obvious.

On the following day, still at Dunstable, the run of flops continued. I had been booked for three horses, and they all ran badly. I spent the whole depressing afternoon apologetically explaining to owner after owner that I had not been able to make their horse go faster. The third horse, in fact, went so badly that I had to pull him up half-way round. He was a slow jumper on the best of days, but on that particular one he took so long putting himself right and so long starting off again when he landed, that the rest of the field were a whole fence ahead by the time we had gone a mile. It was hopeless. When I reined him in he slowed from a reluctant gallop to a walk in a couple of strides, sure sign of a very tired horse. I thought as he was trained by a farmer-owner who might not know better, that he must have been given too stiff a training gallop on the previous day, but the farmer said he was sure he had not.

Runs of bad luck are commoner in racing than good ones, and the fact that six of my mounts in a row had made a showing far below their usual capabilities would not have attracted much notice had it not been for John Ballerton.

I changed into street clothes after the fifth race and strolled out of the weighing-room to find him standing close by with a small circle of cronies. All the heads turned towards me with that sideways, assessing look which meant they had been talking about me, and Ballerton said something forceful to them, of which the word 'disgrace' floated across clearly.

Jockeys being as accustomed as politicians to abuse I gave no sign of having heard what had obviously been intended for my ears, and walked casually off to the stands to watch the last race; but I did wonder how long and how maliciously Ballerton would hold Shantytown's failure against me, and what effect his complaints would have on the number of horses I was asked to ride. He was not a man to keep his grudges to himself, and as a National Hunt Committee member he was not without influence either.

Up on the stands Maurice Kemp-Lore came across to talk to me. We had met briefly on racecourses several times now, and were on superficially friendly terms, but in spite of his charm, or perhaps because it sometimes seemed too polished, I felt his friendship came strictly into the professional, 'might be useful' category. I did not believe that he liked me for my own sake.

He smiled vividly, the charm turned on to full wattage, his slim figure radiating health and confidence and his blue eyes achieving the near impossible of twinkling on a grey January afternoon. I smiled back automatically: one couldn't help it. All his impressive success stemmed from the instantaneous, irresistible feeling of well-being he inspired in whomever he talked to, and there was no one from the Senior Steward downwards who did not enjoy his company, even if, like me, one suspected his unfailing motive was the gathering of material for his programme.

'What bad luck, Rob,' he said cheerfully. 'I hear the good word I put in for you with John Ballerton has gone awry.'

'You can say that again,' I agreed. 'But thanks for trying anyway.'

The blue eyes glimmered. 'Anything to help,' he said.

I could hear distinctly a faint high-pitched wheeze as he drew breath into his lungs, and I realized it was the first time I had encountered him in an asthmatic attack. I was vaguely sorry for him.

The horses for the sixth race cantered past, going down to the start.

'Are James's plans fixed for the Midwinter Cup?' he asked casually, his eyes on the horses. I smiled. But he had his job to do, I supposed, and there was no harm in telling him.

'Template runs, all being well,' I said.

'And you ride him?'

'Yes,' I agreed.

'How is Pip getting along?' he asked, wheezing quietly.

'They think his leg is mending well, but he is still in plaster,' I said. 'It comes off next week, I believe, and he might be ready for Cheltenham, but of course he won't be fit for the Midwinter.'

The race in question was a richly endowed new event at Ascot, introduced to provide a high spot in mid-February, and nicely timed to give three full weeks for recovery and retuning before the Cheltenham Gold Cup. It lay almost a month ahead, on that day at Dunstable, and I was looking forward to it particularly as it seemed possible that it would be my last chance on Template. Pip would do his very best to be fit to ride him in the Gold Cup, and so would I have done in his place.

'What chance do you give Template in the Midwinter?' Maurice asked, watching the start through his race glasses.

'Oh, I hope he'll win,' I said, grinning. 'You can quote me.'

'I probably will,' he agreed, grinning back. We watched the race together, and such was the effect of his personality that I left Dunstable quite cheerfully, the dismal two days' results temporarily forgotten.

CHAPTER EIGHT

It was a false security. My charmed run of good luck had ended with a vengeance, and Dunstable proved to be only the fringe of the whirlpool. During the next two weeks I rode seventeen horses. Fifteen of them finished in the rear of the field, and in only two cases was this a fair result.

I couldn't understand it. As far as I knew there was no difference in my riding, and it was unbelievable that my mounts should all lose their form simultaneously. I began to worry about it, and that didn't help, as I could feel my confidence oozing away as each disturbing and embarrassing day passed.

There was one grey mare I particularly liked riding because of the speed of her reactions: she often seemed to know what I intended to do a split second before I gave her signals, rather as if she had sized up the situation as quickly as I had and was already taking independent action. She was sweet tempered and silken mouthed, and jumped magnificently. I liked her owner too, a short jolly farmer with a thick Norfolk accent, and while we watched her walk round the parade ring before her race he commiserated with me on my bad luck and said, 'Never mind, lad. The mare will put you right. She'll not fail you. You'll do all right on her, never fear.'

I went out smiling to the race because I too believed I would do all right on her. But that week she might have been another horse. Same colour, same size, same pretty head. But no zip. It was like driving a car with four flat tyres.

The jolly farmer looked less jolly and more pensive when I brought her back.

'She's not been last ever before, lad,' he said reproachfully.

We looked her over, but there was nothing wrong with her that we could see, and she wasn't even blowing very hard.

'I could get her heart tested I suppose,' the farmer said doubtfully. 'Are you sure you gave her her head, lad?'

'Yes,' I said. 'But she had no enthusiasm at all today.'

The farmer shook his head, doleful and puzzled.

One of the horses I rode belonged to a tall sharp-faced woman who knew a great deal about racing and had no sympathy with bunglers. She laid straight into me with her tongue after I had eased her ultra-expensive new gelding from last into second last place only feet from the winning post.

'I suppose you realize,' she said in a loud, hard voice, unashamedly listened to by a large group of racegoers, 'that in the last five minutes you have succeeded both in halving the value of my horse and making me look a fool for having paid a fortune for him.'

I apologized. I suggested possibly that her animal needed a little time.

'Time?' she repeated angrily. 'For what? For you to wake up? You speak as if it were my judgement that is at fault, not yours. You lay far too far out of your ground. You should have taken closer order from the beginning...' Her acid lecture went on and on and on, and I looked at the fine head of her glossy black high-bred gelding and admitted to myself that he was probably a great deal better than he had appeared.

One Wednesday was the big day for a ten-year-old schoolboy with sparkly brown eyes and a conspiratorial grin. His wealthy eccentric grandmother, having discovered that there was no minimum age laid down for racehorse owners, had given Hugo a colossal chestnut 'chaser twice his height, and was considerate enough to foot the training bills as well.

I had become firm friends with Hugo. Knowing that I saw his horse most mornings at James's, he used to send me tiny parcels containing lumps of sugar filched from the dining table at his prep. school, which I conscientiously passed on to their intended destination: and I used to write back to Hugo, giving him quite detailed accounts of how his giant pet was progressing.

On that Wednesday Hugo had not only begged a day off from school to see his horse run, but had brought three friends with him. The four of them stood with me and James in the parade ring, Hugo's mother being the rare sort who liked her son to enjoy his limelight alone. As I had walked down from the weighing-room she had smiled broadly to me from her station on the rails.

The four little boys were earnest and excited, and James and I had great fun with them before the race, treating them with seriousness and as man-to-man, which they obviously appreciated. This time, I promised myself, this time, for Hugo, I will win. I must.

But the big chestnut jumped very clumsily that day. On the far side of nearly every fence he ducked his head, and once, to prevent myself being hauled over in a somersault, I had to stretch forward down his neck with one hand only, leaving go of the reins entirely with the other. The free arm, swinging up sideways, helped to bring my weight far enough back to keep me in the saddle, but the gesture known as 'calling a cab' was not going to earn me any bonus points with James, who had denounced it often as the style of 'bad, tired, scared or unfit amateurs'.

Hugo's little face was pink when I dismounted, and the three friends glumly shuffled their feet behind him. With them as witnesses there would be no chance of

Hugo smoothing over the disaster with the rest of his schoolmates.

'I'm very sorry, Hugo,' I said sincerely, apologizing for everything – myself, the horse, the race, and the miserliness of fate.

He answered with a stoicism which would have been a lesson to many of his seniors. 'I expect it was an off day,' he said kindly. 'And anyway, someone always has to be last. That's what Daddy said when I came bottom in History.' He looked at the chestnut forgivingly, and said to me, 'I expect he's keen really, don't you?'

'Yes,' I agreed. 'Keen, very.'

'Well,' said Hugo, turning bravely to his friends. 'That's that, then. We might as well have tea.'

Failures like these were too numerous to escape anyone's attention, but as the days passed I noticed a change in the way people spoke to me. One or two, and Corin in particular, showed something like contempt. Others looked uncomfortable, others sympathetic, others pitying. Heads turned towards me wherever I went, and I could almost feel the wave of gossip I left in my wake. I didn't know exactly what they were saying, so I asked Tick-Tock.

'Pay no attention,' he said. 'Ride a couple of winners and they'll be throwing the laurel wreaths again, and back-pedalling on everything they're saying now. It's badpatchville, chum, that's all.'

And that was all I could get out of him.

One Thursday evening James telephoned to my digs and asked me to go up to his house. I walked up in the dark, rather miserably wondering whether he, like two other trainers that day, was going to find an excuse for putting someone else up on his horses. I couldn't blame him. Owners could make it impossible for him to continue with a jockey so thoroughly in the doldrums.

James called me into his office, a square room joining his house to the stable yard. Its walls were covered with racing photographs, bookshelves, a long row of racing colours on clothes hangers, and filing cabinets. A huge roll-top desk stood in front of the window, which looked out on to the yard. There were three broken-springed armchairs with faded chintz covers, a decrepit Turkish carpet on the floor, and a red-hot coal fire in the grate. I had spent a good many hours there in the past three months, discussing past performances and future plans.

James waited for me and stood aside to let me go in first. He followed me in and shut the door, and faced me almost aggressively across the familiar room.

'I hear,' he said without preamble, 'that you have lost your nerve.'

The room was very still. The fire crackled slightly. A horse in a near-by loose box banged the floor with his hoof. I stared at James, and he stared straight back, gravely.

I didn't answer. The silence lengthened. It was not

a surprise. I had guessed what was being said about me when Tick-Tock had refused to tell me what it was.

'No one is to blame for losing his nerve,' James said non-committally. 'But a trainer cannot continue to employ someone to whom it has happened.'

I still said nothing.

He waited a few seconds, and went on, 'You have been showing the classic symptoms . . . trailing round nearly last, pulling up for no clear reason, never going fast enough to keep warm, and calling a cab. Keeping at the back out of trouble, that's what you've been doing.'

I thought about it, rather numbly.

'A few weeks ago,' he said, 'I promised you that if I heard any rumours about you I would make sure they were true before I believed them. Do you remember?'

I nodded.

'I heard this rumour last Saturday,' he said. 'Several people sympathized with me because my jockey had lost his nerve. I didn't believe it. I have watched you closely ever since.'

I waited dumbly for the axe. During the week I had been last five times out of seven.

He walked abruptly over to an armchair by the fire and sat down heavily.

Irritably he said, 'Oh sit down, Rob. Don't just stand there like a stricken ox, saying nothing.'

I sat down and looked at the fire.

'I expected you to deny it,' he said in a tired voice.
'Is it true, then?'

'No,' I said.

'Is that all you've got to say? It isn't enough. What
has happened to you? You owe me an explanation.'

I owed him much more than an explanation.

'I can't explain,' I said despairingly. 'Every horse
I've ridden in the last three weeks seems to have
had its feet dipped in treacle. The difference is in
the horses... I am the same.' It sounded futile and
incredible, even to me.

'You have certainly lost your touch,' he said slowly.
'Perhaps Ballerton is right...'

'Ballerton?' I said sharply.

'He's always said you were not as good as you were
made out to be, and that I'd pushed you too fast...
given you a top job when you weren't ready for it.
Today he has been going round smugly saying "I told
you so." He can't leave the subject alone, he's so
pleased.'

'I'm sorry, James,' I said.

'Are you ill, or something?' he asked exasperatedly.

'No,' I said.

'They say the fall you had three weeks ago was
what frightened you – the day you got knocked out
and your horse rolled on you. But you were all right
going home, weren't you? I remember you being a bit
sore, but you didn't seem in the least scared of falling
again.'

'I didn't give that fall another thought,' I said.

'Then why, Rob, why?'

But I shook my head. I didn't know why.

He stood up and opened a cupboard which contained bottles and glasses, poured out two whiskies, and handed one to me.

'I can't convince myself yet that you've lost your nerve,' he said. 'Remembering the way you rode Template on Boxing Day, only a month ago, it seems impossible. No one could change so fundamentally in so short a time. Before I took you on, wasn't it your stock in trade to ride all the rough and dangerous horses that trainers didn't want to risk their best jockeys on? That's why I first engaged you, I remember it clearly. And all those years you spent in wherever it was as a stockman, and that spell in a rodeo ... you aren't the sort of man to lose his nerve suddenly and for nothing, and especially not when you're in the middle of a most spectacularly successful season.'

I smiled for almost the first time that day, realizing how deeply I wanted him not to lose faith in me.

I said, 'I feel as if I'm fighting a fog. I tried everything I knew today to get those horses to go faster, but they were all half-dead. Or I was. I don't know ... it's a pretty ghastly mess.'

'I'm afraid it is,' he said gloomily. 'And I'm having owner trouble about it, as you can imagine. All the original doubters are doubting again. I can't reassure them ... it's like a Stock Exchange crash; catching. And you're the bad stock that's being jettisoned.'

'What rides can I still expect?' I said.

He sighed. 'I don't exactly know. You can have all the Broome runners because he's on a cruise in the Mediterranean and won't hear the rumours for a while. And my two as well; they both run next week. For the rest, we'll have to wait and see.'

I could hardly bring myself to say it, but I had to know.

'How about Template?' I asked.

He looked at me steadily. 'I haven't heard from George Tirrold,' he said. 'I think he will agree that he can't chuck you out after you've won so many races for him. He is not easily stampeded, there's that to hope for, and it was he who drew my attention to you in the first place. Unless something worse happens,' he finished judiciously, 'I think you can still count on riding Template in the Midwinter a week on Saturday. But if you bring him in last in that ... it will be the end.'

I stood up and drained the whisky.

'I'll win that race,' I said, 'whatever the cost, I'll win it.'

We went silently together to the races the following day, but when we arrived I discovered that two of my three prospective mounts were mine no longer. I had been, in the expressive phrase, jocked off. The owners, the trainer in question brusquely explained, thought they would have no chance of winning if they put me up as planned. Very sorry and all that, he said, but no dice.

I stood on the stands and watched both the horses run well: one of them won, and the other finished a close third. I ignored as best I could the speculative, sideways glances from all the other jockeys, trainers and pressmen standing near me. If they wanted to see how I was taking it, that was their affair; just as it was mine if I wanted to conceal from them the inescapable bitterness of these two results.

I went out to ride James's runner in the fourth race absolutely determined to win. The horse was capable of it on his day, and I knew him to be a competent jumper and a willing battler in a close finish.

We came last.

All the way round I could barely keep him in touch with the rest of the field. In the end he cantered slowly past the winning post with his head down in tiredness, and mine down too, in defeat and humiliation. I felt ill.

It was an effort to go back and face the music. I felt more like driving the Mini-Cooper at top speed into a nice solid tree.

The freckle-faced lad who looked after the horse deliberately did not glance at me when he took hold of the reins in the paddock. He usually greeted me with a beaming smile. I slid off the horse. The owner and James stood there, their faces blank. No one said anything. There was nothing to say. Finally, without a word, the owner shrugged his shoulders and turned on his heel, and walked off.

I took my saddle off the horse and the lad led him away.

James said, 'It can't go on, Rob.'

I knew it.

He said, 'I'm sorry. I'm very sorry. I'll have to get someone else to ride my horses tomorrow.'

I nodded.

He gave me a searching look in which puzzlement and doubt were tinged for the first time with pity. I found it unbearable.

'I think I'll go to Kensington tonight after the races,' I said, trying to speak evenly. 'Instead of coming back with you.'

'Very well,' he said, obviously relieved at not having to face an embarrassing return journey. 'I really am sorry, Rob.'

'Yes,' I said. 'I know.'

I took my saddle back to the weighing-room, acutely aware of the glances which followed me. The conversation in the changing-room died into an embarrassed silence when I walked in. I went over to my peg and put the saddle on the bench, and began to take off my colours. I looked at the circle of faces turned towards me, reading on some curiosity, on some hostility, on some sympathy, and on one or two,

139

pleasure. No contempt: they would leave that to people who didn't ride, to the people who didn't know at first hand how formidable a big fence can look to a jockey on a bad horse. In the changing-room there was too much consciousness in their minds of 'there but for the grace of God go I,' for them to feel contempt.

They began to talk again, but not much to me. I guessed they didn't know what to say. Nor did I.

I felt neither more nor less courageous than I had done all my life. It was surely impossible, I thought confusedly, to be subconsciously afraid, to keep out of trouble and yet think one was as willing as ever to accept risks. Three weeks earlier, I would have laughed at the idea. But the shattering fact remained that none of the twenty-eight horses I had ridden since I had been knocked out in that fall had made any show at all. They were trained by several different trainers and owned by different owners: all they had had in common was me. There were too many of them for it to be a coincidence, especially as those I had been removed from had done well.

Round and round in a jumble went the profitless thoughts, the hopeless statistics, the feeling that the sky had fallen. I put on my street clothes and brushed my hair, and was surprised to see in the mirror that I looked the same as usual.

I went outside on to the steps outside the weighing-room and heard the normal chatter which my presence had muffled in the changing-room break out cheerfully again as soon as I was gone. No one outside either seemed very anxious to talk to me: no one, that is, except a weedy little ferret of a man, who worked, I knew, for one of the minor sporting papers.

He was standing with John Ballerton, but when he caught sight of me he came directly over.

'Oh, Finn,' he said, taking a notebook and pencil out of his pocket and looking at me with a sly, malicious smile. 'May I have a list of the horses you are riding tomorrow? And next week?'

I looked across at Ballerton. There was a smirk of triumph on his heavy face. I took a great grip on my rising temper and spoke mildly to the pressman.

'Ask Mr Axminster,' I said. He looked disappointed, but he didn't know how close he had come to feeling my fist in his face. I had just enough sense to know that letting fly at him would be the worst thing I could do.

I strode away from him, seething with rage; but the day had not done with me, even yet. Corin, crossing my path purposefully, stopped me and said, 'I suppose you've seen this?' He held out a copy of the paper for which the ferrety little man wrote.

'No,' I said. 'And I don't want to.'

Corin smiled thinly, enjoying himself. 'I think you ought to sue them. Everyone thinks so. You'll have to sue them when you've read it. You can't ignore it, or everyone will think ...'

141

'Everyone can think what they damn well please,' I said roughly, trying to walk on.

'Read it,' insisted Corin, thrusting the paper in front of my eyes. 'Everyone else has.'

It needed only a half glance to see the headline. There was no missing it. In bold type it said, 'Nerve Lost.'

Against my will I began to read.

'Nerve, depending on how it takes you, is either fear overcome by an effort of will, or a total lack of imagination. If you ride steeplechasing it doesn't matter which sort you have, as long as you have one of them.

'Does anyone understand why one man is brave and another is not? Or why a person can be brave at one time and cowardly at another?

'Maybe it is all a matter of hormones! Maybe a bang on the head can destroy the chemical make-up which produces courage. Who knows? Who knows?

'The crumbling of a jumping jockey's nerve is a pathetic sight, as every recent racegoer will realize. But while one may extend sympathy to a man for a state which he cannot help, one must at the same time ask whether he is doing the right thing if he continues to seek and accept rides in races.

'The public deserves a fair run for its money. If a jockey can't give it to them because he is afraid of hurting himself, he is taking fees under false pretences.

'But it is only a matter of time, of course, before owners and trainers withdraw their custom from such a man and, by forcing him into retirement, protect the betting public from wasting any more of its money.

'And a good thing too!'

I gave the paper back to Corin and tried to loosen the clamped tension of my jaw muscles.

'I can't sue them,' I said. 'They don't mention my name.'

He didn't look surprised, and I realized sharply that he had known it all along. He had wanted only the pleasure of watching me read, and there was still about his eyes a remnant of a very nasty smile.

'What did I ever do to you, Corin,' I asked, 'to make you feel the way you do?'

He looked taken aback, and said weakly, 'Er . . . nothing . . .'

'Then I'm sorry for you,' I said stonily. 'I'm sorry for your spiteful, mean, cowardly little soul . . .'

'Cowardly!' he exclaimed, stung and flushing. 'Who are you to call anyone else cowardly? That's a laugh, that really is. Just wait till they hear this. Just wait till I tell . . .'

But I didn't wait. I had had far, far more than enough. I went back to Kensington in as deep and terrible a mood of despair as I ever hope to have to live through.

There was no one in the flat, and for once it was spotlessly tidy. The family, I concluded, were away. The kitchen confirmed it. There was no food or milk in the refrigerator, no bread in the bin, no fruit in the basket.

Back in the silent sitting-room I took a nearly full whisky bottle out of the cupboard and lay down full length on the sofa. I uncorked the bottle and took two large gulps. The neat spirit bit into my gums and scorched down to my empty stomach. I put the cork in the bottle and the bottle on the floor beside me. What is the point of getting drunk, I thought: I'd only feel worse in the morning. I could stay drunk for several days perhaps, but it wouldn't do any good in the end. Nothing would do any good. Everything was finished. Everything was busted and gone.

I spent a long time looking at my hands. Hands. The touch they had for horses had earned me my living all my adult life. They looked the same as always. They were the same, I thought desperately. Nerves and muscles, strength and sensitivity, nothing was changed. But the memory of the last twenty-eight horses I had ridden denied it: heavy, cumbersome and unresponsive.

I knew no other skill but riding, nor had ever wanted any. I felt more than whole on horseback: I felt extended. Four extra limbs and a second brain.

More speed, more strength, more courage ... I winced at the word ... and quicker reactions. A saddle was to me as the sea to a fish, natural and easy. Home. And a racing saddle? I drew in a breath, shivering. For a racing saddle, I thought bleakly, I am not sufficient.

It wasn't enough after all to *want* to race as well as anybody, one had to have the talent and the staying power as well; and I was face to face with the conviction that I was not good enough, that I was never going to be good enough, to take firm hold of the position which had been so nearly in my grasp. I had thought myself capable of seizing the incredible opportunity I had been given. The mess I had made of it, the weak, degrading retreat from the brink of success, was tearing to shreds all I had known or believed about myself.

I picked up the whisky bottle and held it on my chest. It was all the company I had, and it offered sleep, at least. But I suppose old habits cling hard: I held the bottle to my chest like a life-jacket to a drowning man and knew I wouldn't pull the cork out again. Not for a while. Not that night, anyway.

And what of the future? I could return during the next week and race on one or two of James's horses, if he would still let me, and perhaps even on Template in the Midwinter. But I no longer either expected or hoped to do well, and I could feel myself shrink at the prospect of going back to a racecourse to face all those stares and insults again. Better to start a new life at once, perhaps. But a new life doing what?

It couldn't be the old life. Being a stockman might have suited me at twenty, but it was not what I would want at thirty, nor at forty, nor fifty. And whatever I did, wherever I went now, I would drag around with me the knowledge that I had totally failed at what I had tried hardest to do.

After a long time I stood up and put the bottle back into the cupboard.

It was then a good twenty-six hours since I had eaten, and despite everything my stomach was beginning its squeezing routine. On a second inspection the kitchen revealed only some assorted tins of *escargots*, cheese straws and *marrons glacés*; so I went out and along the streets until I came to a decent-looking pub where I was sure I was not known by sight. I didn't want to have to talk.

I ordered ham sandwiches and a glass of beer, but when it came the thick new white bread stuck tastelessly in my mouth and my throat kept closing convulsively against all attempts to swallow. This can't go on, I thought. I've got to eat. If I can't get drunk and I can't have Joanna and I can't ... I can't be a jockey any more ... at least I can eat now as much as I like, without worrying about gaining a pound or two ... but after ten minutes trying I had swallowed only two mouthfuls, and I couldn't manage another bite.

The fact that it was Friday had meant nothing to me all evening, and the approach of 9 o'clock went unnoticed. But just when I pushed away the sandwiches and was eyeing the beer with the beginnings of nausea, someone turned up the volume of the television set which stood at one end of the bar, and the opening bars of the 'Galloping Major' suddenly blared out across the tinkling glasses and the buzzing voices. A large bunch of devotees who had settled themselves with full pint pots in front of the set made shooshing noises to those nearest to them, and by the time Maurice Kemp-Lore's tidy features materialized there was a more or less attentive audience to receive him. My little glass-topped table was as far as it could be from the door, so that it was more because leaving meant weaving my way through the sprawling silent crowd, than from a positive desire to watch, that I stayed where I was.

'Good evening,' Maurice said, the spellbinding smile in place. 'This evening we are going to talk about handicapping, and I have here to meet you two well-informed men who look at weights and measures from opposing angles. The first is Mr Charles Jenkinson, who has been an official handicapper for several years.' Mr Jenkinson's self-conscious face appeared briefly on the screen. 'And the other is the well-known trainer, Corin Kellar.'

Corin's thin face glowed with satisfaction. We'll never hear the last of this, I thought; and then with a stab remembered that I wouldn't be there to hear any of it anyway.

'Mr Jenkinson,' said Maurice, 'will explain how he builds a handicap. And Mr Kellar will tell you how he tries to avoid having his horses defeated by their weights. The battle between handicappers and trainers is none the less fierce for being conducted in gentlemanly and largely uncomplaining reticence, and perhaps tonight you will capture a whiff of that unrelenting struggle.' He smiled engagingly. 'A handicapper's pinnacle of success is for every single runner in a race to pass the winning post in a straight line abreast – a multiple dead-heat – since it is his aim to give each horse an exactly equal chance. It never actually happens, but handicappers dream about it in their softer moments.' He grinned sideways in a friendly fashion towards his guest, and when Mr Jenkinson appeared on the screen one could almost see the self-confidence begin to flow in him as he started to talk about his job.

I listened with only half my mind, the rest being submerged in persistent misery, and Corin had been speaking for some moments before I paid much attention to him. He was being of necessity less than frank, since the bald truth would have lost him his licence very smartly. In practice he felt no qualms at all when giving his jockey orders to start at the back and stay there, but in theory, I was sardonically amused to see, he was righteously on the side of the angels.

'Horses from my stable are always doing their best to win,' he said, lying without a tremor.

'But surely you don't insist on them being ridden hard at the end when they've no chance at all?' said Maurice, reasonably.

'As hard as necessary, yes,' Corin asserted. 'I hate to see jockeys easing up too soon, even if they are beaten. I dismissed a jockey a short while ago for not riding hard enough at the end. He could have come third if he had ridden the horse out ...' his voice droned on, pious and petulant, and I thought of Tick-Tock, thrown to the stewards for obeying his orders too conscientiously and now having trouble getting other trainers to trust him. I thought of Art, nagged and contradicted and driven to death; and the active dislike I already felt for Corin Kellar sharpened in that dim pub corner into hatred.

Maurice dragged him back to handicapping and finally wrung from him a grudging admission that from the point of view of the weight he would be allotted in future, it was better for a horse to win by one length than by ten. Maurice would have done better, I thought, to have chosen almost anyone else to show how to dodge the handicapper; or perhaps he did not know Corin well enough to expect him hypocritically to deny in public what he had said in private. Every jockey who had ridden the Kellar horses had learned it the hard way.

'One is always in the hands of one's jockey,' Corin was saying.

'Go on,' said Maurice encouragingly, leaning forward. A light somewhere in the studio lent his eyes a momentary shimmer as he moved. Corin said, 'You can slave away for weeks preparing a horse for a race and then a jockey can undo it all with one stupid mistake.'

'It does the handicap good though,' Maurice interrupted, laughing. The pub audience laughed too.

'Well . . .' agreed Corin, nonplussed.

'If you look at it that way,' Maurice continued, 'there is always some compensation for a jockey not getting the most out of a horse. Whatever the reason, trivial, like a mistake, or more serious, like a failure of resolution at a crucial point . . .'

'No guts, you mean?' said Corin flatly. 'I'd say that that would be as obvious to a handicapper as to everyone else, and that he'd take it into account. There's a case in point now . . .' he hesitated, but Maurice did not try to stop him, so he went on more boldly, 'a case now where everything a certain jockey rides goes round at the back of the field. He is afraid of falling, you see. Well, you can't tell me any handicapper thinks those particular horses are not as good as they were. Of course they are. It's just the rider who's going downhill.'

I could feel the blood rush to my head and begin

to pulse there. I leaned my elbows on the table and
bit my knuckle. Hard.

The voices went on inexorably.

Maurice said, 'What are your views on that, Mr
Jenkinson?'

And the handicapper, looking embarrassed,
murmured that 'Of course... er... in certain
circumstances, one would... er... overlook the
occasional result.'

'Occasional!' said Corin. 'I wouldn't call nearly
thirty races in a row occasional. Are you going to
overlook them all?'

'I can't answer that,' protested Jenkinson.

'What do you usually do in these cases?' Maurice
asked.

'I... that is... they aren't usually as blatant as this.
I may have to consult... er, others, before coming to
a decision. But it really isn't a thing I can discuss here.'

'Where better?' said Maurice persuasively. 'We all
know that this poor chap took a toss three weeks ago
and has ridden... er... ineffectively... ever since.
Surely you'd have to take that into account when you
are handicapping those horses?'

While the cameras focused on Jenkinson hesitating
over his answer Corin's voice said, 'I'll be interested
to know what you decide. One of those horses was
mine, you know. It was a shocking exhibition. Finn
won't be riding for me again, or for anyone else either,
I shouldn't wonder.'

Jenkinson said uneasily, 'I don't think we should mention names,' and Maurice cut in quickly, saying, 'No, no. I agree. Better not.' But the damage was done.

'Well, thank you both very much for giving us your time this evening. I am sorry to say we have come nearly to the end once again . . .' He slid expertly into his minute of chit-chat and his closing sentences, but I was no longer listening. Between them he and Corin had hammered in the nails on the ruins of my brief career, and watching them at it on the glaring little screen had given me a blinding headache.

I stood up stiffly as the chatter broke out again in the crowded pub and threaded my way a little unsteadily to the door. The bunch of racing enthusiasts were downing their pints and I caught a scrap of their conversation as I squeezed around them.

'Laid it on a bit thick, I thought,' one of them said.

'Not thick enough,' contradicted another. 'I lost a quid on Finn on Tuesday. He deserves all he gets, if you ask me, the windy b—.'

I stumbled out into the street, breathing in great gulps of cold air and making a conscious effort to stand up straight. It was no use sitting down and weeping in the gutter, which would have been easy enough to do. I walked slowly back to the dark, empty flat, and without switching on any lights lay down fully dressed on my bed.

The glow from the street below dimly lit the small room, the window frame throwing an angular distorted shadow on the ceiling. My head throbbed. I remembered lying there like that before, the day Grant's fist pulped my nose. I remembered pitying him, and pitying Art. It had been so easy. I groaned aloud, and the sound shocked me.

It was a long way down from my window to the street. Five storeys. A long, quick way down. I thought about it.

There was a chiming clock in the flat below ours, counting away the quarter-hours, and in the quiet house I could hear it clearly. It struck ten, eleven, twelve, one, two.

The window threw its shadow steadily on the ceiling. I stared up at it. Five storeys down. But however bad things were I couldn't take that way, either. It wasn't for me. I shut my eyes and lay still, and finally after the long despairing hours drifted into an exhausted, uneasy, dream-filled sleep.

I woke less than two hours later, and heard the clock strike four. My headache had gone, and my mind felt as clear and sharp as the starry sky outside: washed and shining. It was like coming out of a thick fog into sunshine. Like coolness after fever. Like being re-born.

Somewhere between sleeping and waking I found I had regained myself, come back to the life-saving certainty that I was the person I thought I was, and not the cracked-up mess that everyone else believed.

And that being so, I thought in puzzlement, there must be some other explanation of my troubles. All – *all* I had to do was find it. Looking back unsympathetically on the appalling desolation in which I had so recently allowed myself to flounder, I began at last, at long last, to use my brain.

Half an hour later it was clear that my stomach was awake too, and it was so insistent to be filled that I couldn't concentrate. I got up and fetched the tins of cheese straws and *marrons glacés* from the kitchen, but not the snails. How hungry would one have to be, I wondered idly, to face those molluscs cold and butterless at five o'clock in the morning?

I opened the tins and lay down again, and crunched up all the cheese straws while I thought, and peeled and chewed half of the syrupy weight-producing chestnuts. My stomach quietened like a dragon fed its daily maiden, and outside the stars faded into the wan London dawn.

In the morning I took the advice I had given to Grant, and went to see a psychiatrist.

CHAPTER NINE

I had known the psychiatrist all my life as he was a friend of my father, and, I hoped, I knew him well enough to ring him up for help on a morning which he always reserved for golf. At eight o'clock I telephoned to his house in Wimpole Street where he lived in a flat above his consulting rooms.

He asked after my father. He sounded in a hurry.

'Can I come and see you, sir?' I said.

'Now? No. Saturday. Golf,' he said economically.

'Please . . . it won't take long.'

There was a brief pause.

'Urgent?' A professional note to his question.

'Yes,' I said.

'Come at once, then. I'm due at Wentworth at ten.'

'I haven't shaved . . .' I said, catching sight of myself in the looking-glass and realizing what a wreck I looked.

'Do you want to shave, or do you want to talk?' he said, exasperated.

'Talk,' I said.

'Then arrive,' he said, and put down his receiver.

I took a taxi, and he opened the door to me with a corner of toast and marmalade in his hand. The eminent Mr Claudius Mellit, whose patients usually saw him in striped trousers and black jacket, was sensibly attired for winter golf in waterproof trousers and a comfortably sloppy Norwegian sweater. He gave me a piercing preliminary glance and gestured, 'Upstairs.'

I followed him up. He finished his breakfast on the way. We went into his dining-room, where he gave me a seat at the oval mahogany table and some lukewarm coffee in a gold-rimmed cup.

'Now,' he said, sitting down opposite me.

'Suppose . . .' I began, and stopped. It didn't seem so easy, now that I was there. What had seemed obvious and manifest at five in the morning was now tinged with doubt. The dawn hours had shown me a pattern I believed in, but in the full light of day I felt sure it was going to sound preposterous.

'Look,' he said, 'if you really need help my golf can go hang. When I said on the telephone that I was in a hurry I hadn't seen the state you are in . . . and if you will excuse my saying so, your suit looks as if you had slept in it?'

'Well, yes, I did,' I said, surprised.

'Relax then, and tell me all.' He grinned, a big bear of a man, fifty years old and formidably wise.

'I'm sorry I look so untidy and unshaven,' I began.

'And sunken-eyed and hollow-cheeked,' he murmured, smiling.

'But I don't feel as bad as I suppose I look. Not any more. I won't keep you away from your golf if you'll just tell me . . .'

'Yes?' he waited for me calmly.

'Suppose I had a sister,' I said, 'who was as good a musician as Mother and Father, and I was the only one in the entire family to lack their talent – as you know I am – and I felt they despised me for lacking it, how would you expect me to act?'

'They don't despise you,' he protested.

'No . . . but if they did, would there be any way in which I could persuade them – and myself – that I had a very good excuse for not being a musician?'

'Oh, yes,' he said instantly, 'I'd expect you to do exactly what you have done. Find something you can do, and pursue it fanatically until in your own sphere you reach the standard of your family in theirs.'

I felt as if I'd been hit in the solar plexus. So simple an explanation of my compulsion to race had never occurred to me.

'That . . . that isn't what I meant,' I said helplessly. 'But when I come to think of it, I see it is true.' I paused. 'What I really meant to ask was, could I, when I was growing up, have developed a physical infirmity to explain away my failure? Paralysis, for instance, so that I simply couldn't play a violin or a piano or any musical instrument? An apparently honourable way out?'

He looked at me for a few moments, unsmiling and intent.

'If you were a certain type of person, yes, it's possible. But not in your case. You had better stop waltzing round it and ask me your question straight out. The real question. I am very well accustomed to hypothetical questions ... I meet them every day ... but if you want a trustable answer you'll have to ask the real question.'

'There are two,' I said. I still hesitated. So very much, my whole life, depended on his answers. He waited patiently.

I said at last, 'Could a boy whose family were all terrific cross-country riders develop asthma to hide the fact that he was afraid of horses?' My mouth was dry.

He didn't answer at once. He said, 'What is the other question?'

'Could that boy, as a man, develop such a loathing for steeplechase jockeys that he would try to smash their careers? Even if, as you said, he had found something else which he could do extremely well?'

'I suppose this man has that sister you mentioned?'

'Yes,' I said. 'She is getting to be the best girl point-to-point rider for a generation.'

He slouched back in his chair.

'It obviously matters so desperately to you, Robert, that I can't give you an answer without knowing more

158

about it. I'm not giving you a couple of casual yeses and find afterwards I've let you stir up disastrous trouble for all sorts of people. You must tell me why you ask these questions.'

'But your golf,' I said.

'I'll go later,' he said calmly. 'Talk.'

So I talked. I told him what had happened to Art, and to Grant, and to Peter Cloony, and Tick-Tock, and myself.

I told him about Maurice Kemp-Lore. 'He comes from a family who ride as soon as walk, and he's the right build for steeplechasing. But horses give him asthma, and that, everyone knows, is why he doesn't race himself. Well ... it's a good reason, isn't it? Of course there are asthmatics who do ride – asthma doesn't stop people who think that racing is worth the wheezing – but no one would dream of blaming a man who didn't.'

I paused, but as he made no comment, I went on, 'You can't help being drawn to him. You can't imagine the spell of his personality unless you've felt it. You can see people wake up and sparkle when he speaks to them. He has the ear of everyone from the stewards down ... and I think he uses his influence to sow seeds of doubt about jockeys' characters.'

'Go on,' Claudius said, his face showing nothing.

'The men who seem to be especially under his spell are Corin Kellar, a trainer, and John Ballerton, a member of the ruling body. Neither of them ever has a good word to say for jockeys. I think Kemp-Lore picked them out as friends solely because they had the right sort of mean-mindedness for broadcasting every damaging opinion he insinuated into their heads. I think all the ruinous rumours start with Kemp-Lore, and that even the substance behind the rumours is mostly his work. Why isn't he content with having so much? The jockeys he is hurting like him and are pleased when he talks to them. Why does he need to destroy them?'

He said, 'If this were a hypothetical case I would tell you that such a man could both hate and envy his father – and his sister – and have felt both these emotions from early childhood. But because he knows these feelings are wrong he represses them, and the aggression is unfortunately transferred on to people who show the same qualities and abilities that he hates in his father. Such individuals can be helped. They can be understood, and treated, and forgiven.'

'I can't forgive him,' I said. 'And I'm going to stop him.'

He considered me. 'You must make sure of your facts,' he said, stroking his thumbnail down his upper lip. 'At present you are just guessing. And as I've had no opportunity to talk to him you'll get no more from me than an admission that your suspicions of Kemp-Lore are *possibly* correct. Not even probably correct. He is a public figure of some standing. You are making a very serious accusation. You need cast-iron facts.

Until you have them, there is always the chance that you have interpreted what has happened to you as malice from outside in order to explain away your own inner failure. Asthma of the mind, in fact.'

'Don't psychologists ever take a simple view?' I said, sighing.

He shook his head. 'Few things are simple.'

'I'll get the facts. Starting today,' I said. I stood up. 'Thank you for seeing me, and being so patient, and I'm sincerely sorry about your golf.'

'I won't be very late,' he reassured me, ambling down the stairs and opening his front door. On the doorstep shaking hands, he said as if making up his mind, 'Be careful, Robert. Go gently. If you are right about Kemp-Lore, and it is just possible that you are, you must deal with him thoughtfully. Persuade him to ask for treatment. Don't drive him too hard. His sanity may be in your hands.'

I said flatly, 'I can't look at it from your point of view. I don't think of Kemp-Lore as ill, but as wicked.'

'Where illness ends and crime begins . . .' he shrugged. 'It has been debated for centuries, and no two people agree. But take care, take care.' He turned to go in. 'Remember me to your parents.' He smiled, and shut the door.

Round a couple of corners, first during a luxurious shave in a fresh-smelling barber's and second over a triple order of eggs and bacon in the café next door, I bent my mind to the problem of how the cast-iron facts were to be dug up. On reflection, there seemed to be precious few of them to work on, and in the digging, to start with at least, I was going to come up against the barrier of pity and contempt which my recent performances had raised. Nasty medicine; but if I wanted a cure, I'd have to take it.

Using the café's telephone, I rang up Tick-Tock.

'Are you riding this afternoon?' I asked.

He said, 'Do me a favour, pal. No unkind questions so early in the day. In a word – negative.' A pause. 'And you?' Innocently, too innocently.

'You're a bastard,' I said.

'So my best friends tell me.'

'I want the car,' I said.

'Not if you're thinking of driving it over Beachy Head.'

'I'm not,' I said.

'Well, I'm relieved to hear it. But if you change your mind, let me know and I'll join you.' His voice was light and mocking; the desperate truth underneath needed no stating.

'I want to call at some stables,' I began.

'Whose?' he interrupted.

'Several people's ... about six altogether, I think, apart from Axminster's. And Kellar's. I'll have to go there as well.'

'You've got a nerve,' said Tick-Tock.

'Thank you,' I said. 'You're about the only person in the country who thinks so.'

'Damn it . . . I didn't mean . . .'

I grinned into the telephone. 'Save it. Where's the car now?'

'Outside the window.'

'I'll come down to Newbury by train and pick it up, if you'll meet me at the station,' I said.

'It's no use going to any stables today,' he said. 'The trainers will all be at the races.'

'Yes, I sincerely hope so,' I agreed.

'What are you up to?' he asked suspiciously.

'Retrieving the fallen fortunes of the House of Finn,' I said. 'I'll catch the 10.10. You meet it. O.K.?' And I put the receiver down, hearing and ignoring, a protesting 'Hey' before I cut him off.

But when I stepped off the train at Newbury he was waiting, dressed in a dandyish waisted riding jacket of almost eighteenth-century length on top of some unbelievably narrow cavalry cord trousers. He enjoyed his moment ironically while I looked him up and down.

'Where's the cravat, the ruffles and the sword?' I asked.

He said, 'You don't get the message. I'm tomorrow's man. My sword will be a do-it-yourself instant anti-radiation kit. You must fit your defence to the danger you meet . . .' He grinned.

Young Tick-Tock, I reflected, not for the first time, took an uncompromisingly realistic view of the world.

He opened the car door and settled himself behind the wheel.

'Where to?' he said.

'You're not coming,' I said.

'I certainly am. This car is half mine. Where it goes, I go.' He was clearly determined. 'Where to?'

'Well ...' I got in beside him, fished out of my pocket a list I had made on the train, and showed it to him. 'These are the stables I want to go to. I've tried to arrange them in order so that there isn't too much back-tracking, but even so it means a lot of driving.'

'Phew,' he said. 'There's a lot of them. Hampshire, Sussex, Kent, Oxford, Leicester, and Yorkshire ... how long will you be staying in each place? We'll never cover this lot in one day. Especially as you look tired already.'

I glanced at him, but he was looking down at the paper. It was true that I felt tired, but disconcerting that it should be so obvious. I had thought that the shave and breakfast and the return of self-confidence would have wiped away the ravages of the previous day and night.

'You needn't come,' I began.

'We've been through all that,' he interrupted. 'We'll start by going to your digs and mine for overnight things, and then make for Kent. And on the way you can tell me why we're going.' He calmly let in the clutch and drove off; and truth to tell I was very glad of his company.

We collected our things, and Tick-Tock pointed the

Mini-Cooper's blunt nose towards the first stable on the list, Corin Kellar's, in Hampshire.

'Now,' he said. 'The works.'

'No,' I said. 'I'm not going to tell you why we're going. Listen and watch, and then you tell me.'

'You're a cagey blighter,' he said, without arguing. He added, 'I suppose you've taken into account all that about saps rushing in where angels wouldn't plonk their holy feet? I mean, to put it mildly, we are neither of us in the red carpet bracket just now. Strictly doomsville, us.'

'You are so right,' I said, smiling.

Tick-Tock turned his head and gave me a surprised stare.

'Keep your eyes on the road,' I said mildly.

'I'll never know you,' he said. 'I'd have thought you'd take it very hard ... what has happened ... but since I picked you up at the station I've felt more cheerful than I have for weeks.' His foot went down on the accelerator and he began to whistle.

We arrived at Corin's extensive, well-groomed stable while the lads were doing up the horses after the second morning exercise. Arthur, the head lad, was crossing the yard with a bucket of oats when we climbed out of the little car, and the crinkling smile with which he usually greeted me got half-way to his eyes before he remembered. I saw the embarrassment take over and the welcome fade away.

'The guvnor isn't here,' he said awkwardly. 'He's gone to the races.'

'I know,' I said. 'Can I speak to Davey?'

Davey was the lad who looked after Shantytown.

'I suppose so,' said Arthur doubtfully, 'but you won't make no trouble?'

'No,' I said. 'No trouble. Where is he?'

'Fourth box from the end over that side,' he said, pointing. Tick-Tock and I walked over, and found Davey tossing and tidying the straw bed round a big chestnut, Shantytown. We leaned over the bottom half of the door, and watched Davey's expression too change from warmth to disgust. He was a short, tough, sixteen-year-old boy with flaming red hair and an intolerant mouth. He turned his back on us and ran his hand down the horse's neck. Then he spat into the straw. Tick-Tock took a sharp breath and his hands clenched into fists.

I said quickly, 'Davey, there's a quid for you if you feel like talking a bit.'

'What about?' he said, without turning round.

'About the day I rode Shantytown at Dunstable,' I said. 'Three weeks ago. Do you remember?'

'I'll say I remember,' he said offensively.

I ignored his tone. 'Well, tell me what happened from the moment you arrived on the course until I got up on Shantytown in the parade ring.'

'What the hell do you mean?' he said, wheeling

round and coming over to the door. 'Nothing happened. What should happen?'

I took a pound note out of my wallet and gave it to him. He looked at it for a second or two, then shrugged, and thrust it into his pocket.

'Start when you set off from here. Don't leave anything out,' I said.

'Are you off your nut?' he said.

'No,' I said, 'and I want my quid's worth.'

He shrugged again, but said, 'We went in the horse box from here to Dunstable, and . . .'

'Did you stop on the way?' I asked.

'Yes, Joe's Caff, same as always when we go to Dunstable.'

'Did you see anyone there you knew?'

'Well . . . Joe, and the girl who pours out the char.'

'No one you wouldn't expect?' I pressed.

'No, of course not. Like I said, we got to the course and unloaded the horses, two of them, in the stables there, and went and got another cuppa and a wad in the canteen, and then I went round the bookies, like, and put ten bob on Bloggs in the first, and went up on the stands and watched it get stuffed . . . sodding animal didn't try a yard . . . and then I went back to the stables and got Shantytown and put on his paddock clothing and led him out into the paddock . . .' His voice was bored as he recited the everyday racing routine of his job.

'Could anyone have given Shantytown anything to

eat or drink in the stables, say a bucket of water just before the race?' I asked.

'Don't be so ruddy stupid. Of course not. Who ever heard of giving a horse anything to eat or drink before a race? A mouthful of water, I dare say, a couple of hours beforehand, but a bucketful . . .' The scorn in his voice suddenly changed to anger. 'Here, you're not suggesting I gave him a drink, are you? Oh no, mate, you're not putting the blame on me for the balls you made of it.'

'No,' I said, 'no, Davey. Calm down. How tight is the security on the Dunstable stables? Would anyone but a lad or a trainer get in there?'

'No,' he said, more moderately, 'it's as tight as a drum. The last gateman got sacked for letting an owner in alone without a trainer, and the new man's as pernickety as they come.'

'Go on, then,' I said. 'We've got you as far as the paddock.'

'Well, I walked the horse round the assembly ring for a bit, waiting for the guvnor to bring the saddle up from the weighing-room . . .' He smiled suddenly, as at some pleasant memory '. . . and then when he came I took Shanty into one of the saddling boxes and the guvnor saddled up, and then I took Shanty down into the parade ring and walked him round until they called me over and you got up on him.' He stopped. 'I can't see what you wanted to hear all that for.'

'What happened while you were walking round the assembly ring?' I asked. 'Something you enjoyed? Something you smile about when you remember it?'

He sniffed. 'It's nothing you'd want to know.'

I said, 'The quid was for telling everything.'

'Oh, very well then, but it's nothing to do with racing. It was that chap on the telly, Maurice Kemp-Lore, he came over and spoke to me and admired the horse. He said he was a friend of the owner, old man Ballerton. He patted Shanty and gave him a couple of sugar knobs, which I wasn't too keen on, mind, but you can't be narky with a chap like him, somehow, and he asked me what his chances were, and I said pretty good ... more fool me ... and then he went away again. That's all. I told you it wasn't anything to do with racing.'

'No,' I said. 'Well, never mind. Thanks for trying.'

I straightened up and turned away from the door, and Tick-Tock had taken a step or two towards the car when Davey said under his breath behind me, 'Trying ... you two could both do a bit more of that yourselves, if you ask me.' But Tick-Tock fortunately didn't hear, and we folded ourselves back into the Mini-Cooper and drove unmourned out of the yard.

Tick-Tock exploded. 'Anyone would think you'd killed your mother and robbed your grandmother, the way they look at you. Losing your nerve isn't a crime.'

'Unless you can put up with a few harmless sneers you'd better get out at the next railway station,' I said cheerfully, having blessedly discovered in the last half-hour that they no longer hurt. 'And I haven't lost my nerve. Not yet, anyway.'

He opened his mouth and shut it again and flicked a glance at me, and drove another twenty miles without speaking.

We reached the next yard on my list shortly before one o'clock, and disturbed the well-to-do farmer, who trained his own horses, just as he was about to sit down to his lunch. When he opened the door to us a warm smell of stew and cabbage edged past him, and we could hear a clatter of saucepans in the kitchen. I had ridden several winners for him in the past two years before disgracing his best horse the previous week, and after he had got over the unpleasant shock of finding me on his doorstep, he asked us, in a friendly enough fashion, to go in for a drink. But I thanked him and refused, and asked where I could find the lad who looked after the horse in question. He came out to the gate with us and pointed to a house down the road.

We winkled the lad out of his digs and into the car, where I gave him a pound and invited him to describe in detail what had happened on the day I had ridden his horse. He was older, less intelligent and less truculent than Davey, but not much more willing. He didn't see no sense in it, he didn't. He said so, several times. Eventually I got him started, and then there was no stopping him. Detail I had asked for, and detail I got, solidly, for close on half an hour.

Sandwiched between stripping off the paddock clothing and buckling up the saddle came the news that Maurice Kemp-Lore had lounged into the saddling box, said some complimentary things to the farmer-owner about his horse, meanwhile feeding the animal some lumps of sugar, and had drifted away again leaving behind him the usual feeling of friendliness and pleasure.

'A proper corker, ain't he?' was how the lad put it.

I waited until he had reached the point when the farmer had given me a leg up on the horse, and then stopped him and thanked him for his efforts. We left him muttering that we were welcome, but he still didn't see the point.

'How odd,' said Tick-Tock pensively as we sped along the road to the next stable, eighty miles away. 'How odd that Maurice Kemp-Lore . . .' but he didn't finish the sentence; and nor did I.

Two hours later, in Kent, we listened, for another pound, to a gaunt boy of twenty telling us what a smashing fellow that Maurice Kemp-Lore was, how interested he'd been in the horse, how kind to give him some sugar, though it wasn't really allowed in his stables, but how could you tell a man like that not to, when he was being so friendly? The lad also treated us with a rather offensive superiority, but even Tick-Tock by now had become too interested to care.

'He drugged them,' he said flatly, after a long silence, turning on to the Maidstone by-pass. 'He drugged them to make it look as if you couldn't ride them ... to make everyone believe you'd lost your nerve.'

'Yes,' I agreed.

'But it's impossible,' he protested vehemently. 'Why on earth should he? It can't be right. It must be a coincidence that he gave sugar to three horses you rode.'

'Maybe. We'll see,' I said.

And we did see. We went to the stables of every horse (other than James's) that I had ridden since Shantytown, talking to every lad concerned. And in every single case we heard that Maurice Kemp-Lore had made the lad's afternoon memorable (before I had blighted it) by admiring the way the lad had looked after his horse, and by offering those tempting lumps of sugar. It took us the whole of Saturday, and all Sunday morning, and we finished the last stable on my list on the edge of the Yorkshire moors at two o'clock in the afternoon. Only because I wanted my facts to be as cast-iron as possible had we gone so far north. Tick-Tock had become convinced in Northampton-shire.

I drove us back to our respective digs in Berkshire, and the following morning, Monday, I walked up to the Axminster stables to see James.

He had just come in from supervising the morning

exercise, and the cold downland air had numbed his toes and fingers.

'Come into the office,' he said when he saw me waiting. His tone was neutral, but his protruding lower jaw was unrelenting. I followed him in, and he turned on an electric heater to warm his hands.

'I can't give you much to ride,' he said, with his back to me. 'All the owners have cried off, except one. You'd better look at this; it came this morning.' He stretched out his hand, picked up a paper from his desk, and held it out to me.

I took it. It was a letter from Lord Tirrold. It said,

'Dear James,
Since our telephone conversation I have been thinking over our decision to replace Finn on Template next Saturday, and I now consider that we should reverse this and allow him to ride as originally planned. It is, I confess, at least as much for our sake as for his, since I do not want it said that I hurried to throw him out at the first possible moment, showing heartless ingratitude after his many wins on my horses. I am prepared for the disappointment of not winning the Midwinter and I apologize to you for robbing you of the chance of adding this prize to your total, but I would rather lose the race than the respect of the racing fraternity.
Yours ever, George.'

I put the letter back on the desk.

'He doesn't need to worry,' I said thickly. 'Template will win.'

'Do you mean you aren't going to ride it?' said James, turning round quickly. There was a damaging note of eagerness in his voice, and he saw that I had heard it. 'I . . . I mean . . .' he tailed off.

'James,' I said, sitting down unasked in one of the battered armchairs. 'There are a few things I'd like you to know. First, however bad it looks, and whatever you believe, I have not lost my nerve. Second, every single horse I have ridden since that fall three weeks ago has been doped. Not enough to be very noticeable, just enough to make it run like a slug. Third, the dope has been given to all the horses on sugar lumps. I should think it was some form of sleeping draught, but I've no way of knowing for sure.' I stopped abruptly.

James stood looking at me with his mouth open, the prominent lower teeth bared to the gums as his lip dropped in shocked disbelief.

I said, 'Before you conclude that I am out of my mind, do me the favour of calling in one of the lads, and listening to what he has to say.'

James shut his mouth with a snap. 'Which lad?'

'It doesn't really matter. Any of them whose horse I have ridden in the last three weeks.'

He paused dubiously, but finally went to the door and shouted for someone to find Eddie, the lad who looked after Hugo's big chestnut. In less than a minute the boy arrived, out of breath, and with his curly hair sticking up in an uncombed halo.

James gave me no chance to do the questioning. He said brusquely to Eddie, 'When did you last talk to Rob?'

The boy looked scared and began to stutter, 'N-not since l-l-last week.'

'Since last Friday?' That was the day James himself had last seen me.

'No sir.'

'Very well, then. You remember the big chestnut running badly last Wednesday week?'

'Yes sir.' Eddie treated me to a scornful glance.

'Did anyone give the chestnut a lump of sugar before the race?' There was now only interest to be heard in James's voice: the severity was masked.

'Yes sir,' said Eddie eagerly. The familiar remembering smile appeared on his grubby face, and I breathed an inward sigh of bottomless relief.

'Who was it?'

'Maurice Kemp-Lore, sir. He said how splendidly I looked after my horses, sir. He was leaning over the rails of the assembly ring and he spoke to me as I was going past. So I stopped, and he was ever so nice. He gave the chestnut some sugar, sir, but I didn't think it would matter as Mr Hugo is always sending sugar for him anyway.'

175

'Thank you, Eddie,' said James, rather faintly. 'No matter about the sugar . . . run along, now.'

Eddie went. James looked at me blankly. The loud clock ticked.

Presently I said, 'I've spent the last two days talking to the lads of all the horses I've ridden for other stables since I had that fall. Every one of them told me that Maurice Kemp-Lore gave the horse some lumps of sugar before I rode it. Ingersoll came with me. He heard them too. You've only to ask him if you can't believe it from me.'

'Maurice never goes near horses at the races,' James protested, 'or anywhere else for that matter.'

'That's precisely what helped me to understand what was happening,' I said. 'I talked to Kemp-Lore on the stands at Dunstable just after Shantytown and two other horses had run hopelessly for me, and he was wheezing quite audibly. He had asthma. Which meant that he had recently been very close to horses. I didn't give it a thought at the time, but it means a packet to me now.'

'But Maurice . . .' he repeated, unbelievingly. 'It's just not possible.'

'It is, however, possible,' I said, more coldly than I had any right to, having believed it myself for twelve awful hours, 'for me to fall apart from a small spot of concussion?'

'I don't know what to think,' he said uncomfortably. There was a pause. There were two things I wanted

176

James to do to help me: but in view of his ingrained disinclination to do favours for anyone, I did not think my requests would be very enthusiastically received. However, if I didn't ask, I wouldn't get.

I said slowly, persuasively, as if the thought had just occurred to me, 'Let me ride a horse for you ... one of your own, if the owners won't have me ... and see for yourself if Kemp-Lore tries to give it sugar. Perhaps you could stick with the horse yourself, all the time? And if he comes up with his sugar lumps, maybe you could manage to knock them out of his hand before the horse eats them. Perhaps you could pick them up yourself and put them in your pocket, and give the horse some sugar lumps of your own instead? Then we would see how the horse runs.'

It was too much trouble; his face showed it. He said, 'That's too fantastic. I can't do things like that.'

'It's simple,' I said mildly, 'you've only to bump his arm.'

'No,' he said, but not obstinately. A hopeful no, to my ears. I didn't press him, knowing from experience that he would irrevocably stick in his toes if urged too vehemently to do anything he did not want to.

I said instead, 'Aren't you friendly with that man who arranges the regular dope tests at the races?' One or two spot checks were taken at every meeting, mainly to deter trainers of doubtful reputation from pepping-up or slowing-down their horses with drugs. At the beginning of each afternoon the stewards decided which horses to test – for example, the winner of the second race, and the favourite in the fourth race (especially if he was beaten). No one, not even the stewards, always knew in advance exactly which horses would have their saliva taken, and the value of the whole system lay in this uncertainty.

James followed my thoughts. 'You mean, will I ask him if any of the horses you have ridden since your fall have been tested for dope in the normal course of events?'

'Yes,' I agreed. 'Could you possibly do that?'

'Yes, I'll do that,' he said. 'I will ring him up. But if any of them have been tested and proved negative, you do realize that it will dispose of your wild accusations absolutely?'

'I do,' I agreed. 'Actually, I've ridden so many beaten favourites that I can't think why such systematic doping has not already been discovered.'

'You really do believe it, don't you?' said James, wonderingly.

'Yes,' I said, getting up and going to the door. 'Yes, I believe it. And so will you, James.'

But he shook his head, and I left him staring frozen-faced out of the window, the incredible nature of what I had said to him still losing the battle against his own personal knowledge of Kemp-Lore. James liked the man.

CHAPTER TEN

Late that Monday evening James rang me up at my digs and told me that I could ride his own horse, Turniptop, which was due to run in the novice 'chase at Stratford-on-Avon on the following Thursday. I began to thank him, but he interrupted, 'I'm doing you no favour. You know it won't win. He's never been over fences, only hurdles, and all I want is for you to give him an easy race round, getting used to the bigger obstacles. All right?'

'Yes,' I said. 'All right.' And he rang off. There was no mention of whether he would or would not contemplate juggling with sugar knobs.

I was tired. I had spent the whole day driving to Devon and back to visit Art Mathews's beautiful widow, the ice maiden. A fruitless journey. She had been as chilly as ever. Widowhood had warmed her no more than wifehood had done. Blonde, well-bred and cold, she had answered my questions calmly and incuriously and with a complete lack of interest. Art had been dead four months. She spoke of him as though she could hardly remember what he had looked like. No, she did not know exactly why Art had quarrelled so continuously with Corin. No, she did not know why Art had thought fit to shoot himself. No, Art had not got on well with Mr John Ballerton, but she did not know why. Yes, Art had once appeared on television on *Turf Talk*. It had not been a success, she said, the shadow of an old grievance sharpening her voice. Art had been made to look a fool. Art, whose meticulous sense of honour and order had earned him only respect on the racecourse, had been made to look a cantankerous, mean-minded fool. No, she could not remember exactly how it had been done, but she did remember, only too well, the effect it had had on her own family and friends. They had, it appeared, loudly pitied her on her choice of husband.

But I, listening to her, inwardly pitied poor dead Art on his choice of wife.

On the following day, Tuesday, I again appropriated the Mini-Cooper, much to Tick-Tock's disgust. This time I went towards Cheltenham, and called at Peter Cloony's neat, new bungalow, turning down the narrow, winding lane from the high main road to the village in the hollow.

Peter's wife opened the door to me and asked me in with a strained smile. She no longer looked happy and rosily content. She was too thin, and her hair hung straight and wispy round her neck. It was very nearly as cold inside the house as it was outside, and she wore some tattered fur boots, thick stockings, bulky clothes, and gloves. With no lipstick and no life in her eyes, she was almost unrecognizable as the loving girl who had put me up for the night four months ago.

'Come in,' she said, 'but I'm afraid Peter isn't here. He was given a lift to Birmingham races ... perhaps he'll get a spare ride ...' She spoke without hope.

'Of course he will,' I said. 'He's a good jockey.'

'The trainers don't seem to think so,' she said despairingly. 'Ever since he lost his regular job, he's barely had one ride a week. We can't live on it, how could we? If things don't change very soon, he's going to give up racing and try something else. But he only cares for horses and racing ... it will break his heart if he has to leave it.'

She had taken me into the sitting-room. It was as bare as before. Barer. The rented television set had gone. In its place stood a baby's cot, a wickerwork basket affair on a metal stand. I went over and looked down at the tiny baby, only a small bump under the mound of blankets. He was asleep. I made admiring remarks about what I could see of him, and his mother's face momentarily livened up with pleasure.

She insisted on making us a cup of tea, and I had to wait until the question of no milk, no sugar, no biscuits had all been settled before asking her what I really wanted to know.

I said, 'That Jaguar – the one which blocked the lane and made Peter late – who did it belong to?'

181

'We don't know,' she said. 'It was very odd. No one came to move it away and it stayed across the lane all that morning. In the end the police arranged for it to be towed away. I know Peter asked the police who owned it, because he wanted to tell the man just what his filthy Jaguar had cost him, but they said they hadn't yet traced him.'

'You don't happen to know where the Jaguar is now?' I asked.

'I don't know if it is still there,' she said, 'but it used to be outside the big garage beside Timberley Station. They're the only garage round here with a breakdown truck, and they were the ones who towed it away.'

I thanked her and stood up, and she came out to the car with me to say goodbye. I had spent some time going through the form book adding up the number of races Peter had ridden during the past few weeks, and I knew how little he had earned. I had brought with me a big box of groceries, butter, eggs, cheese and so on, and a stack of tins, and also a string of plastic ducks for the baby. This collection I carried back into the bungalow and dumped on the kitchen table, ignoring her surprised protest as she followed me in.

I grinned. 'They are too heavy to take back. You'll have to make the best of it.'

She began to cry.

'Cheer up,' I said, 'things will get better soon. But

meanwhile, don't you think the bungalow is too cold for a baby? I read somewhere that some babies die every winter from breathing freezing air, even though they may be as warmly wrapped up as yours is.'

She looked at me aghast, tears trickling down her cheeks.

'You ought to heat that room a little, and especially keep it warm all night too, if he sleeps in there,' I said.

'But I can't,' she said jerkily, 'the payments on the bungalow take nearly all we have . . . we can't afford a fire, except just in the evenings. Is it really true about babies dying?'

She was frightened.

'Yes, quite true,' I said. I took a sealed envelope out of my pocket and gave it to her. 'This is a present for the baby. Warmth. It's not a fortune, but it will pay your electricity bills for a while, and buy some coal if you want it. There's likely to be a lot of cold weather coming, so you must promise to spend most of it on keeping warm.'

'I promise,' she said faintly.

'Good.' I smiled at her as she wiped her eyes, and I went back to the car and drove away up the lane.

The garage at Timberley Station was a modernized affair with the front all snowy plaster and the back, when I walked round there, of badly pointed cheap brickwork. The elderly abandoned Jaguar stood there, tucked away between the burnt-out remains of a Standard 8 and a pile of old tyres. I went back to the front of the garage to talk to the man in charge, and I asked him if I could buy the car.

'Sorry, sir, no can do,' he said breezily. He was a dapper thirtyish man with.no oil on his hands.

'Why not?' I said. 'It doesn't look good for anything but the scrap heap.'

'I can't sell it to you because I don't know who it belongs to,' he said regretfully, 'but,' he brightened, 'it's been here so long now that it might be mine after all ... like unclaimed lost property. I'll ask the police.'

With a bit of prompting he told me all about the Jaguar being stuck across the lane and how his firm had fetched it.

I said, 'But someone must have seen the driver after he left the car?'

'The police think he must have got a lift, and then decided the car wasn't worth coming back for. But it's in good enough order. And it wasn't hot ... stolen, I mean.'

'What's it worth?' I asked.

'To you, sir,' he smiled glossily, 'I'd have let it go for a hundred pounds.'

A hundred. I parted from him and strolled out on to the forecourt. Was it worth a hundred to Kemp-Lore I wondered, to ruin Peter Cloony? Was his obsessive hatred of jockeys so fierce? But then a hundred to Kemp-Lore, I reflected, was probably a lot less than a hundred to me.

Timberley railway station (six stopping trains a day

and twenty-two expresses) lay on my left. I stood and considered it. The station was nearly four miles from the top of the lane leading to Peter's village; say an hour's quick walk. Peter had found the Jaguar across the lane at eleven o'clock, and it had to have been jammed in position only seconds before he came up the hill, as his had been the first car to be obstructed. I had a vivid mental picture of Kemp-Lore parked in the gateway where the lane began to curve downwards, watching Peter's house through binoculars, seeing him go out and get into his car and start on his way to the races. There wouldn't have been much time to force the Jaguar into position, lock its door and disappear before Peter got there. Not much time: but enough.

And then? The one tremendous disadvantage Kemp-Lore had to overcome, I thought, was his own fame. His face was so well known to almost the entire British population that he could not hope to move about the country inconspicuously, and wherever he went he would be noticed and remembered. Surely, I thought, in this sparsely populated area, it should be possible to find someone who had seen him.

As I was there anyway, I started with the station. Outside, I looked up the times of the stopping trains. There was, I found, a down train at twelve-thirty but no up train until five o'clock. The only other trains ran early in the morning and later in the evening. The booking office was shut. I found the clerk-ticket-collector-porter nodding over a hot stove and a racing paper in the parcels office. A large basket of hens squawked noisily in a corner as I walked in, and he woke with a jerk and told me the next train was due in one hour and ten minutes.

I got him talking via the racing news, but there was nothing to learn. Maurice Kemp-Lore had never (more's the pity he said) caught a train at Timberley. If it had happened when he was off-duty, he'd have heard about it all right. And yes, he said, he'd been on duty the day they'd fetched the Jaguar down to the garage. Disgusting that. Shouldn't be allowed, people being rich enough to chuck their old cars in the ditch like cigarette ends.

I asked him if the station had been busy that day: if there had been a lot of passengers catching the midday train.

'A lot of passengers?' he repeated scornfully. 'Never more than three or four, excepting Cheltenham race days . . .'

'I was just wondering,' I said idly, 'whether the chap who left his Jaguar behind could have caught a train from here that morning?'

'Not from here, he didn't,' the railway man said positively. 'Because, same as usual, all the people who caught the train were ladies.'

'Ladies?'

'Yeh, women. Shopping in Cheltenham. We haven't had a man catch the midday – excepting race days of course – since young Simpkins from the garage got sent home with chickenpox last summer. Bit of a joke it is round here, see, the midday.'

I gave him a hot tip for Birmingham that afternoon (which won, I was glad to see later) and left him busily putting a call through to his bookmaker on the government's telephone bill.

Timberley village pub, nearly empty, had never been stirred, they told me regretfully, by the flashing presence of Maurice Kemp-Lore.

The two transport cafés along the main road hadn't heard of any of their chaps giving him a lift.

None of the garages within ten miles had seen him ever.

The local taxi service had never driven him. He had never caught a bus on the country route.

It wasn't hard at each place to work conversation round to Kemp-Lore, but it was never quick. By the time a friendly bus conductor had told me, over a cigarette at the Cheltenham terminus, that none of his mates had ever had such a famous man on board because they'd never have kept quiet about it (look how Bill went on for days and days when Dennis Compton took a tenpenny single), it was seven o'clock in the evening.

If I hadn't been so utterly, unreasonably sure that it was Kemp-Lore who had abandoned the Jaguar, I would have admitted that if no one had seen him, then he hadn't been there. As it was, I was depressed by the failure of my search, but not convinced that there was nothing to search for.

The army tank carrier that had blocked Peter's and my way to Cheltenham was there accidentally: that much was clear. But Peter had got into such trouble for being late that a weapon was put straight into the hand of his enemy. He had only to make Peter late again, and to spread his little rumours, and the deed was done. No confidence, no rides, no career for Cloony.

I found I still hoped by perseverance to dig something up, so I booked a room in a hotel in Cheltenham, and spent the evening in a cinema to take my mind off food. On the telephone Tick-Tock sounded more resigned than angry to hear that he would be car-less yet again. He asked how I was getting on, and when I reported no progress, he said, 'If you're right about our friend, he's as sly and cunning as all get out. You won't find his tracks too easily.'

Without much hope I went down in the morning to the Cheltenham railway station and sorted out, after a little difficulty with old time-sheets and the passing of a pound note, the man who had collected the tickets from the passengers on the stopping train from Timberley on the day the Jaguar was abandoned.

He was willing enough, but he too had never seen Kemp-Lore, except on television; though he hesitated while he said so.

'What is it?' I asked.

'Well, sir, I've never seen him, but I think I've seen his sister.'

'What was she like?' I asked.

'Very like him, of course, sir, or I wouldn't have known who she was. And she had riding clothes on. You know – jodhpurs, I think they're called. And a scarf over her head. Pretty she looked, very pretty. I couldn't think who she was for a bit, and then it came to me, afterwards like. I didn't talk to her, see? I just took her ticket when she went through the barrier, that's all. I remember taking her ticket.'

'When was it that you saw her?' I asked.

'Oh, I couldn't say. I don't rightly know when it was. Before Christmas though, some time before Christmas, I'm certain of that.'

He flipped the pound I gave him expertly into an inner pocket. 'Thank you, sir, thank you indeed,' he said.

I dressed and shaved with particular care on the Thursday morning as, I supposed, a sort of barrier against the reception I knew I was going to meet. It was six days since I had been racing, six days in which my shortcomings and the shreds of my riding reputation would have been brought up, pawed over and discarded. Life moved fast in the changing-room;

today was important, tomorrow more so; but yesterday was dead. I belonged to yesterday. I was ancient news.

Even my valet was surprised to see me, although I had written to say I was coming.

'You are riding today then?' he said. 'I was wondering if you wanted to sell your saddle . . . there's a boy just starting who needs one.'

'I'll keep it a bit longer,' I said. 'I'm riding Turniptop in the fourth. Mr Axminster's colours.'

It was a strange day. As I no longer felt that I deserved the pitying glances to which I was treated, I found that they had, to a great extent, ceased to trouble me, and I even watched with fair equanimity the success of two of my ex-mounts in the first two races. The only thing I worried about was whether or not James would have both sugar lumps in his pocket and willingness in his heart.

He was so busy with his other runners that I did not exchange more than a few words with him during the first part of the afternoon, and when I went out into the parade ring to join him for Turniptop's race, he was standing alone, thoughtfully gazing into the distance.

'Maurice Kemp-Lore's here,' he said abruptly.

'Yes, I know,' I said. 'I saw him.'

'He has given sugar to several horses already.'

'What?' I exclaimed.

'I have asked quite a few people . . . Maurice has been feeding sugar to any number of horses during the past few weeks, not only to the ones you have ridden.'

'Oh,' I said weakly. Cunning as all get out, Tick-Tock had said.

'None of the horses you rode were picked for the regulation dope test,' said James, 'but some of the other horses Maurice gave sugar to were tested. All negative.'

'He only gave doped sugar to my mounts. The rest were camouflage, and he was damn lucky that the horses I rode weren't tested,' I said. It sounded improbable, but I was sure of it.

James shook his head.

'Did you . . .?' I began without much hope. 'Did he . . . Kemp-Lore . . . try to give Turniptop any sugar?'

James compressed his lips and stared into the middle distance. I positively held my breath.

'He did come into the saddling box,' he said grudgingly. 'He admired the horse's coat.'

Turniptop ambled past glowing with good health, but before James could say any more one of the stewards came over to talk to him, and I had no chance to find out about the sugar before it was time to mount and go out for the race.

I knew by the second fence that whether Kemp-Lore had fed him sugar or not, Turniptop was not doped. The leaden sluggishness which had afflicted my last twenty-eight mounts and which I had been forced to believe was due to my own deficiency had lifted like a spent thundercloud.

Turniptop leapt and sprang and surged, pulling like a train and doing his damnedest to run away with me. I could have shouted aloud with relief. He was an untidy jumper with more enthusiasm than judgement, a style which had brought him no especial grief over hurdles; but now, in his first steeplechase, he showed signs of treating fences with the same disrespect. It wouldn't really do; there's a world of difference between a single-thickness, easily knocked-down hurdle and a three-foot-wide fence, solidly built of birch twigs, particularly when an open ditch lies in front of it. But Turniptop did not want to be steadied. He was eager. He was rash.

With things as they were, and with James to be convinced, I must admit that my mood matched Turniptop's exactly. We infected each other with recklessness. We took some indefensible risks, and we got away with them.

I kept him continually on the rails, squeezing forward into tiny openings and letting him take all the bumps that came his way. When he met a fence dead right he gained lengths over it, and when he met one wrong he scrambled through and found a foot to land on somehow. It was more like a roller-coaster ride than the sensible, well-judged race James had indicated, but it taught the tough-minded Turniptop just as much about getting himself out of trouble as going round quietly on the outside would have done.

Coming into the second-to-last fence, I was afraid we would win. Afraid, because I knew James wanted to sell the horse and if he had already won a novice 'chase he would not be as valuable as if he had not. An apparent paradox: but Turniptop, young and still green, showed great promise. Too early a win would disqualify him from entering a string of good novice 'chases in the following season.

It would be far, far better, I knew, to come second. To have shown what he could do but not actually to have won would have put hundreds on his value. But we had run too fierce a race, and at the second-last the disaster of winning seemed unavoidable. There was only one other tiring horse alongside, and I could hear no others on my tail.

Turniptop rose, or rather fell to the occasion. In spite of my urging him to put in another stride, he took off far too soon and landed with his hind feet tangled hopelessly in the birch. His forelegs buckled under the strain and he went down on to his knees, with my chin resting on his right ear and my hands touching each other round his throat. Even then his indomitable sense of balance rescued him, and he staggered back on to his feet with a terrific upthrust of his shoulders, tipping me back into the saddle, and, tossing his head as if in disgust, he set off again towards the winning-post. The horse which had been alongside was now safely ahead, and two that had been behind me had jumped past, so that we came into the last fence in fourth position.

I had lost my irons in the débâcle and couldn't get my feet into them again in time to jump, so we went over the last with them dangling and clanking in the air. I collected him together and squeezed with my legs, and Turniptop, game to the end, accelerated past two of the horses ahead and flashed into second place four strides from the post.

James waited for me to dismount in the unsaddling enclosure with a face from which all expression had studiously been wiped. Poker-faced to match, I slid from the saddle.

'Don't ever ride a race like that for me again,' he said.

'No,' I agreed. I undid the girth buckles and took my saddle over my arm, and at last looked into his eyes.

They gleamed, narrowed and inscrutable. He said, 'You proved your point. But you could have killed my horse doing it.'

I said nothing.

'And yourself,' he added, implying that that was less important.

I shook my head, smiling faintly. 'Not a chance,' I said.

'H'm.' He gave me a hard stare. 'You'd better come up to the stable this evening,' he said. 'We can't talk about ... what we have to talk about ... here. There are too many people about.'

As if to punctuate this remark the owner of the winner leant over the dividing rails to admire Turniptop and I had to loop up the girths and go and weigh in, still without knowing exactly what had happened in the saddling box before the race.

Tick-Tock was standing by my peg in the changing-room, one smoothly shod foot up on the bench and the Tyrolean hat pushed back on his head.

'Before you ride like that again, you might make a will leaving me your half of the car,' he said. 'It would solve so many legal complications.'

'Oh, shut up,' I said, peeling off first the crimson and white sweater, James's colours, and then the thin brown jersey underneath. I took a towel from the valet and went along to the wash-basin.

'A lot of people,' said Tick-Tock in a loud voice across the room, 'are going to have a fine old time eating their words, and I hope it gives them indigestion.' He followed me along and watched me wash, leaning languidly against the wall. 'I suppose you realize that your exploits this afternoon were clearly visible to several million assorted housewives, invalids, babes in arms, and people hanging about on the pavement outside electric shops?'

'What?' I exclaimed.

'It's a fact. Didn't you really know? The last three races are filling up the spare time between *Sex for*

Sixth Forms and *Goggle with Granny*. Universal T. C. Maurice's lot. I wonder,' he finished more soberly, 'what he'll do when he knows you've rumbled the sugar bit?'

'He may not know,' I said, towelling my chest and shoulders. 'He may think it was accidental . . . I haven't heard yet from James what happened before the race.'

'Anyway,' said Tick-Tock confidently, 'his campaign against you is over. He won't risk going on with it after today.'

I agreed with him. It just shows how little either of us understood about obsession.

James was waiting for me in the office, busy with papers at his big desk. The fire blazed hotly and the light winked on the glasses standing ready beside the whisky bottle.

He stopped writing when I went in, and got up and poured our drinks, and stood towering above me as I sat in the battered armchair by the fire. His strong heavy face looked worried.

'I apologize,' he said abruptly.

'Don't,' I said. 'No need.'

'I very nearly let Maurice give Turniptop that damned sugar,' he said. 'I couldn't believe him capable of a scheme as fantastic as doping every horse you ride. I mean, it's . . . it's ridiculous.'

'What happened in the saddling box?' I asked.

196

He took a sip from his glass. 'I gave Sid instructions that no one, absolutely no one, however important they were, was to give Turniptop anything to eat or drink before the race. When I reached the box with your saddle, Maurice was in the box next door and I watched him giving the horse there some sugar. Sid said no one had given Turniptop anything.' He paused and drank again. 'I put on your number cloth, weight pad and saddle, and began to do up the girths. Maurice came round the partition from the next box and said hello. That infectious smile of his . . . I found myself smiling back and thinking you were mad. He was wheezing a bit with asthma . . . and he put his hand in his pocket and brought out three lumps of sugar. He did it naturally, casually, and held them out to Turniptop. I had my hands full of girths and I thought you were wrong . . . but . . . I don't know . . . there was something in the way he was standing, with his arm stretched out rather stiffly and the sugar flat on the palm of his hand, that didn't look right. People who are fond of horses stroke their muzzles when they give them sugar, they don't stand as far away as possible. And if Maurice wasn't fond of horses, why was he giving them sugar? Anyway, I did decide suddenly that there would be no harm done if Turniptop didn't eat that sugar, so I dropped the girths and pretended to trip, and grabbed Maurice's arm to steady myself. The sugar fell off his hand on to the straw on the ground and I stepped on it as if by accident while I was recovering my balance.'

'What did he say?' I asked, fascinated.

'Nothing,' said James. 'I apologized for bumping into him, but he didn't answer. Just for a second he looked absolutely furious. Then he smiled again, and . . .' James's eyes glinted, '. . . he said how much he admired me for giving poor Finn this one last chance.'

'Dear of him,' I murmured.

'I told him it wasn't exactly your last chance. I said you would be riding Template on Saturday as well. He just said "Oh really?", and wished me luck and walked away.'

'So the sugar was crunched up and swept out with the dirty straw,' I said.

'Yes,' he agreed.

'Nothing to analyse. No evidence.' A nuisance.

'If I hadn't stepped on it, Maurice could have picked it up and offered it to Turniptop again. I hadn't taken any sugar with me . . . I hadn't any lumps to substitute . . . I didn't believe I would need them.'

He hadn't intended to bother, I knew. But he had bothered. I would never stop feeling grateful.

We drank our whisky. James said suddenly, 'Why? I don't understand why he should have gone to such lengths to discredit you. What has he got against you?'

'I am a jockey, and he is not,' I said flatly. 'That's all.' I told about my visit to Claudius Mellit and the answers he had given me. I said, 'It's no coincidence that you and most other trainers have had trouble finding and keeping a jockey. You've all been swayed by Kemp-Lore, either by him directly, or through those two shadows of his, Ballerton and Corin Kellar, who soak up his poison like sponges and drip it out into every receptive ear. They've said it all to you. You repeated it to me yourself, not so long ago. Peter Cloony is always late, Tick-Tock doesn't try, Danny Higgs bets too heavily, Grant sold information, Finn has lost his nerve . . .'

He stared at me, appalled. I said, 'You believed it all, James, didn't you? Even you? And so did everyone else. Why shouldn't they, with so much evident foundation for the rumours? It doesn't take much for an owner or a trainer to lose confidence in a jockey. The thought has only to be insinuated, however fleetingly, that a jockey is habitually late, or dishonest, or afraid, and very soon, very soon indeed, he is on his way out . . . Art. Art killed himself because Corin sacked him. Grant had a mental breakdown. Peter Cloony is so broke his wife was starving herself in a freezing cold house. Tick-Tock makes jokes like Pagliacci . . .'

'And you?' asked James.

'I? Well . . . I haven't exactly enjoyed the last three weeks.'

'No,' he said, as if thinking about it from my point of view for the first time. 'No, I don't suppose you have.'

'It's been so calculated, this destruction of jockeys,' I said. 'Every week in *Turf Talk*, looking back on it, there has been some damaging reference to one jockey or another. When he had me on the programme he introduced me as an unsuccessful rider, and he meant me to stay that way. Do you remember that ghastly bit of film he showed of me? You'd never have taken me on if you'd seen that before I'd ridden for you, would you?'

He shook his head, very troubled.

I went on, 'On every possible occasion – when Template won the King 'Chase for instance – he has reminded everyone watching on television that I am only substituting for Pip, and that I'll be out on my ear as soon as that broken leg is strong again. Fair enough, it's Pip's job and he should have it back, but that patronizing note in Kemp-Lore's voice was calculated to make everyone take it for granted that my brief spell in the limelight was thoroughly undeserved. I dare say it was, too. But I think a lot of your owners would have been readier to trust your judgement in engaging me, and less quick to chuck me overboard at the first sign of trouble, if it hadn't been for the continual deflating pin-pricks Kemp-Lore had dealt out all round. And last Friday . . .' I tried, not too successfully, to keep my voice evenly conversational. 'Last Friday he led Corin and that handicapper on until they said straight out that I was finished. Were you watching?'

James nodded, and poured us another drink.

'It's a matter for the National Hunt Committee,' he said firmly.

'No,' I said. 'His father is a member of it.'

James gasped sharply. 'I had forgotten . . .'

I said, 'The whole Committee's a stronghold of pro-Kemp-Lore feeling. They're all sold on Maurice. Most of them wear the same old school tie,' I grinned. James wore it too. 'I would be very glad if you would say nothing to any of them, just yet. They would take even more convincing than you did, and there aren't any facts that Kemp-Lore couldn't explain away. But I'm digging.' I drank. 'The day will come.'

'You sound unexpectedly cheerful,' he said.

'O God, James.' I stood up abruptly. 'I wanted to kill myself last week. I'm glad I didn't. It makes me cheerful.'

He looked so startled that I relaxed and laughed, and put down my glass. 'Never mind,' I said, 'but you must understand I don't think the National Hunt Committee meets the case at the moment. Too gentlemanly. I favour something more in the biter-bit line for dear Maurice.'

But I had as yet no useful plan, and dear Maurice still had his teeth, and they were sharp.

CHAPTER ELEVEN

Although neither Tick-Tock nor I had any rides the next day I pinched the car from him to go to the meeting at Ascot, and walked round the course to get the feel of the turf. There was a bitterly cold north-east wind blowing across the heath and the ground was hard with a touch of frost in the more exposed patches. It had been a surprisingly mild winter so far, but the high clear sky spoke ominously of ice to come. One more day, that was all I asked; only one more day. But prodding the earth on the landing side of the water jump with my heel I felt it jar instead of give.

I finished the circuit, planning the race in my mind as I went. If the ground remained firm it would be a fast run affair, but that suited Template well, especially with top weight to carry. Lugging packets of lead around in the mud was not what his lean streamlined frame was best fitted for.

Outside the weighing-room Peter Cloony stopped me. His face was white and thin and mournful, and lines were developing on his forehead.

'I'll pay you back,' he said, almost belligerently. He seemed prepared to argue about it.

'All right. One day. No hurry,' I said mildly.

'You shouldn't have gone behind my back and given my wife that money and the food. I wanted to send it back at once but she won't let me. We don't need charity. I don't approve of it.'

'You're a fool, Peter,' I said. 'Your wife was right to accept what I gave her, and I'd have thought her a stubborn ass if she hadn't. And you'd better get used to the idea: a box of groceries will be delivered to your house every week until you're earning a decent screw again.'

'No,' he almost shouted, 'I won't have it.'

'I don't see why your wife and baby should suffer because of your misplaced pride,' I said. 'But if it will ease your conscience, I'll tell you why I'm doing it. You'll never get much work as long as you go around with that hang-dog expression. Looking weak and miserable isn't going to persuade anybody to employ you. You need to cheer up, get fit again, and prove you're worth having. Well – all I'm doing is removing one of your worries so that you can think a bit more about racing and bit less about your cold house and empty larder. So now you can get on with it . . . it's all up to you. And don't ever even risk being late.'

I walked off and left Peter standing with his mouth open and his eyebrows half-way to his hair.

What Kemp-Lore had pulled down, I could try to

rebuild, I thought. When I had arrived I had seen him in the distance, talking animatedly to one of the stewards, who was laughing. Slim, vital and wholesome-looking, he seemed to attract the light of the day on to his fair head.

In the weighing-room after the fourth race I was handed a telegram. It said, 'Pick me up White Bear, Uxbridge, 6.30 p.m. Important, Ingersoll.' I felt like cursing Tick-Tock soundly because Uxbridge was in the opposite direction from home. But the car was half his, after all, and I'd had more than my fair share of it during the past week.

The afternoon dragged. I hated having to watch, hated it even more after my reassuring ride on Turniptop, but I tried to take my own advice to Peter and look cheerful: and I was rewarded, as time went on, with a definite thawing of the cold shoulder. It made life much easier not finding everyone still too embarrassed to speak to me; but I was also in no doubt that most final judgements were being reserved until after Template's race. I didn't mind that. I was confident that he was the fastest 'chaser in training and I had James's promise that he would be guarded every second against being doped.

I dawdled after racing ended, with two hours to kill before turning up at Uxbridge to collect Tick-Tock. I watched the men from Universal Telecast erecting their scaffolding towers, ready to televise the Midwinter the next day, and recognized a man directing them as Gordon Kildare, still in navy-blue pinstripe suiting and still looking like a rising young executive who knew the score. He passed by me with the practised half smile which from a man of his sort always means that he doesn't know who he's smiling at, but smiles all the same in case he should later find out it was someone important. However he had only gone two steps past me when he turned and came back.

'We've had you on the programme,' he said pleasantly. 'No don't tell me . . .' His brow furrowed; then he snapped his fingers. 'Finn, that's it, Finn.' But his smile at the triumph of his memory began ludicrously to slip and I knew he was also remembering what had been said about me on his programme a week ago.

'Yes, Finn,' I said, taking no notice. 'All set for tomorrow?'

'Eh, oh, yes. Busy day. Well now, I'm sorry to have to rush off but you know how it is . . . we've got the programme to put out tonight and I'm due back in the studios. Maurice went ages ago.'

He looked at his watch, gave me a noncommittal smile, and gracefully retreated.

I watched him drive off in the latest streamlined Ford, picturing the studio he was going to; the ranks of cameras, the dazzling lights, the plates of sandwiches; they would all be the same. And who, I wondered, who was to be Kemp-Lore's victim this evening? For whom was the chopper poised, the false charm ready?

There was so little I could do against him. Pick up some of the pieces, start some counter rumours? Try to undermine his influence? All that, yes. But I didn't have his sparkle, nor his prestige, nor yet his ruthlessness. I thrust my hands into my pockets, went out to the Mini-Cooper, and drove off to fetch Tick-Tock.

Mine was only the second car in the dark park beside the White Bear. It was one of those disappointing pubs built of tidy pinkish bricks with cold lighting inside and no atmosphere. The saloon bar was empty. The public bar held only a droopy-moustached old man pursing his lips to the evening's first half-pint. I went back to the saloon bar and ordered a whisky. No Tick-Tock. I looked at my watch. Twenty to seven.

The green plastic seats round the walls were so inhospitable that I didn't wonder the pub was empty. The dark-green curtains didn't help. Nor the fluorescent strip-lights on the ceiling.

I looked at my watch again.

'Are you by any chance waiting for someone, sir?' asked the characterless barman.

'Yes, I am,' I said.

'You wouldn't be a Mr Finn?'

'Yes.'

'Then I've a message for you, sir. A Mr Ingersoll

telephoned just now and said he couldn't get here to meet you, sir, and he was very sorry but could you go and pick him up from the station at six fifty-five. The station is just down the road, first turning left and straight on for half a mile.'

Finishing my drink, I thanked the barman and went out to the car. I climbed into the driving seat and stretched my hand out to turn on the lights and the ignition. I stretched out my hand . . . but I didn't reach the lights.

My neck was gripped violently from behind.

There was movement then in the back of the car as the arms shifted to get a better leverage, a rustling of clothes and the scrape of shoe across the thin carpet.

I flung up my hands and clawed but I couldn't reach the face of whoever was behind me, and my nails were useless against his gloves. Thick leather gloves. The fingers inside them were strong, and what was worse, they knew exactly where to dig in and press, each side of the neck, just above the collarbone, where the carotid arteries branched upwards. Pressure on one carotid, I remembered wildly from some distant first-aid course, stops arterial bleeding from the head . . . but pressure on both at once blocked all blood supplies to the brain.

I hadn't a chance. My struggles were hampered by the steering wheel and gained me nothing. In the few seconds before a roaring blackness took me off, I had time for only two more thoughts. First that I should have known that Tick-Tock would never meet me in a dreary pub like that. Secondly, angrily, that I was dead.

I couldn't have been out very long, but it was long enough. When consciousness slowly and fuzzily returned, I found I could open neither my eyes nor my mouth. Both were covered with sticking plaster. My wrists were tied together, and my ankles, when I tried to move them, would only part a foot or two: they were hobbled together, like a gipsy's pony.

I was lying on my side, awkwardly doubled up, on the floor in the back of a car which, from the size and smell and feel, I knew to be the Mini-Cooper. It was very cold, and after a while I realized that this was because I was no longer wearing a jacket or an overcoat. My shirt-sleeved arms were dragged forward between the two front seats so that I couldn't reach the sticking plaster to rip it off, and I was extremely, horribly uncomfortable. I tried once with all my strength to free my arms, lifting and jerking at the same time, but they were securely fastened, and a fist – I supposed – crashed down on them so brutally that I didn't attempt it again. I couldn't see who was driving, and driving fast, but I didn't need to. There was only one person in the world who could have set such a trap; complicated but effective, like the Jaguar in the lane. Only one person who had any reason to abduct me, however mad that reason might be. I had no illusions. Maurice Kemp-Lore did not intend that I should win the Midwinter Cup, and was taking steps to prevent it.

Did he know, I wondered helplessly, that it was no accident that Turniptop had not eaten the doped sugar? Did he guess that I knew all about his anti-jockey activities? Had he heard about my trek round the stables or my enquiries about the Jaguar? If he did know these things, what was he going to do with me? To this last rather bleak question I was in no hurry to discover the answer.

When the journey had been going for some time, the car swung suddenly to the left and bumped on to an unevenly surfaced side road, increasing my discomfort. After a while it slowed, turned again, and rolled to a stop.

Kemp-Lore got out of the car, tipped forward the driver's seat, and tugged me out after him by the wrists. I couldn't get my feet under me because of the hobble, and I fell out on to the back of my shoulders. The ground was hard and gravelly. My shirt tore, and the sharp stones scraped into my skin.

He pulled me to my feet, and I stood there swaying, blinded by the plaster on my eyes and unable to run even if I could have wrenched myself from his grasp. He had some sort of lead fixed to my tied wrists, and he began to pull me forward by it. The ground was uneven and the rope joining my ankles was very short. I kept stumbling, and twice fell down.

It was very unpleasant, falling when I couldn't see, but I managed somehow to twist before hitting the ground, landing on my shoulders instead of my face. Always he pulled my hands so far in front of me that I couldn't reach the sticking plaster: the second time I fell I made a great effort to get it off, but he wrenched my arms roughly over my head and dragged me along the ground on my back for a long way. I very painfully lost a good deal more skin.

At length he paused and let me stand up again. He still didn't speak. Not a word. And I couldn't. There was only the sound of our footsteps on the stony ground and the faint sigh of the sharp north-easter in some near-by trees. My tattered shirt was no shield against that wind, and I began to shiver.

He stopped, and there was the sound of a door being opened, and I was tugged in. This time there was a step up, as I realized a fraction too late to prevent myself falling again. I hadn't time to twist, either. I fell flat on my stomach, elbows and chest. It knocked the wind out of me and made me dizzy.

It was a wooden floor, I thought, with my cheek on it. It smelled strongly of dust, and faintly of horses. He pulled me to my feet again and I felt my wrists being hauled upwards and fastened to something just above my head. When he had finished and stepped away I explored with my fingers to find out what it was; and as soon as I felt the smooth metal hooks, I knew exactly the sort of place I was in.

It was a tack-room. Every stable has one. It is the place where the saddles and bridles are kept, along with all the brushes and straps and bandages and rugs that horses need. From the ceiling of every tack-room hangs a harness hook, a gadget something like a three-pronged anchor, which is used for hanging bridles on while they are being cleaned. There were no bridles hanging from these particular hooks. Only me. I was securely fastened at the point where they branched off their stem.

Most tack-rooms are warm, heated by a stove which dries damp rugs and prevents leather getting mildewed. This tack-room was very cold indeed, and in the air the ingrained smells of leather and saddle soap were overlaid by a dead sort of mustiness. It was an unused room: an empty room. The silence took on a new meaning. There were no horses moving in the boxes. It was an empty stable. I shivered from something more than cold.

I heard him step out into the gritty yard, and presently there was a familiar rattle of bolts and the clang of a stable door being opened. After a few seconds it was shut again, and another one was opened. This again was shut, and another opened. He went on down the row, opening six doors. I thought he must be looking for something, and numbly wondered what it was, and began to hope very much that he wouldn't find it.

After the sixth stable door shut he was gone for

some time, and I couldn't hear what he was doing. But the car had not been started, so I knew he must still be there. I could make no impression at all on the strands of rope twined round my wrists. They were narrow and slippery to touch, and felt like nylon, and I couldn't even find a knot, much less undo one.

Eventually he came back, and dumped down outside the door something that clattered. A bucket.

He stepped into the room and walked softly on the wooden floor. He stopped in front of me. It was very quiet everywhere. I could hear a new sound, the high, faint asthmatic wheeze of the air going into his lungs. Even an empty stable, it seemed, could start him off.

Nothing happened for a while. He walked all round me, slowly, and stopped again. Walked and stopped. Making up his mind, I thought. But to do what?

He touched me once, dragging his gloved hand across my raw shoulders. I flinched, and his breath hissed sharply. He began to cough, the dry difficult asthmatic's cough. And may you choke, I thought.

He went outside, still coughing, and picked up the bucket and walked away across the yard. I heard the bucket clatter down and a tap being turned on. The water splashed into the bucket, echoing in the stillness.

Jack and Jill went up the hill, said my brain ridiculously, to fetch a pail of water. Jack fell down and broke his crown and Jill threw the water all over him.

Oh no, I thought, oh no, I'm so cold already. Part of my mind said I wouldn't mind what he did to me if only he'd let me go in time to ride Template, and the rest said don't be a fool, that's the whole point, he won't let you go, and anyway if you do get away you'll be so cold and stiff after this you won't be able to ride a donkey.

He turned off the tap and came back across the yard, the water splashing slightly as he walked. He brought the bucket with him into the tack-room and stopped behind me. The handle of the bucket clanked. I ground my teeth and took a deep breath, and waited.

He threw the water. It hit me squarely between the shoulder blades and soaked me from head to foot. It was bitterly, icy cold, and it stung like murder on the skinned patches.

After a short pause he went across the yard again and refilled the bucket. I thought I was almost past caring about that. You can't be wetter than wet and you can't be colder than freezing. And my arms, with being hauled up higher than my head, were already beginning to feel heavy and to ache. I began to worry less about the immediate future, and more about how long he intended to leave me where I was.

He came back with the bucket, and this time he threw the water in my face. I had been wrong about not caring. It was at least as bad as the first time, mostly because too much of it went up my nose. Couldn't he see, I thought desperately, that he was drowning me. My chest hurt. I couldn't get my breath. Surely he'd pull the plaster off my mouth, surely . . . surely . . .

He didn't.

By the time a reasonable amount of air was finding its way into my heaving lungs he was across the yard again, with more water splashing into the bucket. In due course he turned the tap off, and his feet began once more to crunch methodically in my direction. Up the step and across the wooden floor. There wasn't anything I could do to stop him. My thoughts were unprintable.

He came round in front of me again. I twisted my face sideways and buried my nose against my upper arm. He poured the whole arctic bucketful over my head. After this, I thought, I am going to have more sympathy for those clowns in circuses. I hoped the poor blighters used warm water, anyway.

It seemed that he now thought that I was wet enough. In any case he dumped the bucket down outside the door instead of going to fill it again, and came back and stood close beside me. His asthma was worse.

He put his hand in my hair and pulled my head back, and spoke for the first time.

He said in a low voice, with obvious satisfaction, 'That should fix *you*.'

He let go of my hair and went out of the room, and I heard him walk away across the yard. His footsteps faded into the distance and after a while there was the distant slam of the Mini-Cooper's door. The engine started, the car drove off, and soon I could hear it no more.

It wasn't very funny being abandoned in a trussed condition soaking wet on a cold night. I knew he wouldn't be back for hours, because it was Friday. From eight o'clock until at least nine-thirty he would be occupied with his programme; and I wondered in passing what effect his recent capers would have on his performance.

One thing was clear, I could not meekly stand still and wait to be released. The first necessity was obviously to get some of the sticking plaster off. I thought that as it was wet it would come away fairly easily, but it was very adhesive, and after a good deal of rubbing my mouth against my arm, I only succeeded in peeling back one corner of it. It was enough to let in a precious extra trickle of air, but no good for shouting for help.

The cold was a serious problem. My wet trousers clung clammily to my legs, my shoes were full of water, and my shirt, what was left of it, was plastered against my arms and chest. Already my fingers were completely numb, and my feet were going through the stage that precedes loss of feeling. He had left the door open on purpose, I knew, and although the biting wind was not blowing straight in there were enough eddies swirling off the walls outside for me to be in a considerable draught. I shivered from head to foot.

Harness hooks. I considered their anatomy. A stem with three upward-curving branches at the bottom. At the top, a ring, and attached to the ring, a chain. The length of chain depended on the height of the ceiling. At the top of the chain, a staple driven into a beam. As the whole thing was solidly constructed to resist years of vigorous stablemen putting their weight on bridles while they cleaned them, it was absolutely hopeless to try and tug it straight out of the ceiling.

I had seen harness hooks which were only hitched on to their chains and would detach easily if lifted instead of being pulled down, but after some fruitless and tiring manoeuvring I knew the one I was fixed to was not so obliging.

But somewhere, I thought, there must be a weak link. Literally a weak link. When they were bought, harness hooks didn't have chains on. Chain was cut to the length needed and added when the hook was installed in the tack-room. Therefore, somewhere there was a join.

The bottom curve of the hooks brushed my hair, and my wrists were tied some three inches above that. It gave me very little leverage, but it was the only hope I had. I started pivoting, leaning my forearms on the hooks and twisting the chain, putting a strain on it and hearing the links rub hollowly together. In two and a half full turns, as near as I could judge, it locked solid. If I could turn it further, the weak link would snap.

The theory was simple. Putting it into operation was different. For one thing, twisting the chain had shortened it, so that my arms were stretched higher above my head and gave me less leverage than ever. And for another, they had begun to ache in earnest.

I pressed round as hard as I could. Nothing happened. I unwound the chain a fraction, and forcefully jerked it tight again. The jolt ran right down my body and threw me off my feet.

I stumbled miserably upright again, and with my legs braced, repeated the process. This time the jolt shook only the top part of my body. I did it again. The chain didn't break.

After that, as a respite from rattling my arms in their sockets, I got back to work on the sticking plaster and a while later dislodged it entirely. It meant that at last I could open my mouth and yell.

I yelled.

No one came. My voice echoed round the tack-room and sounded loud in my ears, but I feared that outside the wind would sweep it away. I shouted, on and off, for a long while. No results.

It was at this point, perhaps an hour after Kemp-Lore had gone, that I became both very frightened and very angry.

I was frightened for my hands, which I could no longer feel. I was now not only shivering but shuddering with cold, and the blood supply to my hands was having, to put it literally, an uphill job; and with the weight of my aching arms to support, the rope tying my wrists was viciously tight.

The dismal fact had to be faced that if I had to stay where I was all night my hands might be dead in the morning. My imagination trotted on unasked with scarifying pictures. Dead. Gangrenous. Amputated.

He can't have meant that, I thought suddenly. Surely he hadn't meant that all along. No one could be so savagely cruel. I remembered the satisfaction in his voice. 'That will fix *you*,' he said. But I'd thought he meant for the next day only. Not for life.

Being angry gave me both strength and resolution. I would not, I absolutely would not let him get away with it. The chain had got to be broken.

I wound it up tight again and jerked. It took my breath away. I told myself not to be a baby. I loosened and jerked, loosened and jerked, pushing against the hooks, trying to twist them round with all my strength. The chain rattled, and held.

I started doing it rhythmically. Six jerks and a rest. Six jerks and a rest. On and on, six jerks and a rest, until I was sobbing.

At least, I thought, with a last flicker of humour, the exercise is making me warmer. But it was little consolation for the cracking pain in my arms and shoulders, or the red-hot pincers which seemed to have attached themselves to the back of my neck, or the bite of the rope into my wrists as the friction rubbed away the skin.

Six jerks and a rest. Six jerks and a rest. The rests got longer. Anyone who has tried crying with sticking plaster over his eyes will know that the tears run down inside the nose. When I sniffed, they came into my mouth. Salty. I got tired of the taste.

Six jerks and a rest. I wouldn't stop. I refused to stop. Six jerks. Rest. Six. Rest.

After a while I unwound the chain by turning round and round where I stood and wound it up again in the opposite direction. I thought that jolting it the other way might both snap it more quickly and be easier on my protesting muscles; but I was wrong on both counts. Eventually, I wound back again.

Time passed. Because I couldn't see I became giddy as I grew tired. I began to sway and buckle at the knees if I didn't concentrate, and neither of these things did my arms any good.

Why – jerk – wouldn't – jerk – the ruddy chain – jerk – jerk – break. I wasn't going to admit it was too much for me without struggling to the end, though the disgusting temptation gradually grew to give up the excruciating wrenching and just hang and faint away and get some peace. A temporary, deceptive, useless, dangerous peace.

I went on jerking for what seemed like hours, sometimes sobbing, sometimes cursing, sometimes maybe praying as well.

I was quite unprepared for it when it happened. One minute I was screwing up the dregs of willpower for another series of jerks, and the next, after a convulsive, despairing heave, I was collapsing in a tumbled heap on the floor with the harness hook clattering down on top of me, still tied to my wrists.

For a moment or two I could hardly believe it. My head was whirling, all sense of direction gone. But the floor was hard beneath my body, dusty smelling and real, damp and reassuring.

After a while, when my head cleared, I rolled into a kneeling position so that the blood was flowing down my arms at last, and put my hands between my thighs to try to warm them. They felt like lumps of frozen meat, with no sensation and no movement. The rope round my wrists didn't cut so much now that it had no weight to support, and there was room for the blood to get back into my hands, I thought, if only it would.

The unimaginable relief of having my arms down made me forget for some time how cold I was, and how wet, and how far still from getting warm and dry. I felt almost cheerful, as if I had won a major battle; and indeed, looking back on it, I know I had.

CHAPTER TWELVE

Kneeling very soon became uncomfortable, so I shuffled across the floor until I came to a wall, and sat with the bottom of my spine propped against it and my knees bent up.

The plaster on my eyes was still stuck tight. I tried to scrape it off by rubbing it against the rope on my wrists, but made no headway. The hooks hindered me and bumped into my face, and in the end I gave it up and concentrated again on warming my hands, alternately cradling them between my thighs and thumping them against my knees to restore the circulation.

After a time I found I could move my fingers. I still couldn't feel them at all, but movement was a tremendous step forward, and I remember smiling about it for at least ten minutes.

I put my hands up to my face and tried to scrape the plaster off with my thumbnail. My thumb slid across my cheek, checked on the edge of the plaster and, when I pushed from the elbow, bent uselessly and

221

slithered away. I tried again. It had to be done, because until I could see where I was going I couldn't leave the tack-room. It was colder outside, and my ankles were still hobbled, and wandering about blind in those conditions did not appeal to me a bit.

I bent my head down and put my right thumb in my mouth, to warm it. Every few minutes I tested the results on the edge of the plaster and at least got to the stage where the thumb would push without bending. I only needed to prise a corner up, but even that took a long time. Eventually, however, my nail had pushed a flap unstuck which was big enough for me to grip between my wrists, and with several false starts and a fair selection of oaths, I managed in the end to pull the obstinate thing off.

Dazzling moonlight poured through the open door and through a window beside it. I was sitting against the end wall with the door away on my left. Above my head and all round the room there were empty wooden supports for saddles and bridles, and bare shelves and a cupboard on the wall facing me. An efficient-looking stove occupied the corner on my right, with a few dead cinders still scattered on the ground beside it.

From the centre of the ceiling, pale in the moonlight, hung twenty inches of sturdy galvanized chain.

I looked down at my hands. The harness hook glinted with reflected light. No wonder it had been so difficult to break. I thought. The chain and the hook were almost new. Not the dark, old, rusty things I had been imagining all along. I swallowed, really shattered. It was just as well I hadn't known.

My hands themselves, including the thumb I had tried to warm, were white. Almost as white as my shirt-sleeves. Almost as white as the nylon rope which wound round the hooks. Only my wrists were dark.

I stretched my feet out. More white nylon rope ran from one ankle to the other, about fifteen inches of it.

My fingers wouldn't undo the knots. My pockets had been emptied; no knife, no matches. There was nothing in the tack-room to cut with. I stood up stiffly, leaning against the wall, and slowly, carefully, shuffled over to the door. My foot kicked against something, and I looked down. On the edge of a patch of moonlight lay the broken link. It was a grotesquely buckled piece of silvery metal. It had given me a lot of trouble.

I went on to the door and negotiated the step. The bucket stood there, dully grey. I looked round the moonlit L-shaped yard. Four boxes stretched away to my right, and at right-angles to them there were two more, on the short arm of the L. Over there too, was the tap; and beside the tap, on the ground, an object I was very glad to see. A boot-scraper made of a thin metal plate bedded in concrete.

With small careful steps I made my way to it across

the hard-packed gravel, the cutting wind ripping the last remnants of warmth from my body.

Leaning against the wall, and with one foot on the ground, I stretched the rope tautly over the boot-scraper and began to rub it to and fro, using the other foot as a pendulum. The blade of the scraper was far from sharp and the rope was new, and it took a long time to fray it through, but it parted in the end. I knelt down and tried to do the same with the strands round my wrists, but the harness hook kept getting in the way again and I couldn't get anything like the same purchase. I stood up wearily. It looked as though I'd have to lug that tiresome piece of ironmongery around with me a while longer.

Being able to move my legs, however, gave me a marvellous sense of freedom. Stiffly, shaking with cold, I walked out of the yard round to the house looming darkly behind it. There were no lights, and looking closer I found the downstairs windows were all shuttered. It was as empty as the stable; an unwelcome but not unexpected discovery.

I walked a bit unsteadily on past the house and down the drive. It was a long drive with no lodge at the gate, only an estate agent's board announcing that this desirable country gentleman's residence was for sale, together with some excellent modern stabling, forty acres of arable land and an apple orchard.

A country lane ran past the end of the drive giving no indication as to which way lay civilization. I tried to remember from which direction the Mini-Cooper had come, but I couldn't. It seemed a very long time ago. I glanced automatically at my left wrist but there was only rope there, no watch. Since it had to be one thing or the other, I turned right. It was a deserted road with open fields on the far sides of its low hedges. No cars passed, and nowhere could I see a light. Cursing the wind and aching all over, I stumbled on, hanging on to the fact that if I went far enough I was bound to come to a house in the end.

What I came to first was not a house but something much better. A telephone box. It stood alone, brightly lit inside, square and beckoning, on the corner where the lane turned into a more main road, and it solved the embarrassing problem of presenting myself at some stranger's door looking like a scarecrow and having to explain how I had got into such a state.

There were a lot of people I could have called. Police, Ambulance or the Fire Brigade for a start; but by the time I had forced my still nearly useless hands to pull the door open far enough for me to get my foot in, I had had time to think. Once I called in authority in any form there would be unending questions to answer and statements to make and like as not I'd end up for the night in the local cottage hospital. I hated being in hospitals.

Also, although I felt so bone cold, it was not, I thought, actually freezing. The puddles at the side of the road had no ice on them. They would be racing at

Ascot the next day. Template would turn up for the Midwinter, and James didn't know his jockey was wandering around unfit to ride.

Unfit ... Between seeing the telephone box and clumsily picking up the receiver I came to the conclusion that the only satisfactory way to cheat Kemp-Lore of his victory was to go and ride the race, and win it if I could, and pretend that tonight's misfortunes had not happened. He had had things his own way for far too long. He was not, he was positively not, I vowed, going to get the better of me any more.

I dialled O with an effort, gave the operator my credit card number, and asked to be connected to the one person in the world who would give me the help I needed, and keep quiet about it afterwards, and not try to argue me out of what I intended to do.

Her voice sounded sleepy. She said, 'Hello?'

'Joanna ... are you busy?' I asked.

'Busy? At this hour?' she said. 'Is that you, Rob?'

'Yes,' I said.

'Well, go back to bed and ring me in the morning,' she said. 'I was asleep. Don't you know what time it is?' I heard her yawn.

'No,' I said.

'Well, it's ... er ... twenty to one. Good night.'

'Joanna, don't go,' I said urgently. 'I need your help. I really do. Please, don't ring off.'

'What's the matter?' She yawned again.

'I ... I ... Joanna, come and help me. Please.'

There was a little silence and she said in a more awake voice, 'You've never said "please" like that to me before. Not for anything.'

'Will you come?'

'Where to?'

'I don't really know,' I said despairingly. 'I'm in a telephone box on a country road miles from anywhere. The telephone exchange is Hampden Row.' I spelled it out for her. 'I don't think it's very far from London, and somewhere on the West, probably.'

'You can't come back on your own?' she asked.

'No,' I said. 'I've no money and my clothes are wet.'

'Oh.' A pause. 'All right, then. I'll find out where you are and come in a taxi. Anything else?'

'Bring a sweater,' I said. 'I'm cold. And some dry socks, if you have any. And some gloves. Don't forget the gloves. And a pair of scissors.'

'Sweater, socks, gloves, scissors. O.K. You'll have to wait while I get dressed again, but I'll come as soon as I can. Stay by the telephone box.'

'Yes,' I said.

'I'll hurry, don't worry,' she said. 'Good-bye.'

'Good-bye . . .' I fumbled the receiver back on to its rest. However quick she was, she wouldn't arrive for an hour. Well, what was one more hour after so many? I had had no idea it was so late: the evening had certainly seemed to me to be going on for an eternity, but I had lost all sense of actual time. And Kemp-Lore hadn't come back. His show had been over for hours, and he hadn't come back. The bloody, murdering bastard, I thought.

I sat down on the floor of the box and leaned gingerly against the wall beside the telephone, with my head resting on the coin box. Exercise and the bitter wind outside, inactivity and shelter inside; one looked as cold a prospect as the other. But I was too tired to walk any more if I didn't have to, so the choice was easy.

I put my hands up to my face and one by one bit my fingers. They were icy cold and yellowish white, and none of them had any feeling. They would curl and uncurl, but slowly and weakly, and that was all. I got to work on them seriously then, rubbing them up and down against my legs, bumping them on my knees, forcing them open and shut, but it seemed to make little difference. I persevered from fear that they should get worse if I didn't, and paid for it in various creaks from my sore and sorely misused shoulders.

There was a good deal to think about to take my mind off my woes. That sticking-plaster for instance. Why had he used it? The strip over my mouth, I had assumed, had been to stop me shouting for help; but when I got it off at last and shouted, there was no one to hear. No one could have heard however loud I yelled, because the stable was so far from the lane.

The strip over my eyes should have been to prevent my seeing where I was going, but why did it matter if I saw an empty yard and a deserted tack-room? What would have happened differently, I wondered, if I had been able to see and talk.

To see... I would have seen Kemp-Lore's expression while he went about putting me out of action. I would have seen Kemp-Lore... that was it! It was himself he had not wanted me to see, not the place.

If that were so it was conceivable that he had prevented me from talking simply so that he should not be trapped into answering. He had spoken only once, and that in a low, unrecognizable tone. I became convinced that he had not wanted me to hear and recognize his voice.

In that case he must have believed I did not know who had abducted me, that I didn't know who he was. He must still believe it. Which meant that he thought James had knocked Turniptop's doped sugar out of his hand by accident, that he hadn't heard about Tick-Tock and me going round all the stables, and that he didn't know that I had been asking about the Jaguar. It gave me, I thought, a fractional advantage for the future. If he had left any tracks anywhere, he would not see any vital, immediate need to obliterate them. If he didn't know he was due for destruction himself, he would not be excessively on his guard.

Looking at my bloodless hands and knowing that on top of everything else I still had to face the pain of their return to life, I was aware that all the civilized brakes were off in my conscience. Helping to build up what he had broken was not enough. He himself had hammered into me the inner implacability I had lacked to avenge myself and all the others thoroughly, and to do it physically and finally and without compunction.

She came, in the end.

I heard a car draw up and a door slam, and her quick tread on the road. The door of the telephone box opened, letting in an icy blast, and there she was, dressed in trousers and woolly boots and a warm blue padded jacket, with the light falling on her dark hair and making hollows of her eyes.

I was infinitely glad to see her. I looked up at her and did my best at a big smile of welcome, but it didn't come off very well. I was shivering too much.

She knelt down and took a closer look at me. Her face went stiff with shock.

'Your hands,' she said.

'Yes. Did you bring the scissors?'

Without a word she opened her handbag, took out a sensible-sized pair, and cut me free. She did it gently. She took the harness hook from between my knees and laid it on the floor, and carefully peeled from my wrists the cut pieces of rope. They were all more brown than white, stained with blood, and where they had been there were big corrugated raw patches, dark and deep. She stared at them.

'More bits of rope down there,' I said, nodding towards my feet.

She cut the pieces round my ankles, and I saw her rubbing my trouser leg between her fingers. The air had been too cold to dry them and my body had not generated enough heat, so they were still very damp.

'Been swimming?' she said flippantly. Her voice cracked.

There was a step on the road outside and a man's shape loomed up behind Joanna.

'Are you all right, miss?' he said in a reliable sounding Cockney voice.

'Yes, thank you,' she said. 'Do you think you could help me get my cousin into the taxi?'

He stepped into the doorway and looked down at me, his eyes on my wrists and my hands.

'Christ,' he said.

'Very aptly put,' I said.

He looked at my face. He was a big sturdy man of about fifty, weather-beaten like a sailor, with eyes that looked as if they had seen everything and found most of it disappointing.

'You've been done proper, haven't you?' he said.

'Proper,' I agreed.

He smiled faintly. 'Come on then. No sense in hanging about here.'

I stood up clumsily and lurched against Joanna, and put my arms round her neck to save myself from falling; and as I was there it seemed a shame to miss the opportunity, so I kissed her. On the eyebrow, as it happened.

'Did you say "cousin"?' said the taxi driver.

'Cousin,' said Joanna firmly. Much too firmly.

The driver held the door open. 'We'd better take him to a doctor,' he said.

'No,' I said. 'No doctor.'

Joanna said, 'You need one.'

'No.'

'That's frostbite,' said the driver pointing to my hands.

'No,' I said. 'It isn't freezing. No ice on the puddles. Just cold. Not frostbite.' My teeth were chattering and I could only speak in short sentences.

'What happened to your back?' asked the driver, looking at the tattered bits of shirt sticking to me.

'I . . . fell over,' I said. 'On some gravel.'

He looked sceptical.

'It's a terrible mess, and there's a lot of dirt in it,' said Joanna, peering round me and sounding worried.

'You wash it,' I said. 'At home.'

'You need a doctor,' said the driver again.

I shook my head. 'I need Dettol, aspirins and sleep.'

'I hope you know what you're doing,' said Joanna. 'What else?'

'Sweater,' I said.

'It's in the taxi,' she said. 'And some other clothes. You can change as we go along. The sooner you get into a hot bath the better.'

'I'd be careful about that, miss,' said the driver. 'Don't go warming those hands up too fast or the fingers will drop off.' A comforting chap. Inaccurate too, I trusted. Joanna looked more worried than ever.

We walked from the telephone box to the taxi. It was an ordinary black London taxi. I wondered what charm Joanna had used to get it so far out into the country in the middle of the night; and also, more practically, whether the meter was still ticking away. It was.

'Get in, out of the wind,' she said, opening the taxi door.

I did as I was told. She had brought a suitcase, from which she now produced a thin, pale blue cardigan of her own, and a padded man-size olive-coloured anorak which zipped up the front. She looked at me judiciously, and out came the scissors. Some quick snips and the ruins of my shirt lay on the seat beside me. She cut two long strips of it and wound them carefully round my wrists. The taxi driver watched.

'This is a police job,' he suggested.

I shook my head. 'Private fight,' I said.

He held up the harness hook, which he had brought across from the telephone box.

'What sort of thing is this?' he asked.

'Throw it in the ditch,' I said, averting my eyes.

'You'll be needing it for the police,' he insisted.

'I told you,' I said wearily, 'no police.'

His disillusioned face showed that he knew all about

people who got themselves beaten up but wouldn't report it. He shrugged and went off into the darkness, and came back without the hook.

'It's in the ditch behind the telephone box, if you change your mind,' he said.

'Thanks,' I said.

Joanna finished the bandages and helped my arms into both the garments she had brought, and fastened the fronts. The next thing the suitcase produced was a pair of fur lined mittens which went on without too much trouble, and after that a thermos flask full of hot soup, and some cups.

I looked into Joanna's black eyes as she held the cup to my mouth. I loved her. Who wouldn't love a girl who thought of hot soup at a time like that?

The driver accepted some soup too, and stamped his feet on the ground and remarked that it was getting chilly. Joanna gave him a pained look, and I laughed.

He glanced at me appraisingly and said, 'Maybe you can do without a doctor, at that.' He thanked Joanna for the soup, gave her back the cup, settled himself in the driving seat and, switching off the light inside the taxi, started to drive us back to London.

'Who did it?' said Joanna.

'Tell you later.'

'All right.' She didn't press. She bent down to the case and brought out some fleecy slippers, thick socks and a pair of her own stretchy trews. 'Take your trousers off.'

I said ironically, 'I can't undo the zip.'

'I forgot . . .'

'Anyway,' I said, 'I'll settle for the socks; can't manage the trousers.' Even I could hear the exhaustion in my voice, and Joanna without arguing got down on her knees in the swaying cab and changed my wet socks and shoes for dry ones.

'Your feet are freezing,' she said.

'I can't feel them,' I said. The moon shone clearly through the window and I looked at the slippers. They were too large for me, much too large for Joanna.

'Have I stepped into Brian's shoes?' I asked.

After a pause she said neutrally, 'They are Brian's, yes.'

'And the jacket?'

'I bought it for him for Christmas.'

So that was that. It wasn't the best moment to find out.

'I didn't give it to him,' she said after a moment, as if she had made up her mind about something.

'Why not?'

'It didn't seem to suit a respectable life in the outer suburbs. I gave him a gold tie-pin instead.'

'Very suitable,' I said dryly.

'A farewell present,' she said quietly.

I said sincerely, 'I'm sorry.' I knew it hadn't been easy for her.

She drew in a breath sharply. 'Are you made of iron, Rob?'

'Iron filings,' I said.

The taxi sped on.

'We had a job finding you,' she said. 'I'm sorry we were so long. It was such a big area, you see.'

'You came, though.'

'Yes.'

I found sitting in the swaying taxi very uncomfortable. My arms and shoulders ached unceasingly and if I leaned back too heavily the raw bits didn't like it. After a while I gave it up, and finished the journey sitting on the floor with my head and my hands in Joanna's lap.

I was of course quite used to being knocked about. I followed, after all, an occupation in which physical damage was a fairly frequent though unimportant factor; and, especially during my first season, when I was a less efficient jockey and most of the horses I rode were the worst to be had, there was rarely a time when some area of my body was not black and blue. I had broken several of the smaller bones, been kicked in tender places, and dislocated one or two joints. On my general sense of well-being, and on my optimism that I wouldn't crash unmendably, none of these things had made the slightest dent. It seemed that in common with most other jockeys I had been born with the sort of resilient constitution which could take a bang and be ready for business, if not the following day, at least a good deal quicker than the medical profession considered normal.

Practice had given me a certain routine for dealing with discomfort, which was mainly to ignore it and concentrate on something else: but this system was not operating very well that evening. It didn't work, for instance, when I sat for a while in a light armchair in Joanna's warm room with my elbows on my knees, watching my fingers gradually change colour from yellowy white to smudgy charcoal, to patchy purple, and finally to red.

It began as a tingle, faint and welcome, soon after we had got back and Joanna had turned both her powerful heaters on. She had insisted at once on removing my clammy trousers and also my pants, and on my donning her black trews, which were warm but not long enough by several inches. It was odd, in a way, letting her undress me, which she did matter-of-factly and without remark; but in another way it seemed completely natural, a throwback to our childhood, when we had been bathed together on our visits to each other's houses.

She dug out some rather powdery-looking aspirins in a bottle. There were only three of them left, which I swallowed. Then she made some black coffee and held it for me to drink. It was stiff with brandy.

'Warming,' she said laconically. 'Anyway, you've stopped shivering at last.'

It was then that my fingers tingled and I told her.

'Will it be bad?' she said prosaically, putting down the empty coffee mug.

'Possibly.'

'You won't want me to sit and watch you then,' she said.

I shook my head. She took the empty mug into the kitchen and was several minutes coming back with a full one for herself.

The tingle increased first to a burning sensation and then to a feeling of being squeezed in a vice, tighter and tighter, getting more and more agonizing until it felt that at any minute my fingers would disintegrate under the pressure. But there they were, harmlessly hanging in the warm air, with nothing to show for it except that they were turning slowly puce.

Joanna came back from the kitchen and wiped the sweat off my forehead.

'Are you all right?' she asked.

'Yes,' I said.

She nodded, and gave me a faint edition of the intimate smile that had had my heart doing flip-flaps from boyhood, and drank her coffee.

When the pulse got going, it felt as though my hands had been taken out of the vice, laid on a bench, and were being rhythmically hammered. It was terrible. And it went on too long. My head drooped.

When I looked up she was standing in front of me, watching me with an expression which I couldn't read. There were tears in her eyes.

'Is it over?' she said, blinking to disguise them.

'More or less.'

We both looked at my hands, which were now a fierce red all over.

'And your feet?' she asked.

'They're fine,' I said. Their awakening had been nothing.

'I'd better wash those grazes on your back,' she said.

'No,' I said. 'In the morning.'

'There's a lot of dirt in them,' she protested.

'It's been there so long already that a few more hours won't hurt,' I said. 'I've had four anti-tetanus injections in the last two years, and there's always penicillin . . . and I'm too tired.'

She didn't argue. She unzipped and helped me take off the anorak, and made me get into her bed, still incongruously dressed in her black trews and blue cardigan and looking like a second-rate ballet dancer with a hangover. The sheets were rumpled from her lying in them before I had woken her up, and there was still a dent in her pillow where her head had been. I put mine there too, with an odd feeling of delight. She saw me grin, and correctly read my mind.

'It's the first time you've got into my bed,' she said. 'And it'll be the last.'

'Have a heart, Joanna,' I said.

She perched herself on the edge of the mattress and looked down at me.

'It's no good for cousins,' she said.

'And if we weren't cousins?'

'I don't know . . .' she sighed. 'But we are.'

She bent down to kiss me good night on the forehead.

I couldn't help it; I put my arms up round her shoulders and pulled her down on to my chest and kissed her properly, mouth to mouth. It was the first time I had ever done it, and into it went all the pent-up and suppressed desire I had ever felt for her. It was too hungry, too passionate, much too desperate. I knew it, but I couldn't stop it. For a moment she seemed to relax and melt and kiss me back, but it was so brief and passing that I thought I had imagined it, and afterwards her body grew rigid.

I let her go. She stood up abruptly and stared at me, her face scrubbed of any emotion. No anger, no disgust; and no love. She turned away without speaking and went across the room to the sofa, where she twisted a blanket around herself and lay down. She stretched out her hand to the table light and switched it off.

Her voice reached me across the dark room, calm, self-controlled. 'Good night, Rob.'

'Good night, Joanna,' I said politely.

There was dead silence.

I rolled over on to my stomach and put my face in her pillow.

CHAPTER THIRTEEN

I don't know whether she slept or not during the next four hours. The room was quiet. The time passed slowly.

The pulse in my hands went on throbbing violently for a while, but who cared? It was comforting, even if it hurt. I thought about all the fat red corpuscles forcing their way through the shrunken capillaries like water gushing along dry irrigation ditches after a drought. Very nice. Very life-giving. By tomorrow afternoon, I thought – correction, this afternoon – they might be fit for work. They'd got to be, that was all there was about it.

Some time after it was light I heard Joanna go into her narrow bathroom-kitchen where she brushed her teeth and made some fresh coffee. The warm roasted smell floated across to me. Saturday morning, I thought. Midwinter Cup day. I didn't leap out of bed eagerly to greet it; I turned over slowly from my stomach on to one side, shutting my eyes against the stiffness which afflicted every muscle from neck to waist, and the sharp soreness of my back and wrists. I really didn't feel very well.

She came across the room with a mug of steaming coffee and put it on the bedside table. Her face was pale and expressionless.

'Coffee,' she said unnecessarily.

'Thank you.'

'How do you feel?' she asked, a little too clinically.

'Alive,' I said.

There was a pause.

'Oh, go on,' I said. 'Either slosh me one or smile . . . one or the other. But don't stand there looking tragic, as if the Albert Hall had burned down on the first night of the Proms.'

'Damn it, Rob,' she said, her face crinkling into a laugh.

'Truce?' I asked.

'Truce,' she agreed, still smiling. She even sat down again on the edge of the bed. I shoved myself up into a sitting position, wincing somewhat from various aches, and brought a hand out from under the bedclothes to reach for the coffee.

As a hand it closely resembled a bunch of beef sausages. I produced the other one. It also was swollen. The skin on both felt very tender, and they were still unnaturally red.

'Blast,' I said. 'What's the time?'

'About eight o'clock,' she said. 'Why?'

Eight o'clock. The race was at two-thirty. I began

counting backwards. I would have to be at Ascot by at the latest one-thirty, preferably earlier, and the journey down, going by taxi, would take about fifty minutes. Allow an hour for hold-ups. That left me precisely four and a half hours in which to get fit enough to ride, and the way I felt, it was a tall order.

I began to consider ways and means. There were the Turkish baths, with heat and massage; but I had lost too much skin for that to be an attractive idea. There was a work-out in a gym; a possibility, but rough. There was a canter in the park – a good solution on any day except Saturday, when the Row would be packed with little girls on leading-reins – or better still a gallop on a racehorse at Epsom, but there was neither time to arrange it nor a good excuse to be found for needing it.

'What's the matter?' asked Joanna.

I told her.

'You don't mean it?' she said. 'You aren't seriously thinking of racing today?'

'I seriously am.'

'You're not fit to,' she said.

'That's the point. That's what we are discussing, how best to get fit,' I said.

'That isn't what I mean,' she protested. 'You look ill. You need a long, quiet day in bed.'

'I'll have it tomorrow,' I said, 'today I am riding Template in the Midwinter Cup.' She began more forcibly to try to dissuade me, so I told her why I was going to ride. I told her everything, all about Kemp-Lore's anti-jockey obsession and all that had happened on the previous evening before she found me in the telephone box. It took quite a time. I didn't look at her while I told her about the tack-room episode, because for some reason it embarrassed me to describe it, even to her, and I knew then quite certainly that I was not going to repeat it to anyone else.

When I had finished she looked at me without speaking for half a minute – thirty solid seconds – and then she cleared her throat and said, 'Yes, I see. We'd better get you fit, then.'

I smiled at her.

'What first?' she said.

'Hot bath and breakfast,' I said. 'And can we have the weather forecast on?' I listened to it every morning, as a matter of routine.

She switched on the radio, which was busy with some sickening matinée music, and started tidying up the room, folding the blanket she had slept in and shaking the sofa cushions. Before she had finished the music stopped, and we heard the eight-thirty news headlines, followed by the forecast.

'There was a slight frost in many parts of the country last night,' said the announcer smoothly, 'and more is expected tonight, especially in exposed areas. Temperatures today will reach five degrees centigrade, forty-one Fahrenheit, in most places, and the north-easterly wind will moderate slightly. It will be bright and sunny in the south. Further outlook: colder weather is expected in the next few days. And here is an announcement. The stewards at Ascot inspected the course at eight o'clock this morning and have issued the following statement. "Two or three degrees of frost were recorded on the racecourse last night, but the ground on both sides of the fences was protected by straw, and unless there is a sudden severe frost during the morning, racing is certain.'

Joanna switched off. She said, 'Are you absolutely determined to go?'

'Absolutely,' I said.

'Well ... I'd better tell you ... I watched that programme last night on television. *Turf Talk*.'

'Did you now!' I said, surprised.

'I sometimes do, since you were on it. If I'm in. Anyway I watched last night.'

'And?' I prompted.

'He,' she said, neither of us needing help to know who she meant, 'he talked about the Midwinter Cup nearly all the time; potted biographies of the horses and trainers, and so on. I was waiting to hear him mention you, but he didn't. He just went on and on about how superb Template is; not a word about you. But what I thought you'd like to know is that he said that as it was such an important race he personally would be commentating the finish today, and that he personally would also interview the winning jockey afterwards. If only you can win, he'll have to describe you doing it, which would be a bitter enough pill, and then congratulate you publicly in full view of several million people.'

I gazed at her, awestruck.

'That's a great thought,' I said.

'Like he interviewed you after that race on Boxing Day,' she added.

'That was the race that sealed my fate with him, I imagine,' I said. 'And you seem to have done some fairly extensive viewing, if I may say so.'

She looked taken aback. 'Well . . . didn't I see you sitting unobtrusively at the back of a concert I gave in Birmingham one night last summer?'

'I thought those lights were supposed to dazzle you,' I said.

'You'd be surprised,' she said.

I pushed back the bedclothes. The black trews looked even more incongruous in the daylight.

'I'd better get going,' I said. 'What do you have in the way of disinfectant and bandages, and a razor?'

'Only a few minute bits of Elastoplast,' she said apologetically, 'and the razor I de-fuzz my legs with. There's a chemist two roads away though, who will be open by now. I'll make a list.' She wrote it on an old envelope.

'And A.P.C. tablets,' I said. 'They are better than just aspirins.'

'Right,' she said. 'I won't be long.'

When she had gone I got out of bed and went into

the bathroom. It's easy enough to say, but it wasn't all that easy to do, since I felt as if some over-zealous laundress had fed me several times through a mangle. It was exasperating, I thought bitterly, how much havoc Kemp-Lore had worked on my body by such simple means. I turned on the taps, took off the trews and socks, and stepped into the bath. The blue cardigan had stuck to my back and the shirt bandages to my wrists, so I lay down in the hot water without tugging at them and waited for them to soak off.

Gradually the heat did its customary work of unlocking the worst of the cramps, until I could rotate my shoulders and turn my head from side to side without feeling that I was tearing something adrift. Every few minutes I added more hot water, so that by the time Joanna came back I was up to my throat in it and steaming nicely, warm to the backbone and beyond.

She had dried my trousers and pants overnight, and she pressed them for me while I eased myself out of the blue cardigan and reluctantly got out of the bath. I put on the trousers and watched her setting out her purchases on the kitchen table, a dark lock of hair falling forward into her eyes and a look of concentration firming her mouth. Quite a girl.

I sat down at the table and she bathed the grazes with disinfectant, dried them, and covered them with large pieces of lint spread with zinc-and-castor-oil ointment which she stuck on with adhesive tape. She was neat and quick, and her touch was light.

'Most of the dirt came out in the bath luckily,' she observed, busy with the scissors. 'You've got quite an impressive set of muscles, haven't you? You must be strong . . . I didn't realize.'

'At the moment I've got an impressive set of jellies,' I sighed. 'Very wobbly, very weak.' And aching steadily, though there wasn't any point in saying so.

She went into the other room, rummaged in a drawer, and came back with another cardigan. Pale green, this time; the colour suited my state of health rather well, I thought.

'I'll buy you some new ones,' I said, stretching it across my chest to do up the fancy buttons.

'Don't bother,' she said, 'I loathe both of them.'

'Thanks,' I said, and she laughed.

I put the anorak on again on top of the jersey and pushed the knitted cuffs up my forearms. Joanna slowly unwound the blood-stained bandages on my wrists. They still stuck a bit in spite of the soaking, and what lay underneath was a pretty disturbing sight, even to me, now that we could see it in daylight.

'I can't deal with this,' she said positively. 'You must go to a doctor.'

'This evening,' I said. 'Put some more bandages on, for now.'

'It's too deep,' she said. 'It's too easy to get it infected. You can't ride like this, Rob, really you can't.'

'I can,' I said. 'I'll dunk them in a bowl of Dettol for a while, and then you wrap them up again. Nice and flat, so they won't show.'

'Don't they hurt?' she said.

I didn't answer.

'Yes,' she said. 'Silly question.' She sighed, and fetched a bowl full of warm water, pouring in Dettol so that it turned a milky white, and I soaked my wrists in it for ten minutes.

'That's fixed the infection,' I said. 'Now . . . nice and flat.'

She did as I asked, fastening the ends of the bandages down with little gold safety pins. When she had finished the white cuffs looked tidy and narrow, and I knew they would be unnoticeable under racing colours.

'Perfect,' I said appreciatively, pulling down the anorak sleeves to cover them. 'Thank you, Florence.'

'And Nightingale to you, too,' she said, making a face at me. 'When are you going to the police?'

'I'm not. I told you,' I said. 'I'm not going at all. I meant what I said last night.'

'But why not; why not?' She didn't understand. 'You could get him prosecuted for assault or for causing grievous bodily harm, or whatever the technical term is.'

I said, 'I'd rather fight my own battles . . . and anyway, I can't face the thought of telling the police what happened last night, or being examined by their doctors, and photographed; or standing up in court, if it came to that, and answering questions about it in public, and having the whole rotten lot printed in gory detail in the papers. I just can't face it, that's all.'

'Oh,' she said slowly. 'I suppose it would be a bit of an ordeal, if you look at it like that. Perhaps you feel humiliated . . . is that it?'

'You may be rather bruisingly right,' I admitted grudgingly, thinking about it. 'And I'll keep my humiliation to myself, if you don't mind.'

She laughed. 'You don't need to feel any,' she said. 'Men are funny creatures.'

The pity about hot baths is that although they loosen one up beautifully for the time being, the effect does not last; one has to consolidate the position by exercise. And exercise, my battered muscles protested, was just what they would least enjoy; all the same I did a few rather half-hearted bend-stretch arm movements while Joanna scrambled us some eggs, and after we had eaten and I had shaved I went back to it with more resolution, knowing that if I didn't get on to Template's back in a reasonably supple condition he had no chance of winning. It wouldn't help anyone if I fell off at the first fence.

After an hour's work, though I couldn't screw myself up to swinging my arms round in complete circles, I did get to the stage where I could lift them above shoulder height without wanting to cry out.

Joanna washed up and tidied the flat, and soon after

ten o'clock, while I was taking a breather, she said, 'Are you going on with this health and beauty kick until you leave for Ascot?'

'Yes.'

'Well,' she said, 'it's only a suggestion, but why don't we go skating instead?'

'All that ice,' I said, shuddering.

She smiled. 'I thought you had to remount at once, after a fall?'

I saw the point.

'Anyway,' she said, 'it's good, warming exercise, and far more interesting than what you've been doing.'

'You're a blooming genius, my darling Joanna,' I said fervently.

'Er . . . maybe,' she said. 'I still think you ought to be in bed.'

When she was ready we went along to my family's flat where I borrowed one of my father's shirts and a tie and also his skates, which represented his only interest outside music. Then we called at the bank, since the taxi ride the night before had taken nearly all Joanna's cash, and apart from needing money myself I wanted to repay her. Lastly, we stopped at a shop to buy me a pair of brown, silk-lined leather gloves, which I put on, and finally we reached the ice rink in Queensway where we had both been members from the days when we were taken there as toddlers on afternoons too rainy for playing in the Park.

We had not skated together since we were sixteen,

and it was fascinating to see how quickly we fell back into the same dancing techniques that we had practised as children.

She was right about the exercise. After an hour of it I had loosened up from head to foot, with hardly a muscle that wasn't moving reasonably freely. She herself, sliding over the ice beside me, had colour in her cheeks and a dazzling sparkle in her eyes. She looked young and vivid.

At twelve o'clock, Cinderella-like, we slid off the rink.

'All right?' she asked, smiling.

'Gorgeous,' I said, admiring the clear, intelligent face turned up to mine.

She didn't know whether I meant her or the skating, which was perhaps just as well.

'I mean . . . how are the aches and pains?'

'Gone,' I said.

'You're a liar,' she said, 'but at least you don't look as grey as you did.'

We went to change, which for me simply meant substituting my father's shirt and tie for the pale green cardigan, and putting back the anorak on top, and the gloves. Necessary, the gloves. Although my fingers were less swollen, less red, and no longer throbbed, the skin in places was beginning to split in short thread-thin cracks.

In the foyer Joanna put the cardigan and my father's skates into her bag and zipped it up, and we went out into the street. She had already told me that she would not come to Ascot with me, but would watch on television. 'And mind you win,' she said, 'after all this.'

'Can I come back to your place, afterwards?' I said.

'Why, yes . . . yes,' she said, as if surprised that I had asked.

'Fine,' I said. 'Well . . . good-bye.'

'Good luck, Rob,' she said seriously.

CHAPTER FOURTEEN

The third cruising taxi driver that I stopped just round the corner in Bayswater Road agreed to take me all the way to Ascot. During the journey, which was quick and skilfully driven, I kept the warmth and flexibility going in my arms by some minor exercises and imaginary piano playing; and if the driver saw me at it in his mirror he probably imagined I was suffering from a sad sort of St Vitus dance.

He announced, when I paid him at the gate, that he thought as it was his own cab that he might as well stay and have a flutter on the races himself, so I arranged for him to drive me back to London again at the end of the afternoon.

'Got any tips?' he said, counting my change.

'How about Template, in the big race?' I said.

'I dunno,' he pursed his lips. 'I dunno as I fancy that Finn. They say as he's all washed up.'

'Don't believe all you hear,' I said, smiling. 'See you later.'

'Right.'

I went through the gate and along to the weighing-room. The hands of the clock on the tower pointed to five-past one. Sid, James's head travelling lad, was standing outside the weighing-room door when I got there, and as soon as he saw me he came to meet me, and said, 'You're here then.'

'Yes,' I said. 'Why not?'

'The governor posted me here to wait for you. I had to go and tell him at once if you came. He's having lunch ... there's a rumour going round that you weren't going to turn up, see?' He bustled off.

I went through the weighing-room into the changing-room.

'Hello,' said my valet. 'I thought you'd cried off.'

'So you came after all,' said Peter Cloony.

Tick-Tock said, 'Where in hell have you been?'

'Why did everyone believe I wouldn't get here?' I asked.

'I don't know. Some rumour or other. Everyone's been saying you frightened yourself again on Thursday and you'd chucked up the idea of riding any more.'

'How very interesting,' I said, grimly.

'Never mind that now,' said Tick-Tock. 'You're here, and that's that. I rang your pad this morning, but your landlady said you hadn't been back all night. I wanted to see if it was O.K. for me to have the car after racing today and for you to get a lift back with Mr Axminster. I have met,' he finished gaily, 'a smashing girl. She's here at the races and she's coming out with me afterwards.'

'The car?' I said. 'Oh . . . yes. Certainly. Meet me outside the weighing-room after the last, and I'll show you where it is.'

'Super,' he said. 'I say, are you all right?'

'Yes, of course.'

'You look a bit night-afterish, to my hawk eyes,' he said. 'Anyway the best of luck on Template, and all that rot.'

An official peered into the changing-room and called me out. James was waiting in the weighing-room outside.

'Where have you been?' he said.

'In London,' I said. 'What's this rumour about me not turning up?'

'God knows,' he shrugged. 'I was sure you wouldn't have stayed away without at least letting me know, but . . .'

'No,' I said. 'Of course not.' Not unless, I thought, I had still been hanging in a deserted tack-room in the process of being crippled for life.

He dismissed the subject and began to talk about the race. 'There's a touch of frost in the ground still,' he said, 'but that's really to our advantage.' I told him I had walked round the course the day before, and knew which parts were best avoided.

'Good,' he said.

I could see that for once he was excited. There was

a sort of uncharacteristic shyness about his eyes, and
the lower teeth gleamed in an almost perpetual half
smile. Anticipation of victory, that's what it is, I
thought. And if I hadn't spent such a taxing night and
morning I would have been feeling the same. As it
was, I looked forward to the race without much joy,
knowing from past experience that riding with injuries
never made them better. Even so, I wouldn't have
given up my place on Template for anything I could
think of.

When I went back into the changing-room to put
on breeches and colours, the jockeys riding in the first
race had gone out, leaving a lot of space and quiet
behind them. I went along to my peg, where all my
kit was set out ready, and sat down for a while on the
bench. My conscience ought to have been troubling
me. James and Lord Tirrold had a right to expect
their jockey to be in tip-top physical condition for so
important a race, and, to put it mildly, he wasn't.
However, I reflected wryly, looking down at my gloved
hands, if we all owned up to every spot of damage,
we'd spend far too much time on the stands watching
others win on our mounts. It wasn't the first time I
had deceived an owner and trainer in this way and yet
won a race, and I fervently hoped it wouldn't be the
last.

I thought about the Midwinter. Much depended on
how it developed, but basically I intended to start
on the rails, sit tight in about fourth place all the way

round, and sprint the last three furlongs. There was a new Irish mare, Emerald, who had come over with a terrific reputation and might take a lot of beating, especially as her jockey was a wily character, very clever at riding near the front and slipping the field by a hard-to-peg-back ten lengths round the last bend. If Emerald led into the last bend, I decided, Template would have to be close to her by then, not still waiting in fourth place. Fast though he was, it would be senseless to leave him too much to do up the straight.

It is not customary for jockeys to stay in the changing-room while a race is on, and I saw the valets looking surprised that I had not gone out to watch it. I stood up, picked up the under-jersey and Lord Tirrold's colours and went to change into them in the washroom. Let the valets think what they like, I thought. I wanted to change out of sight, partly because I had to do it more slowly than usual but mostly so that they shouldn't see the bandages. I pulled down the sleeves of the finely-knitted green and black jersey until they hid those on my wrists.

The first race was over and the jockeys were beginning to stream into the changing-room when I went back to my peg. I finished changing into breeches, nylons and boots and took my saddle and weight cloth along to the trial scales for Mike to adjust the amount of lead needed to bring me to twelve stone.

'You've got gloves on,' he pointed out.

'Yes,' I said mildly, 'it's a cold day. I'd better have some silk ones for riding in, though.'

'O.K.' he said. He produced from a hamper a bundle of whitish gloves and pulled out a pair for me.

I went along to the main scales to weigh out, and gave my saddle to Sid, who was standing there waiting for it.

He said, 'The governor says I'm to saddle Template in the stable, and bring him straight down into the parade ring when it's time, and not go into the saddling boxes at all.'

'Good,' I said emphatically.

'We've had two private dicks and a bloody great dog patrolling the yard all night,' he went on. 'And another dick came with us in the horse-box, and he's sitting in Template's box at this very minute. You never saw such a circus.'

'How's the horse?' I asked, smiling. Evidently James was splendidly keeping his word that Template would not be doped.

'He'll eat 'em,' Sid said simply. 'The Irish won't know what hit them. All the lads have got their wages on him. Yeah, I know they've been a bit fed up that you were going to ride him, but I saw you turn that Turniptop inside out on Thursday and I told 'em they've nothing to worry about.'

'Thanks,' I said, sincerely enough; but it was just one more ounce on a load of responsibility.

The time dragged. My shoulders ached. To take my

mind off that I spent some time imagining the expression on Kemp-Lore's face when he saw my name up in the number frame. He would think at first it was a mistake. He would wait for it to be changed. And at any moment now, I thought maliciously, he will begin to realize that I am indeed here.

The second race was run with me still sitting in the changing-room, the object of now frankly curious looks from the valets. I took the brown gloves off and put on the greyish white ones. They had originally been really white, but nothing could entirely wash out a season's accumulated stains of mud and leather. I flexed my fingers. Most of the swelling had gone, and they seemed to be getting fairly strong again in spite of the cracked and tender skin.

Back came the other jockeys again, talking, laughing, swearing, dealing out friendly and not so friendly abuse, yelling to the valets, dumping down their kit – the ordinary, comradely, noisy changing-room mixture – and I felt apart from it, as if I were living in a different dimension. Another slow quarter of an hour crawled by. Then an official put his head in and shouted, 'Jockeys out, hurry up there, please.'

I stood up, put on the anorak, fastened my helmet, picked up my whip, and followed the general drift to the door. The feeling of unreality persisted.

Down in the paddock where in June the chiffons and ribbons fluttered in the heat stood cold little bunches of owners and trainers, most of them muffled to the eyes against the wind. It seared through the bare branches of the trees beside the parade ring, leaving a uniformity of pinched faces among the people lining the rails. The bright winter sunshine gave an illusion of warmth which blue noses and runny eyes belied. But the anorak, as I had been pleased to discover, was windproof.

Lord Tirrold wore on his fine-boned face the same look of excited anticipation that I could still see on James's. They are both so sure, I thought uneasily, that Template will win. Their very confidence weakened mine.

'Well, Rob,' said Lord Tirrold, shaking me too firmly by the hand, 'this is it.'

'Yes, sir,' I agreed, 'this is it.'

'What do you think of Emerald?' he asked.

We watched her shamble round the parade ring with the sloppy walk and the low-carried head that so often denotes a champion.

'They say she's another Kerstin,' said James, referring to the best steeplechasing mare of the century.

'It's too soon to say that,' said Lord Tirrold: and I wondered if the same thought sprang into his mind as into mine, that after the Midwinter, it might not be too soon, after all. But he added as if to bury the possibility, 'Template will beat her.'

'I think so,' James agreed.

I swallowed. They were too sure. If he won, they

would expect it. If he lost, they would blame me; and probably with good cause.

Template himself stalked round the parade ring in his navy-blue rug, playing up each time as he came face on to the wind, trying to turn round so that it blew on his quarters, with his lad hanging on to his leading-rein like a small child on a large kite.

A bell rang, indicating it was time for the jockeys to mount. James beckoned to the boy, who brought Template across to us and took off his rug.

'Everything all right?' James asked.

'Yes, sir.'

Template's eyes were liquid clear, his ears were pricked, his muscles quivering to be off: the picture of a taut, tuned racing-machine eager to get on with the job he was born for. He was not a kind horse: there was no sweetness in his make-up and he inspired admiration rather than affection: but I liked him for his fire and his aggressiveness and his unswerving will to win.

'You've admired him long enough, Rob,' said James teasingly. 'Get up on him.'

I took off the anorak and dropped it on the rug. James gave me a leg up into the saddle and I gathered the reins and put my feet into the irons.

What he read in my face I don't know, but he said suddenly, anxiously, 'Is anything wrong?'

'No,' I said. 'Everything's fine.' I smiled down at him, reassuring myself as much as him.

Lord Tirrold said, 'Good luck,' as if he didn't think I needed it, and I touched my cap to him and turned Template away to take his place in the parade down the course.

There was a television camera on a tower not far down the course from the starting gate, and I found the thought of Kemp-Lore raging at the sight of me on his monitor set a most effective antidote to the freezing wind. We circled round for five minutes, eleven of us, while the assistant starter tightened girths and complained that anyone would think we were in perishing Siberia.

I remembered that Tick-Tock, the last time we had ridden together on the course on a cold day, had murmured 'Ascot's blasted Heath. Where are the witches?' And I thought of him now, putting a brave face on his inactivity on the stands. I thought briefly of Grant, probably hating my guts while he watched the race on television, and of Peter Cloony's wife, with no set to watch on at all, and of the jockeys who had given up and gone into factories, and of Art, under the sod.

'Line up,' called the starter, and we straightened into a ragged row across the course, with Template firmly on the inside, hugging the rails.

I thought of myself, driven to distraction by having it drummed into me that I had lost my nerve, and I thought of myself dragged over flinty ground and tied to a piece of galvanized chain; and I didn't need any more good reasons for having to win the Midwinter Cup.

I watched the starter's hand. He had a habit of stretching his fingers just before he pulled the lever to let the tapes up, and I had no intention of letting anyone get away before me and cut me out of the position I had acquired on the rails.

The starter stretched his fingers. I kicked Template's flanks. He was moving quite fast when we went under the rising tapes, with me lying flat along his withers to avoid being swept off, like other riders who had jumped the start too effectively in the past. The tapes whistled over my head and we were away, securely on the rails and on the inside curve for at least the next two miles.

The first three fences were the worst, as far as my comfort was concerned. By the time we had jumped the fourth – the water – I had felt the thinly healed crusts on my back tear open, had thought my arms and shoulder would split apart with the strain of controlling Template's eagerness, had found just how much my wrists and hands had to stand from the tug of the reins.

My chief feeling, as we landed over the water, was one of relief. It was all bearable; I could contain it and ignore it, and get on with the job.

The pattern of the race was simple from my point of view, because from start to finish I saw only three other horses, Emerald and the two lightly-weighted animals whom I had allowed to go on and set the pace. The jockeys of this pair, racing ahead of me nose for nose, consistently left a two-foot gap between themselves and the rails, and I reckoned that if they were still there by the time we reached the second last fence in the straight, they would veer very slightly towards the stands, as horses usually do at Ascot, and widen the gap enough for me to get through.

My main task until then was keeping Emerald from cutting across to the rails in front of me and being able to take the opening instead of Template. I left just too little room between me and the front pair for Emerald to get in, forcing the mare to race all the way on my outside. It didn't matter that she was two or three feet in front: I could see her better there, and Template was too clever a jumper to be brought down by the half-length trick – riding into a fence half a length in front of an opponent, causing him to take off at the same moment as oneself and land on top of the fence instead of safely on the ground the other side.

With the order unchanged we completed the whole of the first circuit and swept out to the country again. Template jumped the four fences down to Swinley Bottom so brilliantly that I kept finding myself crowding the tails of the pacemakers as we landed, and had to ease him back on the flat each time to avoid taking the lead too soon, and yet not ease him so much that Emerald could squeeze into the space between us.

From time to time I caught a glimpse of the grimness on Emerald's jockey's face. He knew perfectly well what I was doing to him, and if I hadn't beaten him to the rails and made a flying start, he would have done the same to me. Perhaps I had Kemp-Lore to thank that he hadn't even tried, I thought fleetingly; if the bonfire Kemp-Lore had made of my reputation had led the Irishman to misjudge what I would do, so much the better.

For another half-mile the two horses in front kept going splendidly, but one of the jockeys picked up his whip at the third last fence, and the other was already busy with his hands. They were dead ducks, and because of that they swung a little wide going round the last bend into the straight. The Irishman must have had his usual bend tactics too fixed in his mind, for he chose that exact moment to go to the front. It was not a good occasion for that manoeuvre. I saw him spurt forward from beside me and accelerate, but he had to go round on the outside of the two front horses who were themselves swinging wide, and he was wasting lengths in the process. The mare carried seven pounds less weight than Template, and on that bend she lost the advantage they should have given her.

After the bend, tackling the straight for the last time, with the second last fence just ahead, Emerald was in the lead on the outside, then the two tiring horses, then me.

There was a three foot gap then between the innermost pacemaker and the rails. I squeezed Template. He pricked his ears and bunched his colossal muscles and thrust himself forward into the narrow opening. He took off at the second last fence half a length behind and landed a length in front of the tiring horse, jumping so close to him on one side and to the wings on the other that I heard the other jockey cry out in surprise as I passed.

One of Template's great advantages was his speed away from a fence. With no check in his stride he sped smoothly on, still hugging the rails, with Emerald only a length in front on our left. I urged him a fraction forward to prevent the mare from swinging over to the rails and blocking me at the last fence. She needed two lengths' lead to do it safely, and I had no intention of letting her have it.

The utter joy of riding Template lay in the feeling of immense power which he generated. There was no need to make the best of things, on his back; to fiddle and scramble, and hope for others to blunder, and find nothing to spare for a finish. He had enough reserve strength for his jockey to be able to carve up the race as he wished, and there was nothing in racing, I thought, more ecstatic than that.

I knew, as we galloped towards the last fence, that Template would beat Emerald if he jumped it in anything like his usual style. She was a length ahead and showing no sign of flagging, but I was still holding Template on a tight rein. Ten yards from the fence, I let him go. I kicked his flanks and squeezed with the calves of my legs and he went over the birch like an angel, smooth, surging, the nearest to flying one can get.

He gained nearly half a length on the mare, but she didn't give up easily. I sat down and rode Template for my life, and he stretched himself into his flat-looking stride. He came level with Emerald half-way along the run in. She hung on grimly for a short distance, but Template would have none of it. He floated past her with an incredible increase of speed, and he won, in the end, by two clear lengths.

There are times beyond words, and that was one of them. I patted Template's sweating neck over and over. I could have kissed him. I would have given him anything. How does one thank a horse? How could one ever repay him, in terms he would understand, for giving one such a victory?

The two tall men were pleased all right. They stood side by side, waiting for us in the unsaddling enclosure, the same elated expression on both their faces. I smiled at them, and shook my feet out of the irons and slid off on to the ground. On to the ground: down to earth. The end of an unforgettable experience.

'Rob,' said James, shaking his big head. 'Rob.' He slapped Template's steaming shoulder and watched me struggle to undo the girth buckles with fingers shaking from both weakness and excitement.

'I knew he'd do it,' Lord Tirrold said. 'What a horse! What a race!'

I had got the buckles undone at last and had pulled the saddle off over my arm when an official came over and asked Lord Tirrold not to go away, as the Cup was to be presented to him in a few minutes. To me, he said, 'Will you come straight out again after you have weighed in? There's a trophy for the winning jockey as well.'

I nodded, and went in to sit on the scales. Now that the concentration of the race was over, I began to be aware of the extra damage it had done. Across the back of my shoulders and down my arms to the fingertips every muscle felt like lead, draggingly heavy, shot with stabbing and burning sensations. I was appallingly weak and tired, and the pain in my wrists had increased to the point where I was finding it very difficult to keep it all out of my face. A quick look revealed that the bandages were red again, and so were the cuffs of the silk gloves and parts of the fawn under-jersey. But if the blood had soaked through the black jersey as well, at least it didn't show.

With a broad smile Mike took my saddle from me in the changing-room and unbuckled my helmet and pulled it off my head.

'They are wanting you outside, did you know?' he said.

I nodded. He held out a comb. 'Better smarten your hair a bit. You can't let the side down.'

I obediently took the comb and tidied my hair, and went back outside.

The horses had been led away and in their place stood a table bearing the Midwinter Cup and other trophies, with a bunch of racecourse directors and stewards beside it.

And Maurice Kemp-Lore as well.

It was lucky I saw him before he saw me. I felt my scalp contract at the sight of him and an unexpectedly strong shock of revulsion ran right down my body. He couldn't have failed to understand it, if he had seen it.

I found James at my elbow. He followed my gaze.

'Why are you looking so grim?' he said. 'He didn't even try to dope Template.'

'No,' I agreed. 'I expect he was too tied up with his television work to be sure of having time to do it.'

'He has given up the whole idea,' said James confidently. 'He must have seen there was no chance any more of persuading anyone you had lost your nerve. Not after the way you rode on Thursday.'

It was the reckless way I had ridden on Thursday that had infuriated Kemp-Lore into delivering the packet I had taken on Friday. I understood that very well.

'Have you told anyone about the sugar?' I asked James.

'No, since you asked me not to. But I think

something must be done. Slander or no slander, evidence or not . . .'

'Will you wait,' I asked, 'until next Saturday? A week today? Then you can tell whoever you like.'

'Very well,' he said slowly. 'But I still think . . .'

He was interrupted by the arrival at the trophy table of the day's V.I.P., a pretty Duchess, who with a few well-chosen words and a genuinely friendly smile presented the Midwinter Cup to Lord Tirrold, a silver tray to James, and a cigarette box to me. An enterprising press photographer let off a flash bulb as the three of us stood together admiring our prizes, and after that we gave them back again to the clerk of the course, for him to have them engraved with Template's name and our own.

I heard Kemp-Lore's voice behind me as I handed over the cigarette box, and it gave me time to arrange my face into a mildly smiling blankness before turning round. Even so, I was afraid that I wouldn't be able to look at him without showing my feelings.

I pivoted slowly on my heels and met his eyes. They were piercingly blue and very cold, and they didn't blink or alter in any way as I looked back at them. I relaxed a little, inwardly, thankful that the first difficult hurdle was crossed. He had searched, but had not read in my face that I knew it was he who had abducted me the evening before.

'Rob Finn,' he said in his charming television voice, 'is the jockey you just watched being carried to victory by this wonder horse, Template.' He was speaking into a hand microphone from which trailed yards of black flex, and looking alternately at me and at a camera on a scaffolding tower near by. The camera's red eye glowed. I mentally girded up my loins and prepared to forestall every disparaging opinion he might utter.

He said, 'I expect you enjoyed being his passenger?'

'It was marvellous,' I said emphatically, smiling a smile to outdazzle his. 'It is a great thrill for any jockey to ride a horse as superb as Template. Of course,' I went on amiably, before he had time to speak, 'I am lucky to have had the opportunity. As you know, I have been taking Pip Pankhurst's place all these months, while his leg has been mending, and today's win should have been his. He is much better now, I'm glad to say, and we are all delighted that it won't be long before he is riding again.' I spoke truthfully: whatever it meant to me in fewer rides, it would benefit the sport as a whole to have its champion back in action.

A slight chill crept into the corner of Kemp-Lore's mouth.

'You haven't been doing as well, lately ...' he began.

'No,' I interrupted warmly. 'Aren't they extra-ordinary, those runs of atrocious luck in racing? Did you know that Doug Smith once rode ninety-nine losers in succession? How terrible he must have felt. It makes my twenty or so seem quite paltry.'

'You weren't worried, then, by ... er ... by such a bad patch as you've been going through?' His smile was slipping.

'Worried?' I repeated lightheartedly. 'Well, naturally I wasn't exactly delighted, but these runs of bad luck happen to everyone in racing, once in a while, and one just has to live through them until another winner comes along. Like today's,' I finished with a grin at the camera.

'Most people understood it was more than bad luck,' he said sharply. There was a definite crack in his jolly-chums manner, and for an instant I saw in his eyes a flash of the fury he was controlling. It gave me great satisfaction, and because of it I smiled at him more vividly.

I said, 'People will believe anything when their pockets are touched. I'm afraid a lot of people lost their money backing my mounts ... it's only natural to blame the jockey ... nearly everyone does, when they lose.'

He listened to me mending the holes he had torn in my life and he couldn't stop me without giving an impression of being a bad sport; and nothing kills the popularity of a television commentator quicker than obvious bad-sportsmanship.

He had been standing at right-angles to me with his profile to the camera, but now he took a step towards me and turned so that he stood beside me on my left side. As he moved there was a fleeting set to his mouth that looked like cruelty to me, and it prepared me in some measure for what he did next.

With a large gesture which must have appeared as genuine friendship on the television screen, he dropped his right arm heavily across my shoulders, with his right thumb lying forward on my collar bone and his fingers spread out on my back.

I stood still, and turned my head slowly towards him, and smiled sweetly. Few things have ever cost me more effort.

'Tell us a bit about the race, then, Rob,' he said, advancing the microphone in his left hand. 'When did you begin to think you might win?'

His arm felt like a ton weight, an almost unsupportable burden on my aching muscles. I gathered my straying wits.

'Oh . . . I thought, coming into the last fence,' I said, 'that Template might have the speed to beat Emerald on the flat. He can produce such a sprint at the end, you know.'

'Yes, of course.' He pressed his fingers more firmly into the back of my shoulder and gave me what passed for a friendly shake. My head began to spin. Everything on the edge of my vision became blurred. I went on smiling, concentrating desperately on the fair, good-looking face so close to mine, and was rewarded by the expression of puzzlement and disappointment in his eyes. He knew that under his fingers, beneath two thin jerseys, were patches which must be sore if touched, but he didn't know how much or how little trouble I had had in freeing myself in the tack-room. I wanted him to believe it had been none at all, that the ropes had slipped undone or the hook fallen easily out of the ceiling. I wanted to deny him even the consolation of knowing how nearly he had succeeded in preventing me from riding Template.

'And what are Template's plans for the future?' He strove to be conversational, normal. The television interview was progressing along well-trodden ways.

'There's the Gold Cup at Cheltenham,' I said. I was past telling whether I sounded equally unruffled, but there was still no leap of triumph in his face, so I went on, 'I expect he will run there, in three weeks' time. All being well, of course.'

'And do you hope to ride him again in that?' he asked. There was an edge to his voice which just stopped short of offensiveness. He was finding it as nearly impossible to put on an appearance of affection for me as I for him.

'It depends,' I said, 'on whether or not Pip is fit in time ... and on whether Lord Tirrold and Mr Axminster want me to, if he isn't. But of course I'd like to, if I get the chance.'

'You've never yet managed to ride in the Gold Cup, I believe?' He made it sound as if I had been trying unsuccessfully for years to beg a mount.

'No,' I agreed. 'But it has only been run twice since

I came into racing, so if I get a ride in it so soon in my career I'll count myself very lucky.'

His nostrils flared and I thought in satisfaction, 'That got you squarely in the guts, my friend. You'd forgotten how short a time I've been a jockey.'

He turned his head away from me towards the camera and I saw the rigidity in his neck and jaw and the pulse which beat visibly in his temple. I imagined he would willingly have seen me dead: yet he was enough in command of himself to realize that if he pressed my shoulder any harder I would be likely to guess it was not accidental.

Perhaps if he had been less controlled at that moment I would have been more merciful to him later. If his professionally pleasant expression had exploded into the rage he was feeling, or if he had openly dug his nails with ungovernable vindictiveness into my back, I could perhaps have believed him more mad than wicked, after all. But he knew too well where to stop; and since I could not equate madness with such self-discipline, by my standards he was sane; sane and controlled, and therefore unlikely to destroy himself from within. I threw Claudius Mellit's plea for kid gloves finally overboard.

Kemp-Lore was speaking calmly towards the camera, finishing off his broadcast. He gave me a last, natural-looking little squeezing shake, and let his arm drop away from my shoulders. Slowly and methodically I silently repeated to myself the ten most obscene words I knew, and after that Ascot racecourse stopped attempting to whirl round and settled down again into brick and mortar and grass and people, all sharp and perpendicular.

The man behind the camera on the tower held up his thumb and the red eye blinked out.

Kemp-Lore turned directly to me again and said, 'Well, that's it. We're off the air now.'

'Thank you, Maurice,' I said, carefully constructing one last warm smile. 'That was just what I needed to set me back on top of the world. A big race win and a television interview with you to clinch it. Thank you very much.' I could rub my fingers in his wounds, too.

He gave me a look in which the cultivated habit of charm struggled for supremacy over spite, and still won. Then he turned on his heel and walked away, pulling his black microphone lead along the ground after him.

It is impossible to say which of us loathed the other more.

CHAPTER FIFTEEN

I spent most of the next day in Joanna's bed. Alone, unfortunately.

She gave me a cup of coffee for breakfast, a cosy grin, and instructions to sleep. So I lazily went on snoozing in the pyjamas she had bought me, dreaming about her on her own pillow, doing nothing more energetic than occasionally raise my blood pressure by thinking about Kemp-Lore.

I had arrived in a shaky condition on her doorstep the evening before, having first taken Tick-Tock and his space-age girlfriend by taxi to the boring White Bear at Uxbridge where, as I had imagined, the Mini-Cooper stood abandoned in the car park. It had seemed to me certain that Kemp-Lore had driven to the White Bear in his own car, had used the Mini-Cooper for his excursion to the abandoned stables, and had changed back again to his own car on the return journey. His route, checked on the map, was simple: direct almost. All the same I was relieved to find the little Mini safe and sound.

Tick-Tock's remarks about my carelessness with communal property trickled to a stop when he found my wrist-watch and wallet and the other things out of my pockets on the glove shelf, and my jacket and overcoat and a length of white nylon rope on the back seat.

'Why the blazes,' he said slowly, 'did you leave your watch and your money and your coats here? It's a wonder they weren't pinched. And the car.'

'It's the north-east wind,' I said solemnly. 'Like the moon, you know. I always do mad things when there's a north-east wind.'

'North-east my aunt fanny.' He grinned, picked up the coats, and transferred them to the waiting taxi. Then he surprisingly shovelled all my small belongings back into my trousers pockets, and put my watch into my gloved hand.

'You may have fooled everyone else, mate,' he said lightly, 'but to me you have looked like death inefficiently warmed up all day, and it's something to do with your maulers ... the gloves are new ... you don't usually wear any. What happened?'

'You work on it,' I said amiably, getting back into the taxi. 'If you haven't anything better to do.' I glanced across at his little hep-cat, and he laughed and flipped his hand, and went to help her into the Mini-Cooper.

The taxi-driver, in a good mood because he had backed three winners, drove me back to Joanna's mews without a single complaint about the roundabout journey. When I paid him and added a fat tip on top he said, 'Were you on a winner, too, then?'

'Yes,' I said. 'Template.'

'Funny thing that,' he said. 'I backed him myself, after what you said about not believing all you hear. You were quite right, weren't you? That fellow Finn's not washed up at all, not by a long chalk. He rode a hell of a race. I reckon he can carry my money again, any day.' He shifted his gears gently, and drove off.

Watching his tail-light bump away down the cobbled mews, I felt ridiculously happy and very much at peace. Winning the race had already been infinitely worth the cost, and the taxi-driver, not knowing who he was speaking to, had presented me with the bonus of learning that as far as the British racing public was concerned, I was back in business.

Dead beat but contented, I leaned against Joanna's door-post and rang her bell.

That wasn't quite the end of the most exhausting twenty-four hours of my life, however. My thoughtful cousin, anticipating correctly that I would refuse to turn out again to see a doctor, had imported one of her own. He was waiting there when I arrived, a blunt no-bedside manner Scot with bushy eyebrows and three warts on his chin.

To my urgent protests that I was in no state to withstand his ministrations, both he and Joanna turned deaf ears. They sat me in a chair, and off came my clothes again, the leather gloves and the silk racing ones I had not removed after riding, then the anorak, my father's shirt and the racing under-jersey, also not returned to Mike, then the bits of lint Joanna had stuck on in the morning, and finally the blood-soaked bandages round my wrists. Towards the end of all this rather ruthless undressing, the room began spinning as Ascot had done, and I regrettably rolled off the chair on to the floor, closer to fainting than I had been the whole time.

The Scotsman picked me up and put me back in the chair and told me to pull myself together and be a man.

'You've only lost a wee bit of skin,' he said sternly.

I began to laugh weakly, which didn't go down well, either. He was a joyless fellow. He compressed his mouth until the warts quivered when I shook my head to his enquiries and would not tell him what had happened to me. But he bound me up again comfortably enough and gave me some pain-killing pills which turned out to be very effective; and when he had gone I got into Joanna's bed and sank thankfully into oblivion.

Joanna worked at her painting most of the next day and when I surfaced finally at about four o'clock in the afternoon, she was singing quietly at her easel. Not the angular, spiky songs she specialized in, but a Gaelic ballad in a minor key, soft and sad. I lay and listened with my eyes shut because I knew she would stop if she found me awake. Her voice was true, even at a level not much above a whisper, the result of well-exercised vocal cords and terrific breath control. A proper Finn, she is, I thought wryly. Nothing done by halves.

She came to the end of the ballad, and afterwards began another. 'I know where I'm going, and I know who's going with me. I know who I love, but the dear knows who I'll marry. Some say he's black, but I say he's bonny...' She stopped abruptly and said quietly but forcefully, 'Damn, damn and blast.' I heard her throw down her palette and brushes and go into the kitchen.

After a minute I sat up in bed and called to her, 'Joanna.'

'Yes?' she shouted, without reappearing.

'I'm starving,' I said.

'Oh.' She gave a laugh which ended in a choke, and called, 'All right. I'll cook.'

And cook she did; fried chicken with sweet corn and pineapple and bacon. While the preliminary smells wafted tantalizingly out of the kitchen I got up and put my clothes on, and stripped her bed. There were clean sheets in the drawer beneath, and I made it up again fresh and neat for her to get into.

She carried a tray of plates and cutlery in from the kitchen and saw the bundle of dirty sheets and the smooth bed.

'What are you doing?'

'The sofa isn't good for you,' I said. 'You obviously haven't slept well ... and your eyes are red.'

'That isn't ...' she began, and thought better of it.

'It isn't lack of sleep?' I finished.

She shook her head. 'Let's eat.'

'Then what's the matter?' I said.

'Nothing. Nothing. Shut up and eat.'

I did as I was told. I was hungry.

She watched me finish every morsel. 'You're feeling better,' she stated.

'Oh, yes. Much. Thanks to you.'

'And you are not sleeping here tonight?'

'No.'

'You can try the sofa,' she said mildly. 'You might as well find out what I have endured for your sake.' I didn't answer at once, and she added compulsively, 'I'd like you to stay, Rob. Stay.'

I looked at her carefully. Was there the slightest chance, I wondered, that her gentle songs and her tears in the kitchen and now her reluctance to have me leave meant that she was at last finding the fact of our cousinship more troublesome than she was prepared for? I had always known that if she ever did come to love me as I wanted and also was not able to abandon her rigid prejudice against our blood relationship, it would very likely break her up. If that was what was happening to her, it was definitely not the time to walk out.

283

'All right,' I said smiling. 'Thank you. I'll stay. On the sofa.'

She became suddenly animated and talkative, and told me in great detail how the race and the interview afterwards had appeared on television. Her voice was quick and light. 'At the beginning of the programme he said he thought your name was a mistake on the number boards, because he had heard you weren't there, and I began to worry that you had broken down on the way and hadn't got there after all. But of course you had ... and afterwards you looked like life-long buddies standing there with his arm round your shoulders and you smiling at him as if the sun shone out of his eyes. How did you manage it? But he was trying to needle you, wasn't he? It seemed like it to me, but then that was perhaps because I knew ...' She stopped in mid-flow, and in an entirely different, sober tone of voice she said, 'What are you going to do about him?'

I told her. It took some time.

She was shaken. 'You can't,' she said.

I smiled at her, but didn't answer.

She shivered. 'He didn't know what he was up against, when he picked on you.'

'Will you help?' I asked. Her help was essential.

'Won't you change your mind and go to the police?' she said seriously.

'No.'

'But what you are planning ... it's cruel.'

284

'Yes,' I agreed.

'And complicated, and a lot of work, and expensive.'

'Yes. Will you make that one telephone call for me?'

She sighed and said, 'You don't think you'll relent, once everything has stopped hurting?'

'I'm quite certain,' I said.

'I'll think about it,' she said, standing up and collecting the dirty dishes. She wouldn't let me help her wash up, so I went over to the easel to see what she had been working at all day: and I was vaguely disturbed to find it was a portrait of my mother sitting at her piano.

I was still looking at the picture when she came back.

'It's not very good, I'm afraid,' she said, standing beside me. 'Something seems to have gone wrong with the perspective.'

'Does Mother know you're doing it?' I asked.

'Oh no,' she said.

'When did you start it?'

'Yesterday afternoon,' she said.

There was a pause. Then I said, 'It won't do you any good to try to convince yourself your feelings for me are maternal.'

She jerked in surprise.

'I don't want mothering,' I said. 'I want a wife.'

'I can't . . .' she said, with a tight throat.

I turned away from the picture, feeling that I had

285

pressed her too far, too soon. Joanna abruptly picked up a turpentine-soaked rag and scrubbed at the still wet oils, wiping out all her work.

'You see too much,' she said. 'More than I understood myself.'

I grinned at her and after a moment, with an effort, she smiled back. She wiped her fingers on the rag, and hung it on the easel.

'I'll make that telephone call,' she said. 'You can go ahead with ... with what you plan to do.'

On the following morning, Monday, I hired a drive-yourself car and went to see Grant Oldfield.

The hard overnight frost, which had caused the day's racing to be cancelled, had covered the hedges and trees with sparkling rime, and I enjoyed the journey even though I expected a reception at the end of it as cold as the day.

I stopped outside the gate, walked up the short path through the desolate garden, and rang the bell.

It had only just struck me that the brass bell push was brightly polished when the door opened and a neat dark-haired young woman in a green wool dress looked at me enquiringly.

'I came ...' I said. 'I wanted to see ... er ... I wonder if you could tell me where I can find Grant Oldfield?'

'Indoors,' she said. 'He lives here; I'm his wife. Just a minute, and I'll get him. What name shall I say?'

'Rob Finn,' I said.

'Oh,' she said in surprise; and she smiled warmly. 'Do come in. Grant will be so pleased to see you.'

I doubted it, but I stepped into the narrow hall and she shut the door behind me. Everything was spotless and shining; it looked a different house from the one I remembered. She led the way to the kitchen and opened the door on to another area of dazzling cleanliness.

Grant was sitting at a table, reading a newspaper. He glanced up as his wife went in, and when he saw me his face too creased into a smile of surprised welcome. He stood up. He was much thinner and older-looking, and shrunken in some indefinable inner way; but he was, or he was going to be soon, a whole man again.

'How are you, Grant?' I said inadequately, not understanding their friendliness.

'I'm much better, thanks,' he said. 'I've been home a fortnight now.'

'He was in hospital,' his wife explained. 'They took him there the day after you brought him home. Dr Parnell wrote to me and told me Grant was ill and couldn't help being how he was. So I came back.' She smiled at Grant. 'And everything's going to be all right now. Grant's got a job lined up too. He starts in two weeks, selling toys.'

287

'Toys?' I exclaimed. Of all incongruous things, I thought.

'Yes,' she said, 'they thought it would be better for him to do something which had nothing to do with horses, so that he wouldn't start brooding again.'

'We've a lot to thank you for, Rob,' Grant said.

'Dr Parnell told me,' his wife said, seeing my surprise, 'that you would have been well within your rights if you'd handed him over to the police instead of bringing him here.'

'I tried to kill you,' Grant said in a wondering voice, as if he could no longer understand how he had felt. 'I really tried to kill you, you know.'

'Dr Parnell said if you'd been a different sort of person Grant could have ended up in a criminal lunatic asylum.'

I said uncomfortably, 'Dr Parnell appears to have been doing too much talking altogether.'

'He wanted me to understand,' she said, smiling, 'that you had given Grant another chance, so I ought to give him another chance too.'

'Would it bother you,' I said to Grant, 'if I asked you a question about how you lost your job with Axminster?'

Mrs Oldfield moved protectively to his side. 'Don't bring it all back,' she said anxiously, 'all the resentment.'

'It's all right, love,' Grant said, putting his arm around her waist. 'Go ahead.'

'I believe you were telling the truth when you told Axminster you had not sold information to that professional punter, Lubbock,' I said. 'But Lubbock did get information, and did pay for it. The question is, who was he actually handing over the money to, if he thought he was paying it to you?'

'You've got it wrong, Rob,' Grant said. 'I went over and over it at the time, and I went to see Lubbock and got pretty angry with him . . .' He smiled ruefully, 'and Lubbock said that until James Axminster tackled him about it he hadn't known for sure who he was buying information from. He had guessed it was me, he said. But he said I had given him the information over the telephone, and he had sent the payments to me in the name of Robinson, care of a Post Office in London. He didn't believe I knew nothing about it, of course. He just thought I hadn't covered myself well enough and was trying to wriggle out of trouble.' There was a remarkable lack of bitterness in his voice; his spell in a mental hospital, or his illness itself, seemed to have changed his personality to the roots.

'Can you give me Lubbock's address?' I asked.

'He lives in Solihull,' he said slowly. 'I might know the house again, but I can't remember the name of it, or the road.'

'I'll find it,' I said.

'Why do you want to?' he asked.

'Would it mean anything to you, if I happened to prove that you were telling the truth all along?'

His face came suddenly alive from within. 'I'll say it would,' he said. 'You can't imagine what it was like, losing that job for something I didn't do, and having no one believe in me any more.'

I didn't tell him that I knew exactly what it was like, only too well. I said, 'I'll do my best, then.'

'But you won't go back to racing?' his wife said to him anxiously. 'You won't start all over again?'

'No love. Don't worry,' he said calmly. 'I'm going to enjoy selling toys. You never know, we might start a toy shop of our own, next year, when I've learned the business.'

I drove the thirty miles to Solihull, looked up Lubbock in the telephone directory, and rang his number. A woman answered. She told me that he was not in, but if I wanted him urgently I would probably get hold of him at the Queen's Hotel in Birmingham, as he was lunching there.

Having lost my way twice in the one-way streets, I miraculously found a place to park outside the Queen's, and went in. I wrote a note on the hotel writing-paper, asking Mr Lubbock, whom I did not know even by sight, if he would be so very kind as to give me a few minutes of his time. Sealing the note in an envelope, I asked the head porter if he would have one of the page-boys find Mr Lubbock and give it to him.

'He went into the dining-room with another gentleman a few minutes ago,' he said. 'Here, Dickie, take this note in to Mr Lubbock.'

Dickie returned with an answer on the back of the note: Mr Lubbock would meet me in the lounge at two-fifteen.

Mr Lubbock proved to be a plumpish, middle-aged man with a gingery moustache and a thin section of lank hair brushed across a balding skull. He accepted from me a large brandy and a fat cigar with such an air of surprised irony that I was in no doubt that he was used to buying these things for jockeys, and not the other way about.

'I want to know about Grant Oldfield,' I said, coming straight to the point.

'Oldfield?' he murmured, sucking flame down the cigar. 'Oh yes, I remember, Oldfield.' He gave me a sharp upward glance. 'You ... er ... you still work for the same firm, don't you? Do you want a deal, is that it? Well, I don't see why not. I'll give you the odds to a pony for every winner you put me on to. No one could say fairer than that.'

'Is that what you paid Oldfield?' I said.

'Yes,' he said.

'Did you give it to him personally?' I asked.

'No,' he said. 'But then he didn't ask me personally. He fixed it up on the telephone. He was very secretive: he said his name was Robinson, and asked me to pay him in uncrossed money orders, and to send them to a Post Office for him to collect.'

'Which one?' I asked.

He took a swig at the brandy and gave me an assessing look. 'Why do you want to know?'

'It sounds a good idea,' I said casually.

He shrugged. 'I can't remember,' he said. 'Surely it's unimportant which Post Office it was? Somewhere in a London suburb, I know, but I can't remember where after all this time. NE7? N12? Something like that.'

'You wouldn't have a record of it?'

'No,' he said decisively. 'Why don't you ask Oldfield himself, if you need to know?'

I sighed. 'How many times did he give you information?' I asked.

'He told me the names of about five horses altogether, I should think. Three of them won, and I sent him the money on those occasions.'

'You didn't know it was Oldfield selling you tips, did you?' I asked.

'It depends what you mean by "know",' he said. 'I had a pretty good idea. Who else could it have been? But I suppose I didn't actually "know" until Axminster said "I hear you've been buying information from my jockey," and I agreed that I had.'

'So you wouldn't have told anyone before that that it was Oldfield who was selling you tips?'

'Of course not.'

'No one at all?' I pressed.

'No, certainly not.' He gave me a hard stare. 'You don't broadcast things like that, not in my business, and especially if you aren't dead sure of your facts. Just what is all this about?'

'Well . . .' I said. 'I'm very sorry to have misled you, Mr Lubbock, but I am not really in the market for information. I'm just trying to unstick a bit of the mud that was thrown at Grant Oldfield.'

To my surprise he gave a fat chuckle and knocked half an inch of ash off the cigar.

'Do you know,' he said, 'if you'd agreed to tip me off I'd have been looking for the catch? There's some jockeys you can square, and some you can't, and in my line you get an instinct for which are which. Now you . . .' he jabbed the cigar in my direction . . . 'you aren't the type.'

'Thanks,' I murmured.

'And more fool you,' he said nodding. 'It's not illegal.'

I grinned.

'Mr Lubbock,' I said, 'Oldfield was not Robinson, but his career and his health were broken up because you and Mr Axminster were led to believe that he was.'

He stroked his moustache with his thumb and forefinger of his left hand, wondering.

I went on, 'Oldfield has now given up all thought

of riding again, but it would still mean a great deal to him to have his name cleared. Will you help to do it?'

'How?' he said.

'Wouldn't you just write a statement to the effect that you saw no evidence at any time to support your guess that in paying Robinson, you were really paying Oldfield, and that at no time before James Axminster approached you did you speak of your suspicions as to Robinson's identity.'

'Is that all?' he said.

'Yes.'

'All right,' he said. 'It can't do any harm. But I think you're barking up the wrong tree. No one but a jockey would go to all that trouble to hide his identity. No one would bother, if his job didn't depend on not being found out. Still, I'll write what you ask.'

He unscrewed a pen, took a sheet of hotel writing-paper and in a decisive hand wrote the statement I had suggested. He signed it, and added the date and read it through.

'There you are,' he said. 'Though I can't see what good it will do.'

I read what he had written and folded the paper, and put it in my wallet.

'Someone told Mr Axminster that Oldfield was selling you information,' I said. 'If you hadn't told anyone at all – who knew?'

'Oh.' His eyes opened. 'I see, yes, I see. Robinson

294

knew. But Oldfield would never have let on ... so Oldfield was not Robinson.'

'That's about it,' I agreed, standing up. 'Thank you very much, Mr Lubbock, for your help.'

'Any time.' He waved the diminishing cigar, smiling broadly. 'See you at the races.'

CHAPTER SIXTEEN

On Tuesday morning I bought a copy of the *Horse and Hound* and spent a good while telephoning to a few of the people who had advertised their hunters for sale. With three of them I made appointments to view the animal in question in two days' time.

Next I rang up one of the farmers I rode for and persuaded him to lend me his Land-Rover and trailer on Thursday afternoon.

Then, having borrowed a tape measure out of Joanna's work-box – she was out at a rehearsal – I drove the hired car down to James's stables. I found him sitting in his office dealing with his paper work. The fire, newly lit in the grate, was making little headway against the raw chill in the air, and outside in the yard the lads looked frozen as they scurried about doing up their horses after the second morning exercise.

'No racing again today,' James remarked. 'Still, we've been extraordinarily lucky this winter up to now.'

He stood up and rubbed his hands, and held them out to the inadequate fire. 'Some of the owners have telephoned,' he said. 'They're willing to have you back. I told them . . .' and his lower teeth gleamed as he looked at me from under his eyebrows, '. . . that I was satisfied with your riding, and that you would be on Template in the Gold Cup.'

'What!' I exclaimed. 'Do you mean it?'

'Yes.' The glimmer deepened in his eyes.

'But . . . Pip . . .' I said.

'I've explained to Pip,' he said, 'that I can't take you off the horse when you've won both the King 'Chase and the Midwinter on him. And Pip agrees. I have arranged with him that he starts again the week after Cheltenham, which will give him time to get a few races in before the Grand National. He'll be riding my runner in that – the horse he rode last year.'

'It finished sixth,' I said, remembering.

'Yes, that's right. Now, I've enough horses to keep both Pip and you fairly busy, and no doubt you'll get outside rides as well. It should work out all right for both of you.'

'I don't know how to thank you,' I said.

'Thank yourself,' he said sardonically. 'You earned it.' He bent down and put another lump of coal on the fire.

'James,' I said, 'will you write something down for me?'

'Write? Oh, you'll get a contract for next season, the same as Pip.'

'I didn't mean that,' I said awkwardly. 'It's quite different... would you just write down that it was Maurice Kemp-Lore who told you that Oldfield was selling information about your horses, and that he said he had learned it from Lubbock?'

'Write it down?'

'Yes. Please,' I said.

'I don't see...' He gave me an intent look and shrugged. 'Oh, very well then.' He sat down at his desk, took a sheet of paper headed with his name and address, and wrote what I had asked.

'Signature and date?' he said.

'Yes, please.'

He blotted the page. 'What good will that do?' he said, handing it to me.

I took Mr Lubbock's paper out of my wallet and showed it to him. He read it through three times.

'My God,' he said. 'It's incredible. Suppose I had checked carefully with Lubbock? What a risk Maurice took.'

'It wasn't so big a risk,' I said. 'You wouldn't have thought of questioning what he put forward as a friendly warning. Anyway, it worked. Grant got the sack.'

'I'm sorry for that,' James said slowly. 'I wish there was something I could do about it.'

'Write to Grant and explain,' I suggested. 'He would appreciate it more than anything in the world.'

'I'll do that,' he agreed, making a note.

'On Saturday morning,' I said, taking back Lubbock's statement and putting it with his in my wallet, 'these little documents will arrive with a plop on the Senior Steward's doormat. Of course they aren't conclusive enough to base any legal proceedings on, but they should be enough to kick friend Kemp-Lore off his pedestal.'

'I should say you were right.' He looked at me gravely, and then said, 'Why wait until Saturday?'

'I... er... I won't be ready until then,' I said evasively.

He didn't pursue it. We walked out into the yard together and looked in on some of the horses, James giving instructions, criticism and praise – in that order – to the hurrying lads. I realized how used I had grown to the efficiency and prosperity of his organization, and how much it meant to me to be a part of it.

We walked slowly along one row of boxes, and James went into the tack-room at the end to talk to Sid about the cancellation of the following day's racing. Unexpectedly I stopped dead on the threshold. I didn't want to go in. I knew it was stupid, but it made no difference. Parts of me were still too sore.

The harness hook hung quietly from the centre of the ceiling, with a couple of dirty bridles swinging harmlessly on two of its curving arms. I turned my back on it and looked out across the tidy yard, and wondered if I would ever again see one without remembering.

Up in the rolling, grassy hills a mile or so away from his stable, James owned an old deserted keeper's cottage. In the past it had been the home allotted to the man who looked after the gallops, James had told me once on a journey to the races, but as it had no electricity, no piped water and no sanitation, the new groundsman preferred, not unnaturally, to live in comfort in the village below and go up the hill to work on a motor-bike.

The old cottage lay down an overgrown lane leading off a public but little used secondary road which led nowhere except up and along the side of the hill and down again to join the main road four miles further on. It served only two farms and one private house, and because of its quietness it was a regular route for the Axminster horses on roadwork days.

After leaving James I drove up to the cottage. I had not seen it at close quarters before, only a glimpse of its blank end wall from the end of the lane as I rode by. I now found it was a four-roomed bungalow, set in a small fenced garden with a narrow path leading from the gate to the front door. The neglected grass had been cropped short by sheep. There was one window to each room, two facing the front and two the back.

Getting in without a key presented no difficulty as most of the glass in the windows was broken; and opening one, I climbed in. The whole place smelt of fungus and rot, though faintly, as if the decay were only warming up for future onslaught. The walls and floorboards were still in good condition, and only one of the rooms was damp. I found that all four rooms opened on to a small central hall inside the front entrance; and as I made my tour I reflected that it could not have been more convenient if I had designed it myself.

I let myself out of the front door, and walking round to the back I took out Joanna's inch tape and measured the window frame; three feet high, four feet wide. Then I returned to the front, counted the number of broken panes of glass, and measured one of them. That done, I returned to James and asked him to lend me the cottage for a few days to store some things in for which there was no room at my digs.

'As long as you like,' he agreed absently, busy with paper work.

'May I mend some of the windows, and put on a new lock, to make it more secure?' I asked.

'Help yourself,' he said. 'Do what you like.'

I thanked him, and drove into Newbury, and at a builder's merchants waited while they made me up an order of ten panes of glass, enough putty to put them in with, several pieces of water pipe cut to a specified length, a bucket, some screws, a stout padlock, a bag of cement, a pot of green paint, a putty knife, a screwdriver, a cement trowel and a paint brush. Loaded to the axles with that lot I returned to the cottage.

I painted the weather-beaten front door and left it open to dry, reflecting that no one could blame a keeper, or his wife for that matter, for not wanting to live in that lonely, inconvenient cul-de-sac.

I went into one of the back rooms and knocked out all the panes of glass which still remained in their little oblong frames. Then, outside in the garden, I mixed a good quantity of cement, using water from the rain butt, and fixed six three-foot lengths of water pipe upright in a row across the window. That done, I went round into the hall, and on the doorpost and door of the same room screwed firmly home the fittings for the padlock. On the inside of the door I unscrewed the handle and removed it.

The final job was replacing the glass in the front windows, and it took me longest to do, chipping out all the old putty and squeezing on the new; but at last it was done, and with its whole windows and fresh green door the cottage already looked more cheerful and welcoming.

I smiled to myself. I retrieved the car from where I had parked it inconspicuously behind some bushes, and drove back to London.

The Scots doctor was drinking gin with Joanna when I let myself in.

'Oh no,' I said unceremoniously.

'Oh yes, laddie,' he said. 'You were supposed to come and see me yesterday, remember.'

'I was busy,' I said.

'I'll just take a look at those wrists, if you don't mind,' he said, putting down the gin and standing up purposefully.

I sighed and sat down at the table, and he unwrapped the bandages. There was blood on them again.

'I thought I told you to take it easy,' he said sternly. 'How do you expect them to heal? What have you been doing?'

I could have said 'Screwing in screws, chipping out putty and mixing cement,' but instead I rather uncooperatively muttered, 'Nothing.'

Irritated, he slapped a new dressing on with unnecessary force and I winced. He snorted, but he was gentler with the second one.

'All right,' he said, finishing them off. 'Now, rest them a bit this time. And come and see me on Friday.'

'Saturday,' I said. 'I won't be in London on Friday.'

'Saturday morning then. And mind you come.' He picked up his glass, tossed off the gin, and said a friendly good night exclusively to Joanna.

She came back laughing from seeing him out. 'He isn't usually so unsympathetic,' she said. 'But I think he suspects you were engaged in some sort of sadistic, disgusting orgy last week, as you wouldn't tell him how you got like that.'

'And he's dead right,' I said morosely. He had stirred up my wrists properly, and they hadn't been too good to start with, after my labours at the cottage.

For the third night I went to bed on the sofa and lay awake in the darkness, listening to Joanna's soft sleeping breath. Every day she hesitantly asked me if I would like to stay another night in her flat, and as I had no intention of leaving while there was any chance of thawing her resistance, I accepted promptly each time, even though I was progressively finding that no bread would have been more restful. Half a loaf, in the shape of Joanna padding familiarly in and out of the bathroom in a pretty dressing-gown and going to bed five yards away, was decidedly unsatisfying. But I could easily have escaped and gone to a non-tantalizing sleep in my own bed in my family's flat half a mile away; if I didn't, it was my own fault, and I pointed this out to her when every morning she remorsefully apologized for being unfair.

On Wednesday morning I went to a large photographic agency and asked to see a picture of Maurice Kemp-Lore's sister Alice. I was given a bundle of photographs to choose from, varying from Alice front-view in spotted organza at a Hunt Ball to Alice back-view winning over the last fence in a point to point. Alice was a striking girl, with dark hair, high cheek-bones, small fierce eyes, and a tight aggressive mouth. A girl to avoid, as far as I was concerned. I bought a copy of a waist-length photograph which showed her watching some hunter trials, dressed in a hacking jacket and headscarf.

Leaving the agency, I went to the city offices of my parents' accountants, and talked 'our Mr Stuart' in the records department into letting me use first a typewriter and then his photo-copying machine.

On plain typing paper I wrote a bald account of Kemp-Lore's actions against Grant Oldfield, remarking that as a result of Axminster's relying on the apparent disinterestedness of Kemp-Lore's accusation, Oldfield had lost his job, had subsequently suffered great distress of mind, and had undergone three months' treatment in a mental hospital.

I made ten copies of this statement and then on the photo-copier printed ten copies each of the statements from Lubbock and James. I thanked 'our Mr Stuart' profusely and returned to Joanna's mews.

When I got back I showed her the photograph of Alice Kemp-Lore, and explained who she was.

'But,' said Joanna, 'she isn't a bit like her brother. It can't have been her that the ticket-collector saw at Cheltenham.'

'No,' I said. 'It was Kemp-Lore himself. Could you draw me a picture of him wearing a head-scarf?'

She found a piece of cartridge paper and with

concentration made a recognizable likeness in charcoal of the face I now unwillingly saw in dreams.

'I've only seen him on television,' she said. 'It isn't very good.' She began to sketch in a head-scarf, adding with a few strokes an impression of a curl of hair over the forehead. Then, putting her head on one side and considering her work, she emphasized the lips so that they looked dark and full.

'Lipstick,' she murmured, explaining. 'How about clothes?' Her charcoal hovered over the neck.

'Jodhpurs and hacking jacket,' I said. 'The only clothes which look equally right on men and women.'

'Crumbs,' she said, staring at me. 'It was easy, wasn't it? On with head-scarf and lipstick, and exit the immediately recognizable Kemp-Lore.'

I nodded. 'Except that he still reminded people of himself.'

She drew a collar and tie and the shoulders of a jacket with revers. The portrait grew into a likeness of a pretty girl dressed for riding. It made my skin crawl.

I found Joanna's eyes regarding me sympathetically.

'You can hardly bear to look at him, can you?' she said. 'And you talk in your sleep.'

I rolled up the picture, bounced it on the top of her head, and said lightly, 'Then I'll buy you some ear plugs.'

'He was taking a big risk, all the same, pretending to be a girl,' she said, smiling.

'I don't suppose he did it a minute longer than he

had to,' I agreed. 'Just long enough to get from Timberley to Cheltenham without being recognized.'

I filled ten long envelopes with the various statements, and stuck them down. I addressed one to the Senior Steward and four others to influential people on the National Hunt Committee. One to the Chairman of Universal Telecast, one to John Ballerton, and one to Corin Kellar, to show them their idol's clay feet. One to James. And one to Maurice Kemp-Lore.

'Can't he get you for libel?' asked Joanna looking over my shoulder.

'Not a chance,' I said. 'There's a defence in libel actions called justification, which roughly means that if a man has done something dishonest you are justified in disclosing it. You have to prove it is true, that's all.'

'I hope you are right,' she said dubiously, sticking on some stamps.

'Don't worry. He won't sue me,' I said positively.

I stacked nine of the envelopes into a neat pile on the bookshelf and propped the tenth, the unstamped one for Kemp-Lore, up on end behind them.

'We'll post that lot on Friday,' I said. 'And I'll deliver the other one myself.'

At eight-thirty on Thursday morning Joanna made the telephone call upon which so much depended.

I dialled the number of Kemp-Lore's London flat.

There was a click as soon as the bell started ringing, and an automatic answering device invited us to leave a recorded message. Joanna raised her eyebrows; I shook my head, and she put down the receiver without saying anything.

'Out,' I said unnecessarily. 'Damn.'

I gave her the number of Kemp-Lore's father's house in Essex and she was soon connected and talking to someone there. She nodded to me and put her hand over the mouthpiece, and said, 'He's there. They've gone to fetch him. I . . . I hope I don't mess it up.'

I shook my head encouragingly. We had rehearsed pretty thoroughly what she was going to say. She licked her lips, and looked at me with anxious eyes.

'Oh? Mr Kemp-Lore?' She could do a beautiful cockney-suburban accent, not exaggerated and very convincing. 'You don't know me, but I wondered if I could tell you something that you could use on your programme in the newsy bits at the end? I do admire your programme, I do really. It's ever so good, I always think . . .'

His voice clacked, interrupting the flow.

'What information?' repeated Joanna. 'Oh, well, you know all the talk there's been about athletes using them pep pills and injections and things, well I wondered if you wanted to know about jockeys doing it too . . . one jockey, actually that I know of, but I expect they all do it if the truth were known . . . Which jockey? Oh ... er ... Robbie Finn, you know, the one you talked to on the telly on Saturday after he won that race. Pepped to the eyebrows as usual he was, didn't you guess? You was that close to him I thought you must have ... How do I know? Well I do know ... you want to know how I know ... well ... it's a bit dodgy, like, but it was me got some stuff for him once. I work in a doctor's surgery ... cleaning you see ... and he told me what to take and I got it for him. But now look here, I don't want to get into no trouble, I didn't mean to let on about that ... I think I'd better ring off ... Don't ring off? You won't say nothing about it then, you know, me pinching the stuff?

'Why am I telling you? ... Well, he don't come to see me no more, that's why.' Her voice was superbly loaded with jealous spite. 'After all I've done for him ... I did think of telling one of the newspapers, but I thought I'd see if you were interested first. I can tell them if you'd rather ... Check, what do you mean check? ... You can't take my word for it on the telephone? Well, yes, you can come and see me if you want to ... no, not today, I'm at work all day ... yes, all right, tomorrow morning then.

'How do you get there? ... Well, you go to Newbury and then out towards Hungerford ...' She went on with the directions slowly while he wrote them down. 'And it's the only cottage along there, you can't miss it. Yes, I'll wait in for you, about eleven o'clock, all right then. What's my name? ... Doris Jones. Yes, that's right. Mrs Doris Jones ... Well ta-ta then.' The telephone clicked and buzzed as he disconnected.

She put the receiver down slowly, looking at me with a serious face.

'Hook, line and sinker,' she said.

When the banks opened I went along and drew out one hundred and fifty pounds. As Joanna had said, what I was doing was complicated and expensive; but complication and expense had achieved top-grade results for Kemp-Lore, and at least I was paying him the compliment of copying his methods. I grudged the money not at all: what is money for, it not to get what you want? What I wanted, admirable or not, was to pay him in his own coin.

I drove off to the Bedfordshire farmer who promised to lend me his Land-Rover and trailer. It was standing ready in the yard when I arrived at noon, and before I left I bought from the farmer two bales of straw and one of hay, which we stowed in the back of the Land-Rover. Then, promising to return that evening, I started away to the first of my appointments with the *Horse and Hound* advertisers.

The first hunter, an old grey gelding in Northamptonshire, was so lame that he could hardly walk out of his box and he was no bargain even at the sixty pounds they were asking for him. I shook my head, and pressed on into Leicestershire.

The second appointment proved to be with a brown mare, sound in limb but noisy in wind, as I discovered when I cantered her across a field. She was big, about twelve years old and gawky, but quiet to handle and not too bad to look at, and she was for sale only because she could not go as fast as her ambitious owner liked. I haggled, bringing him from the hundred he had advertised her for down to eighty-five pounds, and clinched the deal. Then I loaded the mare, whose name, her ex-owner said, was Buttonhook, into the trailer and turned my face south again to Berkshire.

Three hours later, at half-past five in the afternoon, I turned the Land-Rover into the lane at the cottage, and bumped Buttonhook to a standstill on the rough ground behind the bushes beyond the building. She had to wait in the trailer while I got the straw and spread it thickly over the floorboards in the room with the water pipes cemented over the window, and again while I filled her a bucket of water out of the rain butt and carried an armful of hay into the room and put it in the corner behind the door.

She was an affectionate old thing, I found. She came docilely out of the trailer and made no fuss when I led her up the little garden path and in through the front door of the cottage and across the little hall into the room prepared for her. I gave her some sugar and rubbed her ears, and she butted her head playfully against my chest. After a while, as she seemed quite content in her unusual and not very spacious loose box, I went out into the hall, shut the door, and padlocked her in. Then I walked round the outside of the cottage and shook the water-pipe bars to see if they were secure, as the frosty air might have prevented the cement from setting properly. But they were all immovably fixed.

The mare came to the window and tried to poke her muzzle through the glassless squares of the window frame and through the bars outside them, but the maze defeated her. I put my hand through and fondled her muzzle, and she blew contentedly down her nostrils. Then she turned and went over to the corner where her hay was, and quietly and trustfully put her head down to eat.

I dumped the rest of the hay and straw in one of the front rooms of the cottage, shut the front door, manoeuvred the trailer round with some difficulty into the lane again, and set off back to Bedfordshire. In due course I delivered the Land-Rover and trailer to their owner, thanked him, and drove the hired car back to Joanna's mews.

When I went in, she kissed me. She sprang up from the sofa where she had been sitting reading, and kissed me lightly on the mouth. It was utterly spontaneous; without thought: and it was a great surprise to both of us. I put my hands on her arms and smiled incredulously down into her black eyes, and watched the surprise there turn to confusion and the confusion to panic. I took my hands away and turned my back on her to give her time, taking off the anorak and saying casually over my shoulder, 'The lodger is installed in the cottage. A big brown mare with a nice nature.'

I hung up the anorak in the cupboard.

'I was just ... glad to see you back,' she said in a high voice.

'That's fine,' I said lightly. 'Can I rustle up an egg, do you think?'

'There are some mushrooms for an omelette,' she said, more normally.

'Terrific,' I said, going into the kitchen. 'Not peeled, by any chance?'

'Damn it, no,' she said, following me and beginning to smile. She made the omelette for me and I told her about Buttonhook, and the difficult moment passed.

Later on she announced that she was coming down to the cottage with me when I went in the morning.

'No,' I said.

'Yes,' she nodded. 'He is expecting Mrs Doris Jones to open the door to him. It will be much better if she does.'

I couldn't budge her.

'And,' she said, 'I don't suppose you've thought of putting curtains in the windows? If you want him to walk into your parlour, you'll have to make it look normal. He probably has a keen nose for smelling rats.' She fished some printed cotton material out of the drawer and held it up. 'I've never used this . . . we can pin it up to look like curtains.' She busily collected some drawing pins and scissors, and then rolled up the big rag rug which the easel stood on and took a flower picture off the wall.

'What are those for?' I said.

'To furnish the hall, of course. It's got to look right.'

'Okay, genius,' I said, giving in. 'You can come.'

We put all the things she had gathered into a tidy pile by the door, and I added two boxes of cubed sugar from her store cupboard, the big electric torch she kept in case of power cuts, and a broom.

After that springing kiss, the sofa was more of a wasteland than ever.

CHAPTER SEVENTEEN

We set off early and got down to the cottage before nine, because there was a good deal to be done before Kemp-Lore arrived.

I hid the car behind the bushes again, and we carried the rug and the other things indoors. Buttonhook was safe and sound in her room, and was delighted to see us, neighing purringly in her throat when we opened her door. While I tossed her straw and fetched her some more hay and water, Joanna said she would clean the windows at the front of the cottage, and presently I heard her humming softly as she wiped away the grime of years.

The putty round the new panes had hardened well, and after I had finished Buttonhook, and Joanna was stepping back admiring the sparkle of the glass, I fetched the paint and began the tedious job of covering the patchwork of old decayed black paint and pale new putty with a bright green skin. Joanna watched me for a while and then went indoors. She put down the rug in the little hall, and I heard her banging a nail into the wall to hang up the picture just inside the front door where no visitor could fail to see it. After that she worked on the inside of the windows while I painted their outsides. She cut the flowery material into lengths and pinned it so that it hung like curtains.

When we had both finished we stood at the gate in front of the cottage admiring our handiwork. With its fresh paint, pretty curtains, and the rug and picture showing through the half-open door, it looked well cared for and homely.

'Has it got a name?' Joanna asked.

'I don't think so. It's always called "The Keeper's Cottage," as far as I know,' I said.

'We should name it Sundew,' she said.

'After the Grand National winner?' I said, puzzled.

'No,' she said soberly, 'the carnivorous plant.'

I put my arm round her waist. She didn't stir.

'You will be careful, won't you?' she said.

'Yes, I will,' I assured her. I looked at my watch. It was twenty minutes to eleven. 'We'd better go indoors in case he comes early.'

We went in and shut the front door and sat on the remains of the hay bale in the front room, giving ourselves a clear view of the front gate.

A minute or two ticked by in silence. Joanna shivered.

'Are you too cold?' I said with concern. There had been another frost during the night and there was, of course, no heating in the cottage. 'We should have brought a stove.'

'It's nerves as much as cold,' she said, shivering again.

I put my arm round her shoulders. She leaned comfortably against me, and I kissed her cheek. Her black eyes looked gravely, warily into mine.

'It isn't incest,' I said.

Her eyelids flickered in shock, but she didn't move.

'Our fathers may be brothers,' I said, 'but our mothers are not related to them or to each other.'

She said nothing. I had a sudden feeling that if I lost this time I had lost for ever, and a leaden chill of despair settled in my stomach.

'No one forbids marriage between cousins,' I said slowly. 'The Law allows it and the Church allows it, and you can be sure they wouldn't if there were anything immoral in it. And in a case like ours, the medical profession raises no objection either. If there were a good genetic reason why we shouldn't marry, it would be different. But you know there isn't.' I paused, but she still looked at me gravely and said nothing. Without much hope I said, 'I don't really understand why you feel the way you do.'

'It's instinct,' she said. 'I don't understand it myself. It's just that I've always thought of it as wrong ... and impossible.'

There was a little silence.

I said, 'I think I'll sleep in my digs down here in

the village tonight, and ride out at exercise with the horses tomorrow morning. I've been neglecting my job this week . . .'

She sat up straight, pulling free of my arm.

'No,' she said abruptly. 'Come back to the flat.'

'I can't. I can't any more,' I said.

She stood up and went over to the window and looked out. Minutes passed. Then she turned round and perched on the window-sill with her back to the light, and I couldn't see her expression.

'It's an ultimatum, isn't it?' she said shakily. 'Either I marry you or you clear out altogether? No more having it both ways like you've given me this past week . . .'

'It isn't a deliberate ultimatum,' I protested. 'But we can't go on like this for ever. At least, I can't. Not if you know beyond any doubt that you'll never change your mind.'

'Before last week-end there wasn't any problem as far as I was concerned,' she said. 'You were just something I couldn't have . . . like oysters, which give me indigestion . . . something nice, but out of bounds. And now'—she tried to laugh—'now it's as if I've developed a craving for oysters. And I'm in a thorough muddle.'

'Come here,' I said persuasively. She walked across and sat down again beside me on the hay bale. I took her hand.

'If we weren't cousins, would you marry me?' I held my breath.

'Yes,' she said simply. No reservations, no hesitation any more.

I turned towards her and put my hands on the sides of her head and tilted her face up. There wasn't any panic this time. I kissed her; gently, and with love.

Her lips trembled, but there was no rigidity in her body, no blind instinctive retreat as there had been a week ago. I thought, if seven days can work such a change, what could happen in seven weeks?

I hadn't lost after all. The chill in my stomach melted away. I sat back on the hay bale, holding Joanna's hand again and smiling at her.

'It will be all right,' I said. 'Our being cousins won't worry you in a little while.'

She looked at me wonderingly for a moment and then unexpectedly her lips twitched at the corners. 'I believe you,' she said, 'because I've never known anyone more determined in all my life. You've always been like it. You don't care what trouble you put yourself to to get what you want ... like riding in the race last Saturday, and fixing up this fly-trap of a cottage, and living with me how you have this week ... so my instinct against blood relatives marrying, wherever it is seated, will have to start getting used to the idea that it is wrong, I suppose, otherwise I'll find myself being dragged by you along to Claudius Mellit to be psychoanalysed or brain-washed, or something.

I will try,' she finished more seriously, 'not to keep you waiting very long.'

'In that case,' I said, matching her lightheartedness, 'I'll go on sleeping on your sofa as often as possible, so as to be handy when the breakthrough occurs.'

She laughed without strain. 'Starting tonight?' she asked.

'I guess so,' I said smiling. 'I never did like my digs much.'

'Ouch,' she said.

'But I'll have to come back here on Sunday evening in any case. As James has given me my job back, the least I can do is show some interest in his horses.'

We went on sitting on the hay bale, talking calmly as if nothing had happened; and nothing had, I thought, except a miracle that one could reliably build a future on, the miracle that Joanna's hand now lay intimately curled in mine without her wanting to remove it.

The minutes ticked away towards eleven o'clock.

'Suppose he doesn't come?' she said.

'He will.'

'I almost hope he doesn't,' she said. 'Those letters would be enough by themselves.'

'You won't forget to post them when you get back, will you?' I said.

'Of course not,' she said, 'but I wish you'd let me stay.'

I shook my head. We sat on, watching the gate. The

minute hand crept round to twelve on my watch, and passed it.

'He's late,' she said.

Five past eleven. Ten past eleven.

'He isn't coming,' Joanna murmured.

'He'll come,' I said.

'Perhaps he got suspicious and checked up and found there wasn't any Mrs Doris Jones living in the Keeper's Cottage,' she said.

'There shouldn't be any reason for him to be suspicious,' I pointed out. 'He clearly didn't know at the end of that television interview with me last Saturday that I was on to him, and nothing I've done since should have got back to him, and James and Tick-Tock promised to say nothing to anyone about the doped sugar. As far as Kemp-Lore should know, he is unsuspected and undiscovered. If he feels as secure as I am sure he does, he'll never pass up an opportunity to learn about something as damaging as pep pills . . . so he'll come.'

A quarter past eleven.

He had to come. I found that all my muscles were tense, as if I were listening for him with my whole body, not only my ears. I flexed my toes inside my shoes and tried to relax. There were traffic jams, breakdowns, detours, any number of things to delay him. It was a long way, and he could easily have misjudged the time it would take.

Twenty past eleven.

Joanna sighed and stirred. Neither of us spoke for ten minutes. At eleven-thirty, she said again, 'He isn't coming.'

I didn't answer.

At eleven-thirty-three, the sleek cream nose of an Aston Martin slid to a stop at the gate and Maurice Kemp-Lore stepped out. He stretched himself, stiff from driving, and glanced over the front of the cottage. He wore a beautifully cut hacking jacket and cavalry twill trousers, and there was poise and grace in his every movement.

'Glory, he's handsome,' breathed Joanna in my ear. 'What features! What colouring! Television doesn't do him justice. It's difficult to think of anyone who looks so young and noble doing any harm.'

'He's thirty-three,' I said, 'and Nero died at twenty-nine.'

'You know the oddest things,' she murmured.

Kemp-Lore unlatched the garden gate, walked up the short path and banged the knocker on the front door.

We stood up. Joanna picked a piece of hay off her skirt, swallowed, gave me a half-smile, and walked unhurriedly into the hall. I followed her and stood against the wall where I would be hidden when the front door opened.

Joanna licked her lips.

'Go on,' I whispered.

322

She put her hand on the latch, and opened the door.

'Mrs Jones?' the honey voice said. 'I'm so sorry I'm a little late.'

'Won't you come in, Mr Kemp-Lore?' said Joanna in her cockney-suburban accent. 'It's ever so nice to see you.'

'Thank you,' he said stepping over the threshold. Joanna took two paces backwards and Kemp-Lore followed her into the hall.

Slamming the front door with my foot, I seized Kemp-Lore from behind by both elbows, pulling them backwards and forcing him forwards at the same time. Joanna opened the door of Buttonhook's room and I brought my foot up into the small of Kemp-Lore's back and gave him an almighty push. He staggered forwards through the door and I had a glimpse of him sprawling face downwards in the straw before I had the door shut again and the padlock firmly clicking into place.

'That was easy enough,' I said with satisfaction. 'Thanks to your help.'

Kemp-Lore began kicking the door.

'Let me out,' he shouted. 'What do you think you're doing?'

'He didn't see you,' said Joanna softly.

'No,' I agreed, 'I think we'll leave him in ignorance while I take you into Newbury to catch the train.'

'Is it safe?' she said, looking worried.

'I won't be away long,' I promised. 'Come on.'

Before driving her down to Newbury I moved Kemp-Lore's car along and off the lane until it was hidden in the bushes. The last thing I wanted was some stray inquisitive local inhabitant going along to the cottage to investigate. Then I took Joanna to the station and drove straight back again, a matter of twenty minutes each way, and parked in the bushes as usual.

Walking quietly I went along the side of the cottage and round to the back.

Kemp-Lore's hands stuck out through the glassless window frames, gripping the water pipe bars and shaking them vigorously. They had not budged in their cement.

He stopped abruptly when he saw me and I watched the anger in his face change to blank surprise.

'Who did you expect?' I said.

'I don't know what's going on,' he said. 'Some damn fool of a woman locked me in here nearly an hour ago and went away and left me. You can let me out. Quickly.' His breath wheezed sharply in his throat. 'There's a horse in here,' he said looking over his shoulder, 'and they give me asthma.'

'Yes,' I said steadily, without moving. 'Yes. I know.'

It hit him then. His eyes widened.

'It was you ... who pushed me ...'

'Yes,' I said.

He stood staring at me through the criss-cross of window frame and bars.

'You did it on purpose? You put me in here with a horse on purpose?' His voice rose.

'Yes,' I agreed.

'Why?' he cried. He must have known the answer already, but when I didn't reply he said again, almost in a whisper, 'Why?'

'I'll give you half an hour to think about it,' I said, turning to walk away.

'No,' he exclaimed. 'My asthma's bad. Let me out at once.' I turned back and stood close to the window. His breath whistled fiercely, but he had not even loosened his collar and tie. He was in no danger.

'Don't you have some pills?' I said.

'Of course. I've taken them. But they won't work with a horse so close. Let me out.'

'Stand by the window,' I said, 'and breathe the fresh air.'

'It's cold,' he objected. 'This place is like an ice house.'

I smiled. 'Maybe it is,' I said. 'But then you are fortunate ... you can move about to keep warm, and you have your jacket on ... and I have not poured three bucketfuls of cold water over your head.'

He gasped sharply, and it was then, I think, that he began to realize that he was not going to escape lightly or easily from his prison.

Certainly, when I returned to him after sitting on

the hay bale for half an hour listening to him alternately kicking the door and yelling for help out of the window, he was no longer assuming that I had lured him all the way from London and gone to the trouble of converting a cottage room into a loose box merely to set him free again at his first squawk.

When I walked round to the window I found him fending off Buttonhook, who was putting her muzzle affectionately over his shoulder. I laughed callously, and he nearly choked with rage.

'Get her away from me,' he screamed. 'She won't leave me alone. I can't breathe.'

He clung on to a bar with one hand, and chopped at Buttonhook with the other.

'If you don't make so much noise she'll go back to her hay.'

He glared at me through the bars, his face distorted with rage and hate and fright. His asthma was much worse. He had unbuttoned the neck of his shirt and pulled down his tie and I could see his throat heaving.

I put the box of sugar cubes I was carrying on the inner window-sill, withdrawing my hand quickly as he made a grab at it.

'Put some sugar on her hay,' I said. 'Go on,' I added, as he hesitated. 'This lot isn't doped.'

His head jerked up. I looked bitterly into his staring eyes.

'Twenty-eight horses,' I said, 'starting with

Shantytown. Twenty-eight sleepy horses who all ate some sugar from your hand before they raced.'

Savagely he picked up the box of sugar, tore it open, and sprinkled the cubes on the pile of hay at the other end of the room. Buttonhook, following him, put her head down and began to crunch. He came back to the window, wheezing laboriously.

'You won't get away with this,' he said. 'You'll go to jail for this. I'll see you're pilloried for this.'

'Save your breath,' I said brusquely. 'I've a good deal to say to you. After that, if you want to complain to the police about the way I've treated you, you're welcome.'

'You'll be in jail so quick you won't know what hit you,' he said, the breath hissing through his teeth. 'Now, hurry up and say whatever it is you want to say.'

'Hurry?' I said slowly. 'Well now, it's going to take some time.'

'You'll have to let me out by two-thirty at the latest,' he said unguardedly. 'I've got rehearsals today at five.'

I smiled at him. I could feel it wasn't a pleasant smile.

I said, 'It isn't an accident that you are here on Friday.'

His jaw literally dropped. 'The programme . . .' he said.

'Will have to go on without you,' I agreed.

'But you can't,' he shouted, gasping for enough breath, 'you can't do that.'

'Why not?' I said mildly.

'It's ... it's television,' he shouted, as if I didn't know. 'Millions of people are expecting to see the programme.'

'Then millions of people are going to be disappointed,' I said.

He stopped shouting and took three gulping, wheezing breaths.

'I know,' he said, with a visible effort at moderation and at getting back to normal, 'that you don't really mean to keep me here so long that I can't get to the studio in time for the programme. All right then,' he paused for a couple of wheezes, 'if you let me go in good time for the rehearsals, I won't report you to the police as I threatened. I'll overlook all this.'

'I think you had better keep quiet and listen,' I said. 'I suppose you find it hard to realize that I don't give a damn for your influence or the pinnacle the British public have seen fit to put you on, or your dazzling, synthetic personality. They are a fraud. Underneath there is only a sick mess of envy and frustration and spite. But I wouldn't have found you out if you hadn't doped twenty-eight horses I rode and told everyone I had lost my nerve. And you can spend this afternoon reflecting that you wouldn't be missing your programme tonight if you hadn't tried to stop me riding Template.'

He stood stock still, his face pallid and suddenly sweating.

'You mean it,' he whispered.

'Indeed I do,' I said.

'No,' he said. A muscle in his cheek started twitching. 'No. You can't. You did ride Template ... you must let me do the programme.'

'You won't be doing any more programmes,' I said. 'Not tonight or any night. I didn't bring you here just for a personal revenge, though I don't deny I felt like killing you last Friday night. I brought you here on behalf of Art Mathews and Peter Cloony and Grant Oldfield. I brought you because of Danny Higgs, and Ingersoll, and every other jockey you have hit where it hurts. In various ways you saw to it that they lost their jobs; so now you are going to lose yours.'

For the first time, he was speechless. His lips moved but no sound came out except the high, asthmatic whine of his breathing. His eyes seemed to fall back in their sockets and his lower jaw hung slack, making hollows of his cheeks. He looked like a death's-head caricature of the handsome charmer he had been.

I took the long envelope addressed to him out of my pocket and held it to him through the bars. He took it mechanically, with black fingers.

'Open it,' I said.

He pulled out the sheets of paper and read them. He read them through twice, though his face showed from the first that he understood the extent of the disaster. The haggard hollows deepened.

'As you will see,' I said, 'those are photostat copies. More like them are in the post to the Senior Steward and to your boss at Universal Telecast, and to several other people as well. They will get them tomorrow morning. And they will no longer wonder why you failed to turn up for your programme tonight.'

He still seemed unable to speak, and his hands shook convulsively. I passed to him through the bars the rolled up portrait Joanna had drawn of him. He opened it, and it was clearly another blow.

'I brought it to show you,' I said, 'so that you would realize beyond any doubt that I know exactly what you have been doing. All along you have found that having an instantly recognizable face was a big handicap when it came to doing things you couldn't explain away, like ramming an old Jaguar across Peter Cloony's lane.'

His head jerked back, as if it still surprised him that I knew so much.

I said calmly, 'A ticket collector at Cheltenham said you were pretty.'

I smiled faintly. He looked very far from pretty at that moment.

'As for that Jaguar,' I said, 'I haven't had time yet to find out where it came from, but it can be done. It's only a question of asking. Advertising its number in the trade papers ... tracing its former owner ... that sort of thing. Tedious, I dare say, but definitely possible, and if necessary I will do it. No one would forget having you for a customer.

'You must have bought it in the week after the tank

carrier blocked Cloony's lane, because that is what gave you the idea. Do you think you can explain away the time sequence of acquiring the Jaguar and abandoning it exactly where and when and how you did? And disappearing from the scene immediately afterwards?'

His mouth hung open and the muscle twitched in his cheek.

'Most of your vicious rumours,' I said, changing tack, 'were spread for you by Corin Kellar and John Ballerton, who you found would foolishly repeat every thought that you put into their heads. I hope you know Corin well enough to realize that he never stands by his friends. When the contents of the letter he will receive in the morning sink into that rat-brain of his, and he finds that other people have had letters like it, there won't be anyone spewing out more damaging truth about you than him. He will start telling everyone, for instance, that it was you who set him at loggerheads with Art Mathews. There won't be any stopping him.

'You see,' I finished after a pause, 'I think it is only justice that as far as possible you should suffer exactly what you inflicted on other people.'

He spoke at last. The words came out in a wheezing croak, and he was past caring what admissions he made. 'How did you find it out?' he said disbelievingly. 'You didn't know last Friday, you couldn't see ...'

'I did know last Friday,' I said, 'I knew just how far you had gone to smash Peter Cloony, and I knew you hated me enough to give yourself asthma doping my mounts. I knew the dope business had gone sour on you when it came to Turniptop at Stratford. And you may care to learn that it was no accident that James Axminster jogged your arm and stepped on the sugar lumps; I asked him to, and told him what you were doing. I knew all about your curdled, obsessive jealousy of jockeys. I didn't need to see you last Friday to know you . . . there wasn't anyone else with any reason to want me out of action.'

'You can't have known all that,' he said obstinately, clinging to it as if it mattered. 'You didn't know the next day when I interviewed you after the race . . .' His voice tailed off in a wheeze and he stared at me hopelessly through the bars.

'You aren't the only one who can smile and hate at the same time,' I said neutrally. 'I learned it from you.'

He made a sound like a high-pitched moan, and turned his back towards me with his arms bent upwards and folded over his head in an attitude of the utmost misery and despair. It may be regrettable, but I felt no pity for him at all.

I walked away from his window, round the cottage and in at the front door, and sat down again on the hay in the front room. I looked at my watch. It was a quarter to two. The afternoon stretched lengthily ahead.

Kemp-Lore had another spell of screaming for help through the window, but no one came; then he tried the door again, but there was no handle on his side of it for him to pull, and it was too solidly constructed for him to kick his way through. Buttonhook grew restive again from the noise and started pawing the ground, and Kemp-Lore shouted to me furiously to let him out, let him out, let him out.

Joanna's great fear had been that his asthma would make him seriously ill, and she had repeatedly warned me to be careful; but I judged that while he had enough breath for so much yelling he was in no real danger, and I sat and listened to him without relenting. The slow hours passed, punctuated only by the bursts of fury from the back room, while I stretched myself comfortably across the hay and day-dreamed about marriage to my cousin.

At about five o'clock he was quiet for a long time. I got up and walked round the outside of the cottage and looked in through the window. He was lying face down in the straw near the door, not moving at all.

I watched him for a few minutes and called his name, but as he still did not stir I began to be alarmed, and decided I would have to make sure he was all right. I returned to the hall, and having shut the front door firmly behind me, I unlocked the padlock on the back room. The door swung inwards, and Buttonhook, lifting her head, greeted me with a soft whinny.

Kemp-Lore was alive, that at least was plain. The sound of his high, squeezed breath rose unmistakably from his still form. I bent down beside him to see into just how bad a spasm he had been driven, but I never did get around to turning him over or feeling his pulse. As soon as I was down on one knee beside him he heaved himself up and into me, knocking me sprawling off balance, and sprang like lightning for the door.

I caught his shoe as it zipped across three inches from my face and yanked him back. He fell heavily on top of me and we rolled towards Buttonhook, with me trying to pin him down on the floor and he fighting like a tiger to get free. The mare was frightened. She cowered back against the wall to get out of our way, but it was a small room and our struggles took us among Buttonhook's feet and under her belly. She stepped gingerly over us and made cautiously for the open door.

Kemp-Lore's left hand was clamped round my right wrist, a circumstance which hindered me considerably. If he'd been clairvoyant he couldn't have struck on anything better calculated to cause me inconvenience. I hit him in the face and neck with my left hand, but I was too close to get any weight behind it and was also fairly occupied dodging the blows he aimed at me in return.

After he had lost the advantage of surprise, he seemed to decide he could only get free of me by lacing his fingers in my hair and banging my head against the wall, for this he tried repeatedly to do. He was staggeringly strong, more than I would have believed possible in view of his asthma, and the fury and desperation which fired him blazed in his blue eyes like a furnace.

If my hair hadn't been so short he would probably have succeeded in knocking me out, but his fingers kept slipping when I twisted my head violently in his grasp, and the third time my ear grazed the plaster I managed at last to wrench my right hand free as well.

After that, hauling off a fraction, I landed a socking right jab in his short ribs, and the air whistled out of his lungs screeching like an express train. He went a sick grey-green colour and fell slackly off me, gasping and retching and clawing his throat for air.

I got to my feet and hauled him up, and staggered with him over to the window, holding him where the fresh cold air blew into his face. After three or four minutes his colour improved and the terrifying heaving lessened, and some strength flowed back into his sagging legs.

I clamped his fingers round the window frames and let go of him. He swayed a bit, but his hands held, and after a moment I walked dizzily out of the room and padlocked the door shut behind me.

Buttonhook had found her way into the front room and was placidly eating the hay. I leaned weakly against the wall and watched her for a while, cursing myself for the foolish way I had nearly got myself locked into my own prison. I was badly shaken, not only by the fight itself but by the strength with which Kemp-Lore had fought and by the shocking effect my last blow had had on him. I ought to have had more sense, I knew, than to hit an asthmatic with that particular punch.

There was no sound from the back room. I straightened up and walked round to the window. He was standing there, holding on to the frames where I had put him, and there were tears running down his cheeks.

He was breathing safely enough, the asthma reduced to a more manageable wheeze, and I imagined it would not get any worse from then on, as Buttonhook was no longer in the room with him.

'Damn you,' he said. Another tear spilt over. 'Damn you. Damn you.'

There wasn't anything to say.

I went back to Buttonhook, and put on her halter. I had meant to deal with her later, after I had let Kemp-Lore go, but in the changed circumstances I decided to do it straight away, while it was still light. Leading her out of the front door and through the gate, I jumped on to her back and rode her away up past the two cars hidden in the bushes and along the ridge of the hill.

A mile further on I struck the lane which led up to the Downs, and turning down that came soon to a gate into a field owned by a farmer I had often ridden for. Slipping off Buttonhook I opened the gate, led her through and turned her loose.

She was so amiable that I was sorry to part with

her, but I couldn't keep her in the cottage, I couldn't stable an elderly hunter in James's yard and expect his lads to look after her, I couldn't find a snap buyer for her at six o'clock in the evening; and I frankly didn't know what else to do with her. I fondled her muzzle and patted her neck and fed her a handful of sugar. Then I slapped her on the rump and watched my eighty-five quid kick up her heels and canter down the field like a two-year-old. The farmer would no doubt be surprised to find an unclaimed brown mare on his land, but it would not be the first time a horse had been abandoned in that way, and I hadn't any doubt that he would give her a good home.

I turned away and walked back along the hill to the cottage. It was beginning to get dark, and the little building lay like a shadow in the hollow as I went down to it through the trees and bushes. All was very quiet, and I walked softly through the garden to the back window.

He was still standing there. When he saw me he said quite quietly 'Let me out.'

I shook my head.

'Well at least go and telephone the company, and tell them I'm ill. You can't let them all wait and wait for me to come, right up to the last minute.'

I didn't answer.

'Go and telephone,' he said again.

I shook my head.

He seemed to crumple inside. He stretched his

hands through the bars and rested his head against the window frames.

'Let me out.'

I said nothing.

'For pity's sake,' he said, 'let me out.'

For pity's sake.

I said, 'How long did you intend to leave me in that tack-room?'

His head snapped up as if I'd hit him. He drew his hands back and gripped the bars.

'I went back to untie you,' he said, speaking quickly, wanting to convince me. 'I went back straight after the programme was over, but you'd gone. Someone found you and set you free pretty soon, I suppose, since you were able to ride the next day.'

'And you went back to find the tack-room empty?' I said. 'So you knew I had come to no harm?'

'Yes,' he said eagerly. 'Yes, that's what happened. I wouldn't have left you there very long, because of the rope stopping your circulation.'

'You did think there was some danger of that, then?' I said innocently.

'Yes, of course there was, and that's why I wouldn't have left you there too long. If someone hadn't freed you first, I'd have let you go in good time. I only wanted to hurt you enough to stop you riding.' His voice was disgustingly persuasive, as if what he was saying were not abnormal.

'You're a liar,' I said calmly. 'You didn't go back to

untie me after your show. You would have found me
still there if you had. In fact it took me until midnight
to get free, because no one came. Then I found a
telephone and rang up for a car to fetch me, but by
the time it reached me, which was roughly two o'clock,
you had still not returned. When I got to Ascot the
following day, everyone was surprised to see me. There
was a rumour, they said, that I wouldn't turn up. You
even mentioned on television that my name in the
number frames was a mistake. Well . . . no one but you
had any reason to believe that I wouldn't arrive at the
races: so when I heard that rumour I knew that you
had not gone back to untie me, even in the morning.
You thought I was still swinging from that hook, in
God knows what state . . . and as I understand it, you
intended to leave me there indefinitely, until someone
found me by accident . . . or until I was dead.'

'No,' he said faintly.

I looked at him without speaking for a moment,
and then turned to walk away.

'All right,' he screamed suddenly, banging on the
bars with his fists. 'All right. I didn't care whether you
lived or died. Do you like that? Is that what you want
to hear? I didn't care if you died. I thought of you
hanging there with your arms swelling and going
black . . . with the agony going on and on . . . and I
didn't care. I didn't care enough to stay awake. I went
to bed. I went to sleep. I didn't care. I didn't care . . .
and I hope you like it.'

His voice cracked, and he sank down inside the room so that all I could see in the gathering dusk was the top of his fair head and the hands gripping the bars with the knuckles showing white through the skin.

'I hope you like it,' he said brokenly.

I didn't like it. Not one little bit. It made me feel distinctly sick.

I went slowly round into the front room and sat down again on the hay. I looked at my watch. It was a quarter-past six. Still three hours to wait: three hours in which the awful truth would slowly dawn on Kemp-Lore's colleagues in the television studio, three hours of anxious speculation and stop-gap planning, culminating in the digging out of a bit of old film to fill in the empty fifteen minutes and the smooth announcement, 'We regret that owing to the – er – illness of Maurice Kemp-Lore there will be no *Turf Talk* tonight.'

Or ever again, mates, I thought, if you did but know it.

As it grew dark the air got colder. It had been frosty all day, but with the disappearance of the sun the evening developed a sub-zero bite, and the walls of the unlived-in cottage seemed to soak it up. Kemp-Lore began kicking the door again.

'I'm cold,' he shouted. 'It's too cold.'

'Too bad,' I said, under my breath.

'Let me out,' he yelled.

I sat on the hay without moving. The wrist which

he had latched on to while we fought was uncomfortably sore, and blood had seeped through the bandage again. What the Scots doctor would have to say when he saw it I hated to think. The three warts would no doubt quiver with disapproval. I smiled at the picture.

Kemp-Lore kicked the door for a long time, trying to break through it, but he didn't succeed. At the same time he wasted a good deal of breath yelling that he was cold and hungry and that I was to let him out. I made no reply to him at all, and after about an hour of it the kicking and shouting stopped, and I heard him slither down the door as if exhausted and begin sobbing with frustration.

I stayed where I was and listened while he went on and on moaning and weeping in desolation. I listened to him without emotion; for I had cried too, in the tack-room.

The hands crawled round the face of my watch.

At a quarter to nine, when nothing could any longer save his programme, and even a message explaining his absence could scarcely be telephoned through in time, Kemp-Lore's decreasing sobs faded away altogether, and the cottage was quiet.

I got stiffly to my feet and went out into the front garden, breathing deeply in the clear air, with an easing sense of release. The difficult day was over, and the stars were bright in the frosty sky. It was a lovely night.

I walked along to the bushes and started Kemp-Lore's car, turning it and driving it back to the gate. Then for the last time I walked round the cottage to talk to him through the window, and he was standing there already, his face a pale blue behind the window frames.

'My car,' he said hysterically. 'I heard the engine. You're going to drive away in my car and leave me.'

I laughed. 'No. You are going to drive it away yourself. As fast and as far as you like. If I were you, I'd drive to the nearest airport and fly off. No one is going to like you very much when they've read those letters in the morning, and it will be only a day or two before the newspapers get on to it. As far as racing goes, you will certainly be warned off. Your face is too well-known in Britain for you to hide or change your name or get another job. And as you've got all night and probably most of tomorrow before the storm breaks and people start eyeing you with sneers and contempt, you can pack up and skip the country quite easily, without any fuss.'

'You mean ... I can go? Just go?' He sounded astounded.

'Just go,' I said, nodding. 'If you go quickly enough, you'll avoid the enquiry the stewards are bound to hold, and you'll avoid any charge they might think of slapping on you. You can get away to some helpful distant country where they don't know you, and you can start again from scratch.'

'I suppose I haven't much choice,' he murmured. His asthma was almost unnoticeable.

'And find a country where they don't have steeplechasing,' I finished.

He moaned sharply, and crashed his fists down on the window frame.

I went round into the cottage and in the light of Joanna's big torch unlocked the padlock and pushed open the door. He turned from the window and walked unsteadily towards me across the straw, shielding his ravaged face from the light. He went through the door, passed me without a glance, and stumbled down the path to his car; and I walked down the path behind him, shining the torch ahead. I propped the torch on top of the gate-post so as to leave my hands free in case I needed to use them, but there didn't seem to be much fight left in him.

He paused when he was sitting in his car, and with the door still wide open looked out at me.

'You don't understand,' he said, his voice shaking. 'When I was a boy I wanted to be a jockey. I wanted to ride in the Grand National, like my father. And then there was this thing about falling off... I'd see the ground rushing past under my horse and there would be this terrible sort of pain in my guts, and I sweated until I could pull up and get off. And then I'd be sick.'

He made a moaning noise and clutched his stomach at the memory. His face twisted. Then he said suddenly, fiercely, 'It made me feel good to see jockeys looking worried. I broke them up all right. It made me feel warm inside. Big.'

He looked up at me with renewed rage, and his voice thickened venomously.

'I hated you more than all the others. You rode too well for a new jockey and you were getting on too quickly. Everyone was saying "Give Finn the bad horses to ride, he doesn't know what fear is". It made me furious when I heard that. So I had you on my programme, remember? I meant to make you look a fool. It worked with Mathews, why not with you? But Axminster took you up and then Pankhurst broke his leg ... I wanted to smash you so much that it gave me headaches. You walked about with that easy confidence of yours, as if you took your strength for granted, and too many people were getting to say you'd be champion one day ...

'I waited for you to have a fall that looked fairly bad, and then I used the sugar. It worked. You know it worked. I felt ten feet tall, looking at your white face and listening to everyone sniggering about you. I watched you find out how it felt. I wanted to see you writhe when everyone you cared for said ... like my father said to all his friends ... that it was a pity about you ... a pity you were a snivelling little coward, a pity you had no nerve ... no nerve ...'

His voice died away, and his hollowed eyes were

wide, unfocused, as if he were staring back into an unbearable past.

I stood looking down at the wreck of what could have been a great man. All that vitality, I thought; all that splendid talent wasted for the sake of hurting people who had not hurt him.

Such individuals could be understood, Claudius Mellit had said. Understood, and treated, and forgiven.

I could understand him in a way, I supposed, because I was myself the changeling in a family. But my father had rejected me kindly, and I felt no need to watch musicians suffer.

Treated . . . The treatment I had given him that day might not have cured the patient, but he would no longer spread his disease, and that was all I cared about.

Without another word I shut the car door on him and gestured to him to drive away. He gave me one more incredulous glance as if he still found it impossible that I should let him go, and began to fumble with the light switches, the ignition, and the gears.

I hoped he was going to drive carefully. I wanted him to live. I wanted him to live for years, thinking about what he had thrown away. Anything else would be too easy, I thought.

The car began to roll, and I caught a last glimpse of the famous profile, the eclipsed, exiled profile, as he slid away into the dark. The brake lights flashed red as he paused at the end of the lane, then he turned out into the road, and was gone. The sound of his engine died away.

I took the torch from the gate-post and walked up the path to the quiet cottage, to sweep it clean.

Forgiveness, I thought. That was something else again.

It would take a long time to forgive.

Visit **www.panmacmillan.com** to read more about all our books and to buy them. You will also find features, author interviews and news of any author events, and you can sign up for e-newsletters so that you're always first to hear about our new releases.